ECHOES OF THE PAST AT ORCHARD COTTAGE HOSPITAL

LIZZIE LANE

Boldwood

First published in Great Britain in 2026 by Boldwood Books Ltd.

Cover Design by Colin Thomas

Cover Images: Colin Thomas

A CIP catalogue record for this book is available from the British Library.

Paperback ISBN 978-1-83656-427-0

Large Print ISBN 978-1-83656-426-3

Hardback ISBN 978-1-83656-425-6

Trade Paperback ISBN 978-1-80656-622-8

Ebook ISBN 978-1-83656-428-7

Kindle ISBN 978-1-83656-429-4

Audio CD ISBN 978-1-83656-420-1

MP3 CD ISBN 978-1-83656-421-8

Digital audio download ISBN 978-1-83656-424-9

This book is printed on certified sustainable paper. Boldwood Books is dedicated to putting sustainability at the heart of our business. For more information please visit https://www.boldwoodbooks.com/about-us/sustainability/

Boldwood Books Ltd, 23 Bowerdean Street, London, SW6 3TN

www.boldwoodbooks.com

PROLOGUE

THE STRANGER

The Great War had been over for twelve years when Harry Hunter took the first step to pulling himself together. He'd been twenty-four years old when demobbed from the army a year after the war had ended, but the memories remained, scouring his head like wire wool scratching the inside of a saucepan.

Getting back – or becoming normal – was an uphill struggle. Every day, trying to forget was a struggle. A lack of purpose gave no reason for living.

The letter from a firm of London solicitors telling him he had inherited a plot of land should have given him hope. The upbeat news made no immediate difference. Instead, it came one night on a dirty road, in a dirty town.

He had been thirty-six years old, lying on the ground, too drunk to move. He heard the laughter of other drunken men and smelled hot urine; one of them had relieved himself close by, the hot liquid splashing over him.

He wasn't there. Not in his mind. Once again, he had slipped back to the battlefields of France, where vile smells from a soup of blood and mud steeled him against any stink that might assail his nostrils nowadays. What was this revolting act in comparison to battling the horrors of bloodied men, starving men, half-dead men going through the motions of being alive whilst broken inside.

They left him in a pool of oblivion, how long he couldn't know. On feeling a warm moistness licking at his eyelids, he'd awoken to find himself looking into the eyes of another lonely soul. The dog was black and white, a collie type, and lying against him, the pleading in its brown eyes begging for help in a world in which they were both strays.

Change hadn't come overnight, but at the heart of his transformation was a promise he'd made a long time ago, one he had pushed aside until now.

Still haunted by the nightmares of that terrible time, he continued travelling the countryside, doing odd jobs for farmers who gave him food, a small wage and a bed for the night.

A little money left from his pension and a little earned had enabled him to invest in a home.

The old narrowboat was a wreck, which had seen better days. Left to rot. The farmer wanted it gone from the riverbank, so she – for boats are always female – came to him as a wage – a bonus in fact.

Then there were the animals. Back in the Great War, he'd been responsible for looking after the mules and horses the army had been so dependent on. His skills grew from there. After all these years, he knew where he was going. The narrowboat was named *Talbot*, the same name he had given his dog. But there was another home, one obscured by the memory of being hard done by. It was mostly to do with a pair of brown eyes as soft and plaintive as his dog's. His mother had told him his history, how she'd borne him out of wedlock and been paid off to keep quiet. Another man, a worker on the estate, had been paid to marry his mother. He'd not been a good man, as rough and ready as many were who had received little education and laboured from dawn to sunset to make a living.

She'd finally succumbed to a fall brought on by a beating. It wasn't long after that he'd run away and joined the army as a bugle boy, a soldier once the war had begun.

The army had been his home. The friends he'd made had helped him heal. One in particular named Ben Tyler.

He'd told Ben everything, told him he would show him the grand house that, in his mind at least, was his birthright. He'd made a promise beneath a starlit sky when they'd shared a barn with several animals they were looking after.

There had been silence. No sound from artillery even though they were only a short way behind the lines.

Peace, perfect peace.

Leaving Ben with the horses, Harry had gone out to stare up at the stars. Whilst doing this, a shell fell on the barn and set it on fire. He'd left the stars to their own devices and ran towards the fire, shouting at Ben to come out. The horses were screaming.

Whizzbangs and shells exploded all around him, yet still he waited for his best friend to emerge from the conflagration. He never came.

Harry was still there the next day when the ash had cooled. Recognising that this was all that was left of his dear friend, he scooped some up into an old biscuit tin, along with several items that had not burned: a watch, an identity tag, a crucifix. All he had left to fulfil the promise he'd made.

That night, he decided he hated the world but would keep his promise to Ben. He would take him to the only other home he had ever known, the one owned by the family who he held responsible for his mother's death.

The state of his mind had intervened. He was lost and groping for the way home.

It took a long time coming, but eventually it did.

1

MAY 1934

Assisted by the dedicated senior nurse, Sister Edith Harrison, Doctor Frances Brakespeare swallowed her feelings. It wasn't her ladyship's fault. Surely not. The Compton-Dixon family owned the mines, though management was nowadays left to an outside corporation.

She'd been asked to attend the Methodist church hall where striking miners had been brought to have their wounds tended. Lady Araminta Compton-Dixon had phoned her earlier that morning, a high-pitched nervousness in her voice.

'I did not order this. Honestly, Doctor. It was not of my doing.'

Strikes were happening throughout the traditional heavy industries on which the British Empire depended. Wages had been cut because exports of coal had been cut. Not only had labourers in coal, steel and shipbuilding been laid off or had their wages cut, the unemployment insurance had too.

Hostile eyes turned their way on entering the Methodist chapel. Frances exchanged a quick look with Sister Harrison before suggesting they get started.

Heads had been cracked. Blood trickled down into faces usually steeped in grime, though today they were surprisingly clean.

Suspecting this would be the case, doctor and nurse had brought an over-abundance of bandages, lint and an interesting salve made by local herbalist, Ma Skittings, from honey.

Bowls of water were demanded of the wives who had appeared to support their men in their struggle for a fair wage – or fair unemployment insurance.

There were ten men in all.

'Thought me skull was cracked,' said one man, who showed more gratefulness than some.

Hoping to take advantage of the medical presence, some of the women had brought their children along, skinny children with bare feet, eyes set in deep hollows on pale faces. Some had scabs around their mouths. The clothes they wore were patched hand-me-downs from older siblings or cut down from adult clothing.

A small child threw itself into its father's arms, straggly hair hiding both their faces.

Sister Harrison jerked her chin at the flea clinging to a spiky tress of hair.

Frances grimaced but held her hand steady, cleaning and binding wounds, lancing the odd boil, even sewing an earlobe back in place. She told the man beforehand that it was going to hurt. He'd replied that he could bear it. He clenched his jaw so tightly, she thought she could hear his teeth grinding.

Bread and cheese rind were handed out by the wives. Some of the men gave half of their meagre meal to their children – though, in some cases – depending on how many children – it was barely a mouthful.

The church minister, a Mr Cedric Rogers, asked in a booming voice if there was anything he could do to help.

Frances cut the cotton from the needle she'd been using and got to her feet.

Her gaze travelled swiftly over the children and the shabbily dressed women, their clothes hanging on thin frames.

'These people look very hungry.'

Without answering, the minister bent from the waist, hands clasped behind his back and asked one of the women what she'd had to eat that morning.

'A slice of fried bread.'

'And what will you have for this evening's meal?'

He smiled as he said it, the look in his eyes partly hidden behind the thick lenses of his spectacles.

'Potatoes,' came the reply.

'Just potatoes?'

A sullen and somewhat hostile nod. 'All there is.'

'The children too,' said the minister, looking directly at Frances. 'Right,' he bellowed. 'How many of you children would like a cup of something hot and warming?'

There was instant interest.

'I can work magic. Did any of you know that?'

As intrigued as anyone, Frances watched before her jaw dropped at the sight of him holding high a jar of beef tea – Bovril.

'I'll put the kettle on. I'm certain we have enough cups for everyone!'

Having finished forming a sling, Sister Harrison checked there was no one else awaiting attention before she offered to help the minister.

'If that's all right with you, Doctor.'

Frances said that it was.

Sister Harrison saw the minister with his sleeves rolled up, a tea towel thrown over his shoulder. He looked capable, but all the same, she decided to give him a helping hand. She was like a whirlwind. Not only was she handing out cups of beef tea, but she was tending ailments as she went, dabbing at the crusts on children's lips, pulling the tooth of a drained-looking mother.

Frances felt an overwhelming sense of hopelessness. When men were out of work and food was scarce, it was women who went without. The direct result of that was their health suffered the most. Some of these women couldn't be more than thirty years old, but missing teeth, lank hair and grey skin made them look older.

'We must do something,' she murmured.

Misinterpreting, Sister Harrison asked her what she meant, after all they had dealt with the injuries.

'The women and children are starving.'

Sister Harrison snorted. 'That's hardly unusual.'

She was right. Working men believed it their right to spend half their wages on beer and tobacco. Wives and families got the rest. Such as it was.

'We have to do something.'

Sister Harrison took in Doctor Brakespeare's concerned expression. She'd worked with her long enough to recognise when she was planning something. 'What have you in mind?'

'A soup kitchen. I intend setting up a soup kitchen. I'm sure I can find some willing hands to help out.'

That look again. Sister Harrison knew she was being challenged to rise to the occasion.

'I'm sure we can.'

2

The windows of St Michael's vicarage reflected the early-morning sunshine.

The Reverend Gregory Sampson, who still awaited Doctor Frances Brakespeare to consent to marry him, had arranged most of the May Day celebrations. He'd been a captain in the army during the Great War and once it had ended had decided he preferred to serve God rather than military might. Becoming the vicar of St Michael's, in the country town of Norton Dene, suited him very well indeed. It was a while into his time here that he'd been seconded onto the committee of the Orchard Cottage Hospital. A few years ago, following the retirement of the old doctor, applications had been invited for the vacant position and along had come Doctor Frances Brakespeare.

The committee had presumed they were getting a Doctor FRANCIS Brakespeare, a male doctor. A female doctor had come as something of a surprise. She'd fulfilled her duties admirably at the same time as acquiring a special place in his heart.

They'd become a couple, become engaged, and, he hoped, in time they would marry. It was just a case of finding time in their busy schedules; both were committed to their professions.

And of course, they supported each other – as with the May Day fair.

He'd helped Frances load what she needed to run the first-aid post at the May Day festivities. He had been set the task of overseeing everything went smoothly. Part of that entailed making sure everyone had put up their stalls in the right place the day before.

Frances had also had him making sandwiches and cutting up a walnut cake made only the day before by his housekeeper, Mrs Cross.

'Not everyone is going to visit the first-aid tent with an injury. Some are going to be starving.'

He'd helped her with the baskets and boxes containing most of the contents of his personal pantry – and more besides. Ma Skittings had come in to help the night before and had added jars of honey and apple jam to the feast. The first-aid tent would also be handing out free food.

He didn't need to be told that many of the miners' families were finding it difficult. The men had gone back to work. An agreement had been reached, but not yet finalised.

It surprised him that Araminta, Lady Compton-Dixon, had taken such action. She'd always been a fair but firm employer.

'Things have been difficult. Not only here. Everywhere. The export market for coal has crashed.' She'd shrugged. 'What am I to do? Countries who used to buy coal are no longer doing so.'

Her patrician face, taut features above a high neckline of cream lace and mauve silk, had creased with worry and guilt.

'I'm a little short of funds,' she'd added. 'My late husband took some advice that was far from genuine.' She'd sighed.

And now Frances had mentioned her plan to provide a soup kitchen. 'It's going to be a while before they can make up for what they've lost. It's the women and children that worry me. I have to do something. Anything!'

He watched her drive away, his heart seeming to drive off with her. How long had they known each other? However long, the time had passed in a blur of memorable instances. There was always something going on in their world and, for the most part, they were on the same page. On occasion it was as though they were reading totally different books!

Beams of sunlight were piercing more forcibly through the wall of trees surrounding the vicarage garden. Revelling in the air, the sight of greenery and the carpet of bluebells nodding beneath the trees, Gregory retreated to the top of the three steps set before the vicarage entrance.

Up here he felt like a monarch surveying his realm, small as it might be –

and full of shadows over a lawn wet with dew. Everything was so still, not a breath of wind, yet he felt a sudden draught.

His eyes followed the garden boundary and then the path leading down to the coach house. His abode was the vicarage. Hers was the coach house; thus they maintained a propriety the town's matriarchs would approve of.

The coach house once been home to the coachman, the carriage and the horses, converted a while back into a cottage. It looked what it had been, nowhere near as majestic as the vicarage, but solid and humble. Its dormer windows reflected the sky, at times seeming to be winking at the world.

The Reverend Gregory Sampson liked having Frances close at hand. Of course he did. It meant he could gradually wear down her resistance and set a date to marry. Any date. A date he would gladly agree to.

The feeling of unease, that he was not alone, did not go away.

Instinct had been learned back in the Great War when sometimes it was all that kept you alive, hearing the whistling of a shell when it was only halfway to the target – and the target was you.

He felt that instinct now but was not inclined to dive for cover. It wasn't that sort of threat that shifted the air.

There was no sign of another soul. He blamed his imagination, the effect of getting up early this morning.

He might have been convinced until a blackbird broke cover from a rowan tree. He recognised its high-pitched shriek as a warning. Something had disturbed it.

His head snapped round so that he was facing the direction it had come from.

A squirrel perhaps? A bird of prey.

He looked skywards. Buzzards flew high. Thanks to the cliffs and crevices of the local quarries, they were common, though not today. The sky was empty, and yet the feeling of not being alone remained.

3

The feeling was accompanied by an odd sound, like an apple makes when falling from the trees in autumn.

But it wasn't autumn and there were no apple trees in the vicarage garden.

Alert to danger, Gregory's gaze swept over the black shadows lying in dark oblongs thrown by the boundary wall.

He was finally convinced. 'Who's there?'

There was a legend about a wandering green man who lived in the woods. That was who this man reminded him of. A tall man, broad in the shoulders, a solid force against the background of trees.

Gregory took in the unkempt details, a mass of hair on head and chin. A tramp with a black and white dog at his side.

Without hesitation, the man stepped forward.

Not sensing an aura of aggression, Gregory stood his ground. It wouldn't be the first time that an itinerant traveller had approached him for alms or somewhere to stay, to rest in order to regain the energy to travel to wherever they were going.

'Can I help you?' His voice rang out confidently, cloaking the apprehension he felt inside.

Man and dog took two more steps towards him. From this distance, Gregory could see that the dog was held on a piece of rope. He could also see that the man's abundant hair resembled a lion's mane, the beard as thick as a clump of grass. It was the eyes peering out from that hirsute face that drew him, as piercingly blue as his own in a face weathered by sun and snow.

Definitely termed by many as a tramp, though in his generous heart the man was no more than a wanderer, someone whose life had become aimless following the trauma of the Great War, and he'd seen many. Jobless men searching for work or lost souls who had come home from the war to end all wars and found that few promises that were given had been kept.

Once a soldier, always a soldier. That was the familiar saying. From experience, he knew this man had once been part of the army that had expected a short war and found themselves in a very long one.

He perceived all the signs. The man's shoulders were laid back, his head held high. A military bearing.

The old images resurfaced, the backdrop of springtime greenery warping into muddy fountains accompanied by the sound of shell fire.

He shook the vision from his head. Normality returned. The greenery returned. He was back in the here and now. The unease remained.

'You're the vicar?'

Gregory managed a smile as he indicated his dog collar. 'My badge of office.'

'I'm hungry,' he said. 'Do you have anything to eat?'

Gregory thought of the few items left in the larder. 'Bread and cheese. That's about it.'

The man stared at him. 'Have you been here long?'

'About ten years. I came here a few years after the end of the war.'

A look of consternation passed over the man's face, as though he'd expected someone else.

'It was the Reverend Julian Blackwood before me. He retired.'

An enlightened nod, as though that explained something.

It occurred to Gregory that the traveller might have visited here before.

Gregory waited for him to continue; when he didn't, he suggested that he come inside for some bread and cheese.

'Or, if you're in no hurry, there's food at the May Day fair. It's being held on the town green around the war memorial. If you've not much money, there's free food at the first-aid tent.'

He reminded him that bread and cheese was on offer in the vicarage kitchen.

'But if you want a bit of company and free food, the war memorial and the green is that way.'

He pointed out the direction. 'Straight ahead. Just follow the road.'

A silent nod and the tramp returned to the shadows.

Gregory narrowed his eyes but saw nothing now except shadows.

He shuddered. The man had been real, flesh and blood real. So why the premonition that the man had brought something with him – not a disease, but a malignancy that was deeply worrying.

Take a deep breath and clear your head. That's what he told himself as he fetched his bicycle and checked the bicycle saddlebag to see that everything was there.

It was. Pushing off firmly, Gregory headed for the May Day fair, determined to enjoy the day and not dwell on either the man or his feeling of unease. Besides that, he was also feeling a determination to finally pin his colours to the mast and press Frances into setting a date. After all, that was far more important – at least to him.

4

Doctor Frances Brakespeare had broken the rules that nothing was available before the official opening at ten o'clock. A group of children with grubby faces and bare feet had heard a rumour about walnut cake and sandwiches. By the time they'd finished, she was left with only half of what she'd arrived with.

'You do know we're not really open yet,' she'd said to them, then frowned. 'I thought everything was fenced off and you had to come through the gate.'

She guessed by their cheeky grins that the chicken wire fencing had been easily traversed by those determined to take full advantage of the jolly affair.

Sister Harrison had the day off and Nancy Skittings had stepped in.

'I want to keep my hand in, and besides, the kids are out playing – thank goodness they're old enough. And Ned's got the day off.'

'So have I,' Frances had answered. 'Doctor Roberts was more than keen to take over at the hospital, and Sister Peebles is there to keep an eye on everything.'

Even this distance from the gate, gasps of delight from small voices waiting outside were easily heard. She imagined them pointing at the treats they could shortly enjoy. Swing boats, a roundabout, a coconut shy, a stall selling home-made jams, cakes and potted plants. There were also donkey rides, their velvety lips tugging at the grass, their harnesses polished for the occasion, collars of home-made bunting strung around their necks.

The striped awnings flapped in a spring breeze. Both men and women held onto their hats, their colours like a field of flowers as they congregated before a silken ribbon stretched across the entrance.

Hush was called for as Lady Araminta Compton-Dixon, dressed in lavender silk, stepped forward to make a short speech before cutting the ribbon.

Despite her age, reputed to be close to seventy-seven, her voice was loud and sharp enough to cut through the hubbub. Not that there was much. As the doyenne of Orchard Manor, owner of mines and quarries on which the local workforce depended, her voice, and her presence, demanded their attention.

'I do believe that this is my sixtieth May Day. Thank you all for taking the trouble to come. Enjoy everything that's on offer. I know I shall. Do try to visit the flower competition if you can. I've entered my best roses this year.'

A slight titter ensued. It was well known that she entered her best roses every year – and won.

But there was also something else, a rumble of criticism running just beneath the surface from those whose wages had been cut.

'And now. Without more ado, I declare this fair open.'

No sooner had the ribbon been cut asunder and fallen, the crowd surged forward, the children heading for the penny rides, the women for the stalls brimming with home-made fare.

Some men threw her ladyship dark looks. Others, not affected by wage cuts and unemployment, held onto their hats as they cantered to the beer tent, where casks of beer and cider were ranged behind a make-do bar which constituted three trestle tables on loan from the church hall.

There was something for everyone, which included a circular tent sited next to the war memorial, its drab colour and foreboding history offset by golden letters, stars and crescent-shaped moons against a blue background.

From Egypt she comes with all the secrets of the past and the future.
Madame Nefertiti – Fortune Teller to Pharaohs, Kings and Queens.

Inside the tent, unseen by the crowds, Ma Skittings was metamorphosing into Queen Nefertiti. Sporting a huge pair of brass earrings, once used with others to slide along a curtain rail, she wound a piece of dark red cloth around her head. Like the brass curtain rings, the piece of chenille had been appropriated from something more humdrum. The turban had once been a portion of tablecloth and was large enough to wind around her head and cover the lower half of her face – very necessary if she was not to be recognised. Her floaty skirt and gypsy-style blouse had taken a bit more thought. Discarded heavy lace curtains that had once graced the dining-room windows at Orchard Manor were gathered at the waist and neck with lengths of elastic.

Aware of the need to check her appearance, she'd had the foresight to bring a hand mirror. Not only did she need to check her rather heavyweight veil, but also whether her face was still in need of walnut juice. Gypsy fortune tellers were expected to be dark-skinned and mysterious – after all, didn't they originally come from Egypt?

Opening her eyes wide, she stared hard into the mirror. Were her eyes deep enough, mysterious enough? Along with the mirror, she'd brought along a small pot of soot she'd spooned from her chimney. After applying a smudge on each eyelid and beneath each eye, she covered the bottom half of her face with a portion of the scarf, holding it there with a safety pin.

She giggled at her reflection and adopted what she considered a deep and husky voice.

'Madame Nefertiti will look into your future.'

She stifled a girlish giggle with her hand in case a potential customer waiting outside might be put off seeking the advice of someone less than mysterious.

Rosie Crane's advice was that being a fortune teller was a serious business – even when you were lying.

Ma had asked Rosie, a real gypsy fortune teller, to explain herself. 'You're allowed to lie?'

'It depends. Just say whatever comes into your head. You needs to make them think that they're of such importance that the universe has their future mapped out. Even when they asks daft questions, don't give a daft answer or they'll only cross your palm with sixpence rather than half a crown. Or nothing at all.'

It was Rosie that should have been doing this, but she'd cried off, she was off to a wedding – a big gypsy one.

'Wouldn't go for anyone else, but it is me daughter getting wed.' Youngest of eight, daughter Blanche was marrying a bigwig in the gypsy community. Not only did he deal in horses in the traditional way, but he also had land and a fertile brain by the sound of it. 'He's got a few acres of land overlooking the sea in Norfolk. Got plans to set up a site for caravans and tents. People are going big into that kind of thing of late. Out to enjoy themselves. Did all right last summer. Expects even better this year. Making good money too.'

Rosie's eyes had glittered like gold sovereigns caught in a ray of sunlight. But that was Rosie. She always had plans about how best to turn a shilling – and the more shillings the better, though sovereigns for preference.

'Sorry, love. I did tell the vicar, but he must have forgot. Anyways, you're known for old lore and cures 'round 'ere and is good at convincing people what's good for them. There ain't much of a difference between the two,' Rosie had sniffed. 'They'll believe you cos they want to believe. That's the secret, see? At the end of the day, it's all about hope. Hoping for something better than what they've got.'

Thinking what a crafty old biddy was Rosie Crane, Ma Skittings spat on the crystal ball she'd loaned her. With the trailing corner of her veil, she gave it a quick polish. At least her identity and any hesitation she might feel would be hidden behind the piece of old chenille tablecloth.

By way of getting herself in the right frame of mind, she began tidying the baize-covered table loaned by the vicar, usually used in the church hall for the weekly whist drive. She shuffled the Tarot cards, split and then shuffled an ordinary deck, then placed both into two separate piles in front of her.

Besides the items loaned from Rosie – at a price – was a silver dish she owned which was deep enough to take coins and perhaps even a ten-shilling note.

Next, she pulled the small oil lamp close to her and put out the larger one. The little one would further cloak her identity, its meagre glow flickering in a magical kind of way, throwing waves of light around the tent and away from her.

Lifting the flap that hid the doorway, she peeped out from her tent in time to see her ladyship cut the ribbon.

As the applause died and the crowd milled onto the green, she dived back inside, made sure the safety pin held and waited for her first customer.

5

Sister Edith Harrison was dressed in her Sunday best, her mint green dress coupled with a tan-coloured hat, soft kid gloves and ankle-strap shoes. She fancied other women were eyeing her enviously but also with respect. Many of them had occasion to thank her for her sterling service at the hospital, where she assisted babies entering the world and the departure of older people. She was also there for all those moments in between when exemplary care and firm discipline was called for. Edith was rigid when it came to discipline. In her opinion, good health was only achieved by a strict regime of neat beds, fresh air and plenty of sleep. Old-fashioned enemas also helped encourage bodily balance – a bit like a train timetable.

Mr March, the chemist and a bachelor, had suggested they share a cream tea. Although she looked for him, she could see no sign, which she found quite disappointing. That sister of his must have had a hand in persuading him otherwise. Sharp of features and flint-eyed, Dorothy March treated her younger brother as though he was still in short trousers and a school cap. *Well, I would soon alter that*, thought Sister Harrison, *but of course, Dorothy must know that*. Her control would be broken, her little brother would finally grow up. And that was the problem. His sister didn't want him to grow up and certainly wouldn't allow the poor man to run his own life – or get married.

So why was she bothering?

An easy answer. The fact was Edith was growing older and reading about romance was no longer quite enough. She had had a fling a while back with the manager of the quarry, but he was now working some distance away. He'd also been unfaithful. She'd found out he'd been having relationships with other women at the same time as dallying with her.

Sister Edith Harrison had a high opinion of herself. As senior sister at the Orchard Cottage Hospital, she was second to none. Greatly respected, though to say she was loved might be taking it too far. Was it also the same with romance? Was she too unapproachable? If so, was it possible that she might relax a bit more? She chewed her bottom lip as she thought how she might act sillier, like most women who wanted a man in their life. It wasn't in her nature to be silly.

Out of the corner of her eye, she espied movement and instantly knew it was Toby Sledge, the blacksmith. Big, sweaty and not known to read a newspaper, let alone a book, he was interested in her, but she was not interested in him.

His voice carried across the heads of the laughing, chattering crowds, the brass band and the guttural voices of the Punch and Judy characters.

'Sister Harrison!'

Pretending not to notice, she quickened her pace, her eyes ardently seeking the place where tea and scones were available. Perhaps she would find Mr March – Gerald – there.

Unfortunately, it was located on the other side of the green, which meant she would have to head towards where Toby stood next to the test your strength machine. Due to his muscular build and the fact that the hammer and machine belonged to him, Toby Sledge was inviting people to swing the hammer and send the leaded weight flying upwards to ring the bell at the top.

A detour was needed.

Skirting round the back of some of the lesser booths seemed the way to go. Chief amongst them and offering to hide her completely from her ardent admirer, she ducked into the dense fabric of the tent closest to the war memorial.

So swift was her decision and action, that she had only given a cursory glance at the placard advertising what was on offer, replete with the sparkly moon and stars and the outlandish name of the fortune teller.

Madame Nefertiti – a ridiculous name if ever there was.

Never mind, any port in a storm, she thought as she heaved aside the heavy khaki flap and almost fell inside.

After the glare of the bright spring day outside, the gloomy interior took some getting used to.

Rumour had it that Madame Nefertiti was a genuine Romany and knew her business. Not that Edith really cared – she wasn't one for such hocus pocus, but escaping Toby Sledge was a priority.

His moony adoration had started when his hand had been burned by the red-hot horseshoe he'd been manoeuvring towards the rear hoof of the coalman's horse. Whilst applying balm and sympathy, Toby had told her in detail how he'd received the injury. The coalman's horse was named Bertha and she'd always been of a skittish and temperamental disposition.

'So we used a switch.'

She hadn't known what a switch was, but he'd elaborated.

It seemed that a length of rope was wound tightly around the horse's muzzle and held firmly. The idea was that the animal concentrated more on the immediate pain of the switch rather than the inconvenience of a hoof being lifted for an iron shoe to be fitted.

Sister Edith Harrison, in her crisply pressed uniform and starched apron, had applied iodine and a dressing.

Toby had gazed at her as though she was an angel come down from heaven. His very own angel.

It was rumoured that he'd once been married, but Gertrude had run away with a salesman who had sold brushes from door to door. Apparently, it had been going on for quite a while before she absconded with her slick and slender lover. Toby had not suspected the salesman of being a regular caller, though the evidence of innumerable sweeping brushes, yard brushes and dustpan and brush sets, should have set alarm bells ringing.

He lived alone in the rooms above the smithy, him and his former wife never having had children.

Shortly following her treatment of his burn, he'd declared himself available.

'You's like me, getting on a bit, and though I can't offer you a smart house and all that, we'd be good company as we get older. What do you say?'

Getting on a bit! He didn't seem to have a clue how insensitive he'd been in daring to touch on her age. Forty was not ancient! And didn't he know that they were far from being equals. What would they talk about sitting on a quiet evening? Certainly not books. The man was ill read, and she certainly had no wish to hear about how many horses' hooves he'd shoed that day.

Her thoughts were jerked back to the present as a brown hand with a very white palm invited her to take a seat. The chair looked very similar to one of many available in the public bar of the Golden Lion.

Relieved to find somewhere Toby Sledge couldn't find her, Edith sat down. Having her fortune told would be entertaining if nothing else.

The hand remained poised, reaching out to her, the white palm, furrowed with wrinkles, upwards.

Ma Skittings hid her amusement well. Sister Edith Harrison was her first customer. What a surprise!

Seeing no movement from her and determined to get what was due, Ma Skittings explained, 'If you want to see your future, you must cross my hand with silver. Half a crown is the usual,' she said without giving Edith time to ask how much.

It crossed Sister Harrison's mind to refuse and leave, but if she lingered a while, Toby might be gone, and she could meet up with Gerald March, who, to her mind, seemed a far better prospect. By virtue of his profession, he was a clean man. No calluses on his hands and he didn't smell of sweat and horses.

Due to the gloom, it was difficult to see what coin she had fumbled from her purse. It turned out to be a shilling.

'Half a crown,' the fortune teller repeated in a nasally voice, her fingers making wiggling engagingly.

After a bit more fumbling, Sister Harrison brought out a florin and a sixpenny piece. 'There you are. Half a crown.'

Brown fingers folded over the lighter coloured palm. The coins slid from the fortune teller's closed palm and into a silver dish.

Edith's eyes followed the crystal ball as it was positioned between them in the centre of the table. Once it was where she wanted it, both of the fortune teller's hands formed a kind of arch over the object.

Sister Harrison told herself that this was all bunkum. On the other hand, she ached to have a knight in shining armour rescue her from a tall tower or a Regency dandy to fall at her feet as he declared his love for her. At the very least, she would like to be told that she had a local admirer who would offer her marriage. Even if it was only Mr March the chemist. Not that she would admit to having any faith in all this malarkey. Truth be told, she wanted to feel her heart race, and she wouldn't experience such a thing with the likes of Toby Sledge.

Not that she would admit to being so needy. It wasn't part of her persona, and she certainly did not want to be regarded as a fool. To that end, she tossed her head and declared with aloofness, 'I don't really believe in this, you know.' She gave a light laugh. 'It's just a bit of fun. I thought I might try it, seeing as it's May Day.'

She looked into the fortune teller's face as if to emphasise what she'd said – not that there was much to see. Just a pair of eyes looking out from deep black pits above a close-fitting veil too dense to see through. The blackened skin around the eyes suggested the fortune teller might have been looking up a chimney or poking her head out of a train carriage window and her face getting covered in smuts from the steam engine up front.

'Look into the crystal ball,' the woman demanded, slicing into her thoughts. 'I might see a tall, dark stranger, who just might be the man you're going to marry.'

Sister Harrison's jaw had dropped on hearing about a possible suitor, exactly the scenario she'd envisaged in her mind. She found herself doing as asked, because for all the men she'd known and all the romance novels she'd read, she was still unmarried. And Mr March was a widower and had his own business. They had so much in common. She had high hopes.

'Yes. I would like that.'

A small oil lamp was pulled closer, its flickering light beneath a purple glass shade throwing odd patches of shadow and light.

Ma Skittings readjusted the lamp so that more light was trained on Edith's face than on hers. It wouldn't do to be recognised. How could she convince her of anything if her identity was exposed?

Her beringed fingers passed over the crystal ball. She repeated the process three times.

'You're a woman of passion.' She was just about to call her by name, until reminding herself that they were supposed to be unknown to each other. 'You are a dutiful woman. You have great responsibility, and yet...' She let her words drift as though another message was coming through. The truth was, she was thinking of anything that might enhance Edith's life, give her the comfort that she wasn't yet past marriageable age. 'The future is not always ours to see, and the spirits are sometimes reluctant to open the door to the future. But...' She let the single word hang in the air, like a morsel of cheese in a mousetrap. 'One of the spirits tells me that there is the possibility of romantic involvement with someone close at hand, someone who lives in this town...'

'Stop right there.' Edith leaned forward, her expression a mixture of interest and scepticism. 'Don't tell me it's the blacksmith,' she declared in a no-nonsense fashion. 'If it is Toby Sledge, you can tell that spirit or whatever that I'm not interested.' She got up to go.

'No!' Ma Skittings' response hung in the air, loud and adamant. Toby Sledge was exactly who she'd had in mind, thought it a dead cert coupling. Obviously, Sister Harrison was not of that mind. Another option was needed, some possibility that might have her looking elsewhere. Forget Gerald March. His sister kept an iron grip on the poor man.

Her hands took a few more passes of the crystal ball. Her eyes opened wide as a flicker of light from the lamp shone through the dense glass.

'No. Not the blacksmith. Not a man called Toby Sledge.'

Her interest piqued just in case it was Gerald March, Edith asked, 'Do you see this man in that bauble you have in front of you?'

Ma Skittings did not voice that Sister Edith Harrison had always been demanding. Perhaps that was why no man had stayed with her for long. But she had to maintain the mystery of the fortune teller, even though she was but an amateur.

She cupped the crystal ball in her hands, which made it seem as though the reflection of the lamp was girded by two definite shadows.

One of the dark shadows seemed to move into the middle of the glass ball momentarily smothering the light.

'The spirits are with us,' she said with great aplomb.

Edith leaned closer. 'Is it someone I might know?'

Although she was tempted to come out with a load of old tripe that the chemist was the man for her, Ma Skittings held back. There was little chance of getting Gerald March away from his sister's grim grasp. There was about as much chance of snaring him as riding a unicorn to the moon. Sheer fantasy.

And that's the course she would follow. Fantasy.

'I see a man. A travelling man. Perhaps a sailor?'

Sister Edith was a nurse and therefore trained in facts, not fancies. Or that was the impression she liked to give, and why not? Her inner thoughts and lonely heart were her business, nobody else's.

Disbelief was instantly suspended. She let out a happy sigh. 'Well, that's something.' She got to her feet. 'I think I've had my half-crown's worth. Still, it's all in a good cause, isn't it. Thank you, Mrs Skittings. It was fun.' The stiff expression lapsed into a grin. 'You did a very good job.'

'Did you know it was me from the very start?' Ma Skittings sounded quite dejected. She'd put so much into playing the part.

'Not at first until I recognised the brass earrings. They came with that brass curtain rail I gave you after my mother died. Don't you remember?'

The tent flap fell behind her.

Ma Skittings dropped the piece of chenille tablecloth covering her dropped jaw. Her sigh was deep but not long lasting. She was disappointed that the senior hospital sister had seen through her disguise. But that wasn't the only surprise. There were moving patterns in the crystal ball and was something she'd not been prepared for. Trick of the light, she reckoned. To clarify matters, she took up a duster and gave it a good polish. The patterns remained. A figure evolved at the centre of what she saw there, a weary man tramping through a dark and desolate landscape.

It was not in her to condemn this vision as fanciful. After all, she was the wise woman who kept bees and made medicines from wild herbs. Should she tell Edith?

No. She'd already fled the tent and anyway there was a right time for everything. A time to live and a time to die. A time to believe and a time to... She couldn't think of what else. A time to love? To believe that anything was possible even in the shoulder years of life.

'Leave it to the spirits,' she murmured to herself and gave the crystal ball another good polish before calling for her next customer to come in.

6

Once all the fun of the fair was over, it was back to serious day-to-day business. The district nurse had voiced her concerns about miners' families not getting enough food and plans were swiftly coming together. First, they needed a team of people willing to cook the food, others to serve it out to those in need.

A soup kitchen! Old Walter, the gardener, had put the word around in town that volunteers were needed. The news spread as far as Orchard Manor. Lucy Compton-Dixon, who had been Lucy Daniels before marrying Devlin, her ladyship's son and heir, was one of the first to volunteer, arriving in her ladyship's chauffeur-driven car. She expressed her intention of getting involved.

Frances thanked her, though pointed out that she was as yet unsure of the logistics of her plan. Volunteers had come forward even at this early stage, but where would the soup kitchen be sited? It had to be a place where it would do the most good.

In order to restrict infection, it wasn't a good idea to have malnourished people come to the hospital.

Lucy suggested St Michael's church hall.

Sister Harrison shook her head at that suggestion, claiming, quite rightly, that it was at the wrong end of town for the miners and their families. A long walk.

Frances agreed with her. 'We need to be close to where the needy live.'

Heads were scratched and a few suggestions made, none of which proved suitable.

It was Sister Peebles, their regular district nurse, who came up with a solution. 'Lower Foxford might be suitable. The Methodist church hall, not the church itself. It's got a tin roof and is a bit draughty when the wind blows, but it might suit?'

Frances observed the district nurse's questioning expression. She could have kissed her. 'In the heart of where it's needed.'

Sister Peebles mentioned there being an old washhouse there, complete with a copper, the name given to a deep receptacle used for boiling laundry.

'Mind you, it's not very modern. Not gas heated. There's a little fire bed beneath it. Wood, lots of wood, will be needed. But ideal for boiling up a hearty stew, enough to feed a hundred people if needed.'

Frances beamed. 'I presume we need to approach the Methodist minister to see if we can use it. I believe that would do very well. Does he have a phone? I'll make arrangements straight away.'

Sister Peebles informed her that he did not, but that she would call in on him when she was doing her rounds either this afternoon or tomorrow.

Doctor Roberts, a new addition to the hospital staff, popped his head round the door and announced that the vicar had arrived.

'He went straight into your office,' he said to Frances and sounded a little surprised. Doctor Roberts had a very formal attitude – rather old-fashioned for a young man not yet thirty years of age. Frances's impression was that he would like some kind of waiting room between the outside world and hospital staff. If he had his way, he'd also segregate the staffroom into a section for nurses and one for doctors, but seeing as there was only him, such an idea was not feasible. Of course, he should be entitled to join Frances in her office. She didn't mind that at all. Nursing sisters shared tea and biscuits with her, and she'd assured him that he was welcome to join them.

'And that concludes our meeting,' Frances said, not without amusement.

Sister Harrison and Sister Peebles went off to their duties.

Lucy hung back. The car was waiting outside for her, but she couldn't help look around the staffroom with a nostalgic moistness in her eyes.

'I do miss it you know. I loved it here.'

Frances smiled. Lucy had been a good nurse, but she was married now with a small child and another on the way.

'Of course you do, but you have a new love now. Two in fact, plus...' She looked down at Lucy's growing middle. 'Another to come.'

Frances walked with her to the exit, watched the car drive away. Was that a tinge of envy she was feeling that Lucy had found a man she loved? If so it had come as something of a surprise.

The Reverend Gregory Sampson had lit the small gas ring in the corner. A wisp of steam was already rising from the spout of the little kettle, an item added only recently to save anyone else having to make and serve her tea.

'It may surprise you to know that I'm quite capable of making and serving tea myself,' she exclaimed.

Gregory was standing with his back to her, looking down at the kettle. Even without seeing his face, she detected an air of solemnity in his demeanour.

Oh-oh. He was about to indulge in serious discussion. She thought she knew what it might be about.

When he turned round, he was smiling. She guessed it was a smile swiftly applied once he'd chosen the right words to say. But right for who?

She swallowed any sign of having guessed what this sudden meeting was all about. She'd left early this morning and had not expected to see him until this evening.

But here he was.

'Tea?'

'Please.'

Looking preoccupied with what was waiting for her on the desk rather than him, she made herself comfortable in the oak swivel chair behind her desk.

The tea was set in front of her.

Gregory stood before her, the desk between them The way he was fixing her with those intensely blue eyes filled her with apprehension. He was going to say something seriously personal. She could feel it in her bones. She fiddled with paperwork that only needed filing, not the close attention she was pretending to give it.

'I think it's time,' he said.

She wasn't so churlish as to ask him what he meant. He wasn't a child. Neither was she.

Taking a deep breath, her hands left the paperwork. Folding them in front of her, she looked up at him.

'You've avoided deciding for long enough. I know you've been engrossed in your work, but we have to give some time to us – to each other – to our future.'

Her calm grey eyes fixed on his blue ones. She didn't need to ask him what he meant. She knew he was referring to their very long and rather casual engagement.

'This wasn't just about my work. It's yours too. We both follow a vocation.'

'Yes. And sometimes it's like a treadmill that doesn't stop turning. We're neither of us getting any younger.' He took a breath. 'I'd like children.'

'Ah!' Frances looked down at her hands. She wasn't beyond the age of having children, and her hands were smooth, the flesh firm. Still, he had a point. The problem was, did she want the same as he did? It was a difficult question, with a number of answers.

She thought it through, then nodded. 'Yes. I understand your concern.' Her eyes opened wide. 'I'm not getting any younger.'

'Sorry. It shouldn't have come out like that.'

She smiled, her eyelids fluttering. 'It wasn't very flattering, but let's face it…' Did he flinch when she looked at him? It did seem so. 'This is the year when I must make my mind up. And I will, Gregory. I promise I will.'

Their sojourn together was interrupted by Sister Harrison. 'Sorry, Vicar.' She turned to Frances. 'It's time for your ward round, Doctor.'

'I'll come now.'

Gregory's eyes followed her out of the door. If Sister Harrison hadn't been there, she would have kissed his cheek. It was something of a relief that she didn't have to.

As they made their way to the wards, a thought came to Frances's mind that immediately transformed into words.

'Sometimes I wish I could see into the future,' she said somewhat pensively. 'It would make my life – anyone's life – so much easier, don't you think?'

'Poppycock!' exclaimed Sister Harrison. 'I was told by Ma Skittings – when she was doing her fortune telling – that I would meet a tall, dark stranger.'

'And you haven't?' Frances maintained a serious expression.

'No one has blown into my life who wasn't there already.' Her sigh was heavy with feeling. 'And none of them are tall and dark!'

* * *

The Reverend Gregory Sampson was of a pragmatic disposition but, because of his profession, did believe in the power of prayer. This year, he sincerely prayed that he would marry Frances and they would become a family. He had no objection to her continuing her profession. By virtue of their individual vocations, he believed their lives dovetailed pretty well. They'd travelled a long way; some progress had been made. Now it was just a case of pushing her over the finish line.

Deciding to confront her had disturbed his sleep, but he'd determined that the subject must be faced. He'd faced it, mentioned it, but still it seemed they were no further along the line.

And for the rest of the day?

He felt unsettled, decided he needed some fresh air and some thinking time. A bicycle ride and a walk along the canal, perhaps as far as Lower Foxford. Perhaps even a pint in the Jolly Boatman.

He had a plan. The day awaited.

7

As was his usual habit, Harry Hunter was sitting on the roof of *Talbot*, his narrowboat, which had the same name as his dog. Keep things simple. That was Harry's motto. Live simply.

Grassy banks dipped into the water. Tall reeds and forests of bullrushes hid shy moorhens. Green and blue iridescence flashed from the wings of a kingfisher.

On the first night there, he had leaned on the five-bar gate, ivy and other wild climbers entwined around its rotting wood.

A row of cottages some way back clustered at the bottom of the lane that wound upwards to the main road. In the past, those cottages had been inhabited by boatmen who had plied their trade along the canal and across to the river back towards the town. Two up and two down, these hard-working men and their wives had raised a litter of children, some who'd lived beyond their second birthday and some who had not.

The remaining inhabitants whose work had depended on the canal were the lockkeepers. Like the boatmen, they had been the last breath of a dying era. The old boatmen had been on a par with the smoke evidencing the whereabouts of a gypsy encampment, another lifestyle that was slowly disappearing.

Dark, dank places where only poor people lived, those at rock bottom, poor people, downtrodden people. This was where he had lived with his mother, and much as the memory pained him, he had to walk along there, look at those cottages, pick out the one that had been home. Though warm and cosy, home it had never been. There had been only violence in that cottage when it should have been a refuge. The family who lived up at Orchard Manor House were responsible for that.

It didn't matter that the old man – his lordship – had left him a piece of land. He'd seethed for years about the attempt to make up for what had happened. His mother had been promised safety in the marriage arranged for her. The husband chosen had been more interested in the monetary allowance that had come with her.

All his memories brought him was pain. A piece of land left in a dead man's will could not make up for the death of his mother by a violent hand.

He was alone except for his dog and his violin and the murmurs of injured wildfowl or small animals abandoned on the riverbank. It was amazing how many he'd rescued in the space of three days. Most of them were found by his dog and hospitalised in cardboard boxes that had once held packets of soap powder or tins of Brasso.

Mid-morning, a mug of tea flavoured with condensed milk, the dog at his side, he returned to the roof of the boat and reached for his violin. The notes rose plaintively on the air, mixing with the soughing of reeds and the rippling of water.

Even when he saw the tall figure approaching, he did not cease playing. Not until he was standing before him, looking as though he would not shift until exchanging a few words.

He recognised the vicar but still kept playing. Let him speak first.

'You live here alone?'

'It's just me and Talbot the dog and *Talbot* the boat.'

'They're both named Talbot. Isn't that a bit confusing?'

'Not to me. I like to keep things simple.' Gregory took in the details of the waterside mooring, the willows tearfully dipping the tips of their branches into the water, the total silence except for the quacking of mallards, the disturbance of water as a water rat slid into it.

He remarked that it must be a lonely life.

Laying down his violin and reminding himself that he'd adopted the name Ben, Harry Hunter made a so-so movement with his head. 'I sometimes have visitors.'

'Do you indeed.'

'Yes.'

'Interesting visitors? Welcome visitors?'

In response, Harry went on to talk about the injured animals and birds he took on board.

'Animals make me smile and fill me with warm feelings. I can't say the same for humans. They're not friendly towards men who look like me... who live like me.'

His voice dropped as his inner thoughts darkened his eyes.

Gregory could well imagine that his long hair and beard singled him out as different.

As though reading his thoughts, Harry recounted how boys on bridges shouted names and threw stones at him.

'I turn the other cheek.' He grinned at Gregory as he said it. 'Just as the likes of you say we should do.' He shrugged. 'It matters not. I make no attempt to stop and give chase. A few more chugs of the faithful engine and I'm miles further on, beyond the towns, beyond the stones and insults, in secret places where the wild thyme grows and moorhens build their nests.'

Gregory asked why the name Talbot was so important.

'I found the name in a book. Talbot was a Norman breed of war dog.' He fondled between the dog's ears. 'A war dog. Just like me. Just like us,' he added, raising eyes full of meaning to Gregory. 'This dog's even got grey hairs like me,' he finished laughingly.

There was an Irish lilt to the deep voice, just a gentle smidgen adding a sing-song element so that his speech was almost poetic.

'We both do,' Gregory remarked laughingly. 'Don't tell me that your name's Talbot as well?'

Sunlight caught the red amongst the grey as the man shook his head.

'Ben Tyler.'

'Reverend Gregory Sampson. Pleased to meet you.'

Ben nodded but did not offer to shake hands.

Gregory merely smiled.

His eyes raked the man who sat so still and staring. He definitely had the look of an ex-military man. A good physique coupled with a haunted look in his eyes.

Should he mention the war?

It was always a difficult decision. Mentioning too much of the past might provoke an unwelcome reaction in this man who had once been a warrior? He wouldn't be the first Gregory had come across who shunned mixing with his fellow man.

He was unprepared for what happened next.

Laying his fiddle to one side, the man he knew as Ben picked up the tin mug containing his hot drink and pointed his finger. 'Come aboard.'

'That's very kind of you. I've never been aboard one of these barges.'

'Boat. It's not a barge. It's a narrowboat.'

'Thank you. I feel honoured.'

'You should do. There's few I honour with an invitation.'

Gregory let his gaze travel all along the side of the boat, seeking the best way to board. He'd never been keen on boats but wasn't about to admit it.

'Don't be slow making up your mind or I might change mine. Come aboard. I might be able to find you another mug.'

Springing deftly up from the towpath, Gregory cocked his leg over the side and into the cockpit, which was barely big enough for Ben's bulk, let alone two men.

There was a three-step ladder down into the cabin. The richness of polished wood gave it a warm feel. At one end was a curtained single bed clinging tight against the far wall. A tiny table was folded against the right-hand wall beneath a tier of narrow shelving. Two tin cups hung from hooks. Two plates behind them tilted on edge.

To the left was the smallest coal-fired range Gregory had ever seen, a kettle hanging from a hook above it, a saucepan sitting on a cast iron hob.

'You have it very comfortable here.'

He was handed a brew of dark tea whether he wanted it or not. To Gregory's relief, it went from treacle-coloured to toffee when a dash of condensed milk was added. It didn't taste too bad once that was done.

The space was small, a cabin barely eight feet by eight. He perched on the narrow bench, the only seating area.

After a sip, he said, 'Have you travelled far?'

'All over.'

'It seems something of a precarious existence.'

'My needs are small. Fuel for the boat. Food for the dog and me. I tie up anywhere I please.'

'You haven't told me exactly why you're here.'

Deep-set eyes became hooded as he contemplated his answer.

'I received a letter from a firm of London solicitors. Years ago now, just after the war. Harry Hunter had inherited a plot of land. Like many others at the front, we made our wills. Harry left me that piece of land. Not that I cared much when I found out. The past and his death were too raw. I put it to one side, telling myself I would act on it someday, and anyway, what did I want with a piece of land?' That dismissive shrug again accompanied by a shaking of his head.

Gregory had no reason for disbelief; he was used to people unloading their experiences on him, relating what had happened to them. But he wasn't sure about this man. He asked, 'So why now?'

Work-worn hands spread in an inconsequential manner, as though it didn't matter a jot. 'I'd been everywhere else. Thought I might as well claim the land and put it to good use.'

'And what would that be?'

A big draught of air expanded the broad chest. 'That field over there.' He jerked his head. 'I've a mind to set up an animal sanctuary.'

'Do you have experience with animals?'

'I looked after the horses and mules – back then. Sometimes all I had to put them out of their misery was a bullet. They hadn't joined up voluntarily. They'd had no choice. They were the real innocents in that war.'

Gregory felt an involuntary shudder at a recollection of dead animals amongst those of dead soldiers. 'I can only imagine.'

'I'm haunted by what I saw.'

'We all are,' said Gregory. He paused. He'd winkled out some information that would allow him to evaluate this man, but there must be more. He sensed a cast-iron barrier that was as yet unbroken. Time had not yet healed this man. 'Would you like to tell me more? It might help.'

He waited, unsure whether the time was right for talking things through.

Harry nodded thoughtfully, his rough hands tightening around the mug of dark brown tea. 'The horses were stabled in a barn. A shell – more than one – fell on that barn. What remained of the rotten roof timbers caught fire. The horses were screaming. We went back in. Tried to get them out.' He slapped his hands over his ears and shook his head. 'For years after I was still hearing those screams. My mate never came out.'

Gregory frowned. 'Your friend, Harry.'

Harry nodded and felt no guilt in lying. Pretending to be Ben Tyler was like a shield against the peacetime England, an antidote to his inner pain.

Ben's name and that of Harry Hunter meant little to Gregory. There were so many men in those trenches, faces and names that had not in the context of being closely acquainted. He didn't think he'd ever met either of them. Imagination working overtime, he saw in his head a lone figure silhouetted against the burning building. It wasn't that difficult to visualise. He'd seen plenty.

'I had to bring him home,' he said suddenly as though reading Gregory's thoughts. 'I couldn't leave him there in bits. I used to be based with the army in India. I saw the reverence they placed on the dead before they distributed their ashes into the Ganges, the sacred river.'

Gregory patted his shoulder reassuringly. 'You did what you thought was right.'

'I thought you being a vicar would disapprove.'

'Not at all. Cremation is becoming more popular. Even bishops are opting to be cremated.' Gregory tried to put what had happened into context – not viewed as it was now, but as it had been back then. 'We all did what we had to do.'

'Even putting your mate's ashes into a biscuit tin?'

The black humour was obvious. Gregory could not condemn.

'What will you do with his remains?'

Gregory waited for the answer, fully expecting that he would be asked for space in St Michael's churchyard.

There was a bitter twist to his mouth that made Gregory shudder. 'I promised Harry I would follow his wishes. It's only right that he should be buried in the family mausoleum.'

Gregory's eyebrows rose. 'Family?'

'The Compton-Dixon crypt. Harry was a bastard, but he was still part of the family. That's why the land was left to him. An attempt to placate the family conscience.'

Gregory's eyes narrowed. There was just something here that wasn't quite gelling. He took most people at face value. In this instance, he wasn't quite so sure. In order to be convinced, he kept the conversation going.

'I know something of Harry's history. There were rumours.'

'The illegitimate son of the lord of the manor.' The sarcasm was self-evident. He went on, 'The black sheep of the family, not by his deeds, but because he was born on the wrong side of the blanket.'

'Yesss...' He said it slowly, thoughtfully. Was it his imagination or was this man avoiding looking at him?

'I would have to get her ladyship's consent to open the crypt and inter Harry's remains there.'

A slow smile stretched the profuse hair growth. It was difficult to see the emotion that might be behind it.

'That seems to me a very odd thing to do.'

'It's a matter of honour.'

Gregory wasn't sure about that. 'She'll be shocked. She is getting on in years.'

'It has to be done.' His voice was sharp and to Gregory's ears seemed angry with untapped bitterness. 'Nevertheless, I will be visiting her.'

Gregory nodded. The mug was taken from his hands, a sure sign of dismissal. The treacle-coloured tea no more than residue at the bottom.

In a flurry of dark coat that reached to his knees, his companion took the lead back up the narrow ladder and onto the roof of the boat.

'That's the field,' he said, pointing to the mangled gate and abundance of wild climbers. 'Not much of a place and something of a challenge.'

'You'll be staying on then.'

He stared at the gate for a while before saying, 'I think I might. All being well. Do you think her ladyship will object?'

There was a certain malice in the way the question was asked.

Most people in Norton Dene knew of her late husband's philandering.

'I've always found her ladyship to be both pragmatic and generous.'

'She'll let bygones be bygones?'

'You should meet her yourself. I can made the preliminary move, but ultimately it should be you.'

'She'll object. I know she'll object.'

Gregory found his outburst quite extraordinary. It made his mind up about this man and his plans. The details of his story just didn't sit well. 'I don't believe a single word you say. If I was a Catholic priest, I'd be taking your confession.'

There was no joviality to the way he phrased and said it.

At his words, the man turned abruptly. 'I know you're not Catholic. All the same, if I swore you to secrecy, you would take the oath and keep it to yourself.'

Gregory flinched. He thought he knew where this was going.

'Harry Hunter was born out of wedlock, but his father took care of the woman he had seduced. Married her off to a man who welcomed the allowance she was given. Not so much her and certainly not me. He killed her that man. Made her life a misery.' His voice hardened. 'I want to needle that family. See if they can be as charitable as some think they are.'

Gregory stared as he took in what was being said, the secret he was being entrusted with. 'Your name's not Ben Tyler. It's Harry Hunter. Is that what you're telling me?'

There was a coolness in those eyes when they met his. It was hard to discern if he was smiling. All Gregory knew was that he'd been entrusted with a secret he did not want to know about.

'Are you so sure that I won't divulge who you really are?'

'You're an honourable man. I know you won't.'

He was right, of course. Behind him, the man he now knew was Harry Hunter stood like a colossus on the cabin roof, his hair billowing out, his eyes staring in the direction of the piece of land for which he had a dream.

As he pedalled back to the vicarage, Gregory wondered at her ladyship's reaction when Harry turned up on her doorstep bearing the tin biscuit box containing all that remained of his friend, passing him off as her husband's bastard son. It was all very confusing and an odd way to take revenge. But there, the war. Blame the war!

8

As expected, the soup kitchen set up at the Methodist church hall was well attended. The faces of scruffy children lit up the moment they smelled the rich stew that had been cooked in the galvanised boiler intended to wash laundry.

There were also older men, those not yet back down the mines and others retired and barely able to make ends meet on their frugal pension or unemployment payout.

Most of them looked down-at-heel, the women drained of energy, the men no longer capable of doing a hard day's work.

Heads were soon bent over bowls of hot food. Spoons dipped swiftly into the rich stew of beef, carrots, potatoes and parsnips. Loaves of bread had been donated by the bakers' shops in town. Tea by the grocer and milk direct from a churn supplied by a farmer on the edge of town.

Sister Edith Harrison and Sister Gwen Peebles were overseeing the volunteers.

'Some of these could do with a good wash,' Sister Harrison remarked.

'Only after a good feed, eh?' added Sister Peebles with a merry laugh.

Her relationship with Sister Harrison was easy-going, mainly because she took everything her colleague said with a pinch of salt. She might have a crabbed exterior at times, but Gwen Peebles was convinced there was a heart of gold beneath the surface. It did occur to her that she might have made a good wife if the right man had come along.

'What are you reading at the moment?' she asked during a lull in hungry people coming through the door. She knew Sister Harrison was a keen romance reader.

'*Honoria and the Pirate*. She gets kidnapped by a pirate who looks a bit like Blackbeard, all straggly black hair, broad shoulders and a merry twinkle in his eye.'

'A bit like him?'

Sister Harrison followed the direction of her compatriot's curt nod. The man was tall enough and broad enough to fill the space in the doorway. As for his hair... Her jaw dropped. 'My word.'

'Quite a sight, don't you think?'

A tall, dark stranger. Just like the one Ma Skittings had claimed to see in the crystal ball.

Sister Harrison was so taken aback, that the ladle she'd been holding slipped from her grasp and landed in the stew.

'Lovely, are you all right?' Sister Peebles was immediately concerned.

'I'm fine.'

'You've gone quite pale.'

'I'm fine,' Sister Harrison returned, more firmly this time.

She was far from that. Especially when she saw that he was heading in her direction.

'Excuse me,' he said, bowing his head apologetically.

'Do you want some stew?' asked Sister Peebles.

He shook his head. 'No. I'm just enquiring whether I'm going the right way for Orchard Manor House.'

Just as Sister Peebles prepared to give him directions, Sister Harrison jumped in.

'I'll come outside with you and point you in the right direction. Then you'll be sure.'

Sister Peebles looked from her superior to the big man with the hair of a lion. Had she missed something?

'That's a good smell coming from this place. I smelled it outside and thought I might get good directions here.'

She fancied he was looking at her a little strangely as she brushed a few breadcrumbs from her ultra white cuffs and straightened her collar.

It was difficult to look him in the eyes unless she looked up at him.

'Now,' Edith said in her most superior voice, which was as crisp as her uniform. 'If you follow this road…'

He listened to her intensely, so intensely that she began to wither beneath his gaze.

'Is something wrong?' she asked.

He stared before shaking his head. 'You're very clean.' He tossed his head and laughed. 'But then nurses always are.'

He went off whistling, a black and white dog loping at heel.

Gwen Peebles joined her at the door, looking to where she was looking.

'That's the man who lives on a boat down at Lower Foxford. He's very big. Lovely head of hair. Wish mine was as glossy as that.'

Sister Harrison didn't respond, just made a small grunt of acknowledgement. Never mind Mr March the chemist. Never mind Toby Sledge – not that he'd been in with a chance anyway. Daft as it might seem, she was sure she'd found her tall dark stranger. And she wanted to meet him again.

* * *

Doctor Brakespeare was packing up for the evening, relieved to be leaving the hospital and putting her feet up. In case of emergency, Doctor Roberts was on call.

She clipped her bag medicine bag shut and fastened the buckle, rubbing it nervously as she thought about what lay ahead.

Gregory would have supper cooking in the oven, a bottle of wine uncorked and a look in his eyes that would set the tone for the evening. She thought of that look as she headed out of the door.

'Have a good evening, Doctor.'

'Thank you.'

The car started first time. Frances took a deep breath as she contemplated what lay ahead.

Gregory was becoming more adamant regarding the subject matter they'd touched on but not concluded. The matter of marriage.

She questioned her attitude, why she couldn't quite commit herself when other women would jump at the chance.

Never mind what other people want, she said to herself as she pulled up outside the coach house. *What is it you want?*

* * *

The evening was much as Frances had expected it to be. She picked at the pie with her fork, making little clearings in the gravy, whilst Gregory gently laid out the advantages of them 'plighting their troth', as he put it.

Finally, the decision made, they stood outside at the top of the steps leading to the front door. The silver moon of late May peeped from between ragged strips of misty cloud.

Neither moved, standing rigidly some distance apart.

Gregory turned to face her. 'It's done.'

She remained looking straight ahead, taking in the black outline of the trees surrounding the vicarage garden. After short contemplation, she said, 'Yes. For better or worse. But...'

'I know.' He smiled. His face was silvered by moonlight. The light from the hallway behind him was like a halo. 'We keep it to ourselves for now. Just in case someone wants to convince us that marriage isn't all it's cracked up to be.'

It was hard not to respond to his humour. Laughter erupting from her throat, she slapped at his shoulder. 'Gregory Sampson, you're a rogue!'

'But a loveable one,' he said, taking her into his arms. 'And that's the way I intend to stay.'

9

Sister Peebles tried to ignore her aching hip, a short sharp injury from two days ago when she'd fallen off her bicycle.

Sister Harrison noticed and asked if she'd like two aspirin.

'I've already taken two. Whether I'll be able to ride that bicycle tomorrow is another matter.'

Gwen enjoyed going out and about in the town and the surrounding villages. A bicycle was a necessity. Who'd ever heard of a district nurse without a trusty bicycle?

The baby and family planning clinic was going full throttle. Babies were crying, mothers were gossiping. There were also some who were only here for the tea and biscuits. That was the way it was hereabouts, so she turned a blind eye to those without babies or in need of family planning advice.

Mrs Newman, who she knew from visiting in Fisherman's Row cottages, was a case in point. Claiming to be widowed, it was rumoured that she was living in sin with a man nobody had a good word for. She lived in one of the damp, cottages with her son, Tommy.

She was far from the only one to have hooked up with a violent man.

'Hello, Mrs Newman. How are you today?' It was hard not to make her welcoming smile turn into a grimace, but that was what Gwen firmly believed was for the best. A little something to make this woman feel that life might be worth living after all.

June Newman, her lip slightly swollen and a yellow stain beneath one eye, responded that she was fine.

It would not do to respond that she didn't look fine.

'What beautiful hair you have.'

A little reassurance went a long way in Gwen's estimation.

Mrs Newman looked surprised at the unexpected flattery but thanked her anyway.

District Nurse Gwen Peebles kept her fixed smile. Besides the swollen lip and leftover bruising beneath her eye, the bald patches advertised the fact that she'd been in a fight and there had only been one winner. Gwen knew an abused wife when she saw one.

'Is there anything I can do for you?'

The woman shook her head and gulped back the hot tea and biscuits. 'I must go. I've a bus to catch.' She laid aside the empty teacup and got to her feet, eyes downcast, unwilling to meet those of the district nurse.

Gwen knew she was lying. Judging by the shabby dress and worn shoes, she didn't look as though she had two pennies to scratch together – not even enough for a bus fare.

'Do you have enough for the bus fare. I've got a few spare coppers in my purse that's going begging...'

'No need. I've got some.'

'Perhaps another time,' Gwen called brightly after her.

June Newman did not look round.

Around eleven o'clock, when it was time for the staff to have a cup of tea, Sister Edith Harrison asked if she could have a word with Gwen in the staffroom.

'Oh. Yes.' What had she done wrong? That was the first thing that came to her.

In her mind, she went through everything she'd done that morning. Had she made any dreadful mistake?

She winced before taking a seat in the staffroom. Her hip was still hurting.

It was nigh on impossible to read Sister Harrison's expression.

First, she received a kindly smile. After that, she was handed a cup of tea and an invitation to choose a biscuit from Sister Harrison's private supply, which was totally unexpected. Bourbons and custard creams were not handed around indiscriminately. Loving anything chocolaty, she took a bourbon.

Settled comfortably, Gwen thanked her for the biscuit.

'Bourbons are my favourite,' she added.

Sister Harrison asked her how things had gone that morning.

Sister Peebles assured her that everything had gone well whilst also mentioning the woman who only came for tea. She frowned as a second thought came to her. 'I think she tucked a few biscuits into her pocket before leaving. More than a few, in fact. I don't think she even had enough for the bus fare home to Lower Foxford. I did offer her the fare, but she wouldn't take it. Dashed off without a backward glance.'

Sister Harrison's eyebrows rose. 'I take it she was also at the soup kitchen.'

Sister Peebles nodded. 'I do believe she was.' She laughed as a thought came to her. 'I think it's becoming something of an event. Our fame is spreading.'

'It doesn't surprise me. The minister must have been surprised too. There were more people there than attend his church.'

'Even a man who was asking for directions,' Sister Peebles reminded her. 'The tall dark stranger,' she added with a laugh.

Sister Harrison flinched. Gwen wasn't to know that she'd heard the same words uttered over a crystal ball. She placed her cup firmly into its saucer. Not willing to continue discussing him, she turned the conversation in another direction.

'And how's your hip, Sister Peebles? I saw you rubbing it.'

'It aches.' Gwen Peebles frowned. 'If it doesn't get better overnight, I'm going to be in agony riding that bicycle tomorrow.'

Sister Harrison offered her another biscuit, which she gladly accepted. It was the last bourbon, which she knew were also Sister Harrison's favourites.

She accepted but couldn't help thinking that something was afoot. Sister Harrison did nothing without a reason.

A sip, a smile and, 'I was thinking that you might manage the baby clinic tomorrow – by way of a change – and I'll take over your beat in Lower Foxford. Let me have your list. It'll make a nice change for both of us.'

Gwen grimaced and rubbed at her hip, wincing as she leaned forward to place the cup and saucer onto the table. 'I think that would be a very sensible arrangement.' Glad of a break from cycling, Gwen pressed her advantage and went on to elaborate one of her most upsetting cases.

'The woman I mentioned, Mrs June Newman, is one of my patients. Her son is about eight years old and is called Tommy. He's got a bad chest. That's usually why I call in on her. Can't remember the husband's name, but then, he wasn't there that often – if there was one,' she added. A knowing look was exchanged between them. 'She's the one with the bruises. There is a man, I think, but not her husband.'

'I assume I can borrow your bicycle?'

Welcoming a break from pedalling the two miles or so to Lower Foxford, Gwen said that she could.

'It's said that cycling is good exercise, but not when your hip starts playing up.'

Unwilling to look a gift horse in the mouth, Gwen Peebles finished her tea. Her aching hip seemed to respond to the news, not aching so much as she made her way back to the clinic. She tried to recall the last time Sister Harrison had left the hospital to do anything else. Only emergencies, she thought. This, she decided, was a one-off. Whatever the true reason was, she couldn't believe it had anything to do with her hip. But never mind. Sister Harrison was in charge. If she wanted a change, then who was she to argue?

10

Harry Hunter had no doubt whatsoever that the vicar would not betray him. Priests, vicars. There was little difference.

One thing he knew for sure was that there would be no good or bad time to descend on Lady Araminta Compton-Dixon and tweak her pompous nose. That's how he regarded her, a snobbish, spoilt woman, not at all like his sainted mother. Rather than dive right in and introduce himself, he wanted to irritate her. That's what he told himself, though could not – would not admit – that he was slightly afraid of finally confronting his origins and those he was related to. In a strange way, he felt that he owed it to his mother. In retrospect, it was her revenge, not his.

He finished drip-feeding milk from a rubber-ended eyedrop dispenser into the gaping mouth of a baby squirrel. The whole process was soothing. He felt as though he was doing something worthwhile. The most worthwhile things he'd ever done in his life were with regard to animals.

When least expected, his conscience whispered that his dream of setting up an animal sanctuary wouldn't be possible if his dead sire had not bequeathed him a piece of land.

The solicitor's letter, soiled and faded from age and long periods of being folded and kept in a trouser pocket, had been quite explicit.

> Lord Compton-Dixon, who fully acknowledges you as his son, has left you a piece of land close to the canal.
>
> Although it is overgrown and not what one would regard as prime pasture, he considers that if you are anything like the young man he once was, you will turn it to worthwhile purpose.
>
> Thus, I enclose a plan of the field which is the subject of that inheritance.
>
> Please give notice of safe receipt of this missive.

He had been swift to send back a short telegram confirming receipt. The firm of solicitors had written back to thank him and to advise that his lordship had died in the space of return of post.

He wondered how he had died. One part of him wanted his death to have been painful, but seeing as he'd never known him, only as a name that had some influence on his past, what should it matter?

After that, he'd done nothing. He still had the letter and the plan. But his heart had been feeling an intense emptiness at the time he'd received it, his mind in turmoil following his wartime experiences. Some days he was still there. Some nights too.

Even his own history had been smothered by the craziness that had lingered in his mind. And there was nobody he could run to and unload his feelings. His mother had died before he was twelve years old.

Perhaps he had inherited an air of authority from the father he had never known, but whatever it was, raw recruits had looked to him for guidance. He'd done his best with all the young lads, only slightly younger than him. A close friendship had developed between him and Ben Tyler, the persona he was now impersonating. They'd laughed together and sang and danced to the creaky note of the old fiddle left to him by his grandfather. His best friend had had the voice of an angel, clear fresh notes that still echoed in his head.

In the cold, terror-filled hours of night, they'd discussed the war; what they were doing there, what was the tinderbox that had erupted into a conflagration that was devouring men's lives like a threshing machine devours sheaves of corn.

In his dreams, he and Ben were talking, laughing, betting which of them would survive the next day.

Keep your head down! That was what they all said was the secret. But there were limits.

At one point he thought he would never find peace ever again, yet here he was. The canal was peaceful. He knew he slept surprisingly well compared to some, but it had taken time to get to this happy occasion.

Despite it being the merry month of May, smoke curled from a few chimneys, but they were far enough distant not to notice the smoke that curled from his own.

A footbridge meandered over the top of the weir to the fields on the other side. At the far end of the field, a railway embankment reared steeply from blankets of corn and wheat, their budding heads currently green but in August would be golden. Corn and wheat closest to the embankment curved like waves on the sea as a train rumbled past, slowing where the line bent to cross the railway bridge some way in the distance.

He took a short walk in order to gather his thoughts, kicking at the loose stones of the towpath, throwing a stick for his dog.

He was on his way back when he saw a man in a bowler hat knocking on the side of the hull of the boat. He was using the point of his umbrella on the fresh paintwork. That act alone annoyed him.

'Are you wanting something?' There was no note of welcome in his voice.

An alarmed expression came and went from the pale face beneath the stiff bowler hat.

'Mr Hunter?' An authoritative tone of a man who had perfected the art of talking down to lesser men.

A quick clutching of fingers into his palm betrayed the man's reluctance to shake hands.

He grunted a wary response and nodded curtly.

The man hooked the handle of his umbrella over his arm. His spectacles were round. His shirt collar was of the stiff old-fashioned sort and looked tight enough to choke him.

'My name is Archibald Weaver of Weaver, Grimes and Porter.'

He did not recognise the name. It certainly wasn't the one on the letter he'd received.

He gave no care to politeness. 'So?'

Seemingly unperturbed, Mr Weaver cleared his throat. He did not look a well man. His complexion was pasty, and his flesh seemed to barely hang onto his bones. 'I understand you have been bequeathed a piece of land. That one in fact.' He jerked his pointed chin in the direction of a marshy field. It was empty except for scrubby vegetation and a tumbledown shack in one corner.

Harry stopped himself from asking how he knew that. Solicitors could be like old ladies – chatting and sharing information within their uptight brotherhood. No matter how much the higher strata of society might prefer to keep their business private, it was also the case that there were few secrets in a small town. Servants and employees of every ilk were likely to know.

He observed Mr Weaver's shiny brogues and found himself wondering if he'd learned how to do that in the army. Perhaps not. Perhaps he'd been an officer and had a member of the lower ranks to clean his shoes. Perhaps his wife did it now.

'Yes.'

A lofty toss of the head. Mr Weaver continued. 'You do not have the looks of a settled man, Mr Hunter, not really the sort for being confined to a piece of land, no matter where it comes from.' He sounded smugly confident that he was right.

Without saying a word, Harry kept his eyes trained on Mr Weaver, leaving him to carry on with whatever he wanted to say.

Perturbed by the intense look for only a moment, Mr Weaver recovered and held his head high like a pointer that's just espied a partridge about to take flight.

'I take it you're a man of few words and look to be something of a wanderer, in which case I will take it as read that you are not really that interested in the property. If this is the case, I can tell you here and now that there is an interested party willing to give you a good price for the land. All you have to do once you have accepted your inheritance is accept a handsome sum from my client for the freehold. I will do the rest.'

'You seem to know a lot about it. Who is this person?' He skewered the man with a piercing look.

Mr Weaver shook his head. 'I cannot possibly divulge—'

A sudden thought caused Harry to interrupt. 'Are you also working for her ladyship – as an agent of the London firm of solicitors?'

He knew he'd hit the nail on the head when a deep flush coloured Mr Weaver's pasty face.

To his credit, he recovered quickly. 'I don't exactly work for her legal advisors, but I do act in her best interests.'

'Does she know you're playing a double game?'

His sheepishness was swiftly discarded as he shook his head. 'You own the land now. It's long gone as far as she's concerned.'

Harry had always been a good judge of men. He'd had to be. Here before him was a man he wouldn't trust. 'And this other party – what do they intend doing with the land?'

'Just look at it.' He extended his umbrella, stabbing its point in the general direction of the field and the tumbledown dwelling place. 'It's inclined to flood so obviously not fit for grazing. You do know that, don't you? It's quite worthless as a piece of land, not that it would matter to a traveller like yourself. There are those who could tend it properly – drain it perhaps. Build something on it.'

'How much do you want to give me?'

Weaver looked taken aback. 'You misunderstand. It's not I who will be paying you. I am merely acting on behalf...'

'Of a man keen to turn a profit on a plot of waterlogged ground. Just goes to show it's not beyond redemption.'

A plumy pinkness suffused Mr Weaver's cheeks. He read annoyance as well as embarrassment that this vagabond of a man had sussed him out.

He was quite right.

'You've said enough.'

Weaver licked his lips, his eyelids half closed as though veiling a secret. 'I urge you to consider this matter most seriously. The land has no value, but the interested party is willing to pay a fair market value. Serious money.'

'But you've just said that it's worthless or are you not aware that you're repeating and contradicting yourself?'

'I'm quite willing to walk it with you, explain its shortcomings, the area of alluvial mud deposited on the bank by flooding on a regular basis. I can also point out the boundary lines.'

'No need.'

'Still, you might be interested in taking a closer look. Not everyone is capable of reading plans – and I do have a set of plans with me.' The soft flesh of his face stiffened with the smug superiority of a man who knows more than most – though not for long.

'I was trained in orienteering. The army relied on me not getting them lost.' The horses too, he thought, but kept their trust in his heart.

'Oh. Indeed.' Sensing he might have overstressed remuneration for the land, Weaver changed tack onto a more personal level. 'Have you met her ladyship before?'

Harry shook his head. 'No.'

The colourless eyes looked him up and down. 'Perhaps you should think of having a shave and a haircut before doing so.' His tone was contemptuous.

Harry's expression hardened. 'I am who I am. My personal habits and appearance are none of your business.'

'All the same…'

'All the same,' he said through gritted teeth.

Wincing beneath the wild-looking man's fierce gaze, Mr Weaver tucked his umbrella beneath his arm and, with an air of finality, tapped the brim of his bowler hat.

'I would appreciate you keeping our meeting a secret. After all, it's early days. The possibility of our doing business in future is just that, a possibility. I wouldn't want anyone getting the wrong end of the stick.'

'Why?'

'Well. They might misconstrue my intentions; think that I am taking advantage of the situation.'

'Isn't that exactly what you're doing?'

Weaver breathed an impatient breath, unclipped his briefcase, rummaged around and brought out a business card. 'Just in case we can do business. In case you wish to sell the lot.'

Harry made no move to take the card. 'The lot?'

'Yes. The land. It's sometimes referred to as a lot, especially in auction catalogues.' He sounded as though he were speaking to a child or a fool. 'In this case, it is your lot. For the moment at least until you've come to a decision.'

He awaited a response.

'Well? Can I give you my card in case you decide to sell? Will you contact me in due course?'

Strands of dark hair momentarily shrouded Harry's eyes, drifting across his face like particularly long seaweed.

He took the card and sent it flying. It landed in the water.

'No.'

It was as if his voice had come from the bottom of the sea. Archibald Weaver felt an involuntary shiver run between his shoulder blades. Was there any chance of this man conforming to standard procedure of negotiation? Could he be bought, or, more specifically, could the land be bought?

* * *

'The man is obtuse.'

That's what he relayed to Clifford Fletcher, owner of the Jolly Boatman, the terrace of run-down cottages and the handsome boathouse where he lived with his wife.

Weaver was presently sitting with Clifford in the boathouse. Set apart from the Jolly Boatman, the boathouse was a handsome building that had once belonged to Lord Compton-Dixon and his family. Ownership had been negotiated and settled once the old lord had died. A deathbed purchase. Clifford had visited the sick man pretending sympathy. His true mission had been to purchase the boathouse, which he had done.

Clifford clenched the tumbler of whisky more tightly as he frowned into its amber hued depths. 'Obtuse? If you mean you failed to persuade him, bloody well say so, why don't you!'

Archibald Weaver restrained from blanching and protested that wasn't his exact meaning. 'I was inferring that he might be a bit stupid and unable to understand how much money he would be given if he sells to you.'

'If you meant stupid, why didn't you say stupid?'

Archibald kept up the pretence of being nothing but a minor pawn in Clifford's plans. Inside, he felt superior. Clifford Fletcher had made a packet flogging off lorries used in war for peaceful purposes – like hauling coal and other goods. On their return from war, enterprising men snapped them up and Clifford had duly obliged in providing them – at a price that suited him rather than them. He'd bribed his way into procuring a goodly supply of those trucks, sold them on and then looked elsewhere to invest the funds he'd accumulated.

Buying the row of cottages had been his first venture. Bought cheaply he had immediately increased the rents. Anyone who couldn't pay was out. What did he care if their families had lived there, the canal traffic and the surrounding farms providing them with work?

Playing at being mine host behind his own bar had been a life's ambition, thus his second purchase had been the Jolly Boatman. The boathouse had followed, the upstairs converted for his own use, the boathouse beneath housing a motorboat.

Archibald admired anyone who had brushed themselves off and rebuilt their life after the war. Most of them were to be admired and even liked. He didn't like Clifford. The man was a boor, not the sort to be invited into the higher echelons of society. He had money, but no finesse.

Still, he was being paid for this.

'Mr Fletcher, I can make another visit if you so wish, but I have to say—'

The response was clipped. 'No need!'

Clifford swigged back the remainder of his drink and immediately poured himself another. He drank the lot, his ruddy cheeks round as apples before he swallowed.

'I've done it the nice way, Mr Weaver. Now I'll do it the other way.'

Archibald pursed his lips. He would not ask what that other way might entail. He didn't want to know.

'Whatever you think best, Mr Fletcher.'

'I'll get the better of that... that... tramp! Just you wait and see.'

Declining a snifter to see him on his way, Archibald left the inn and the village behind. As he drove his little black car, he thought on what Mr Fletcher had said. There was no doubt in his mind that he would use violence against Mr Hunter if he had to. What he wasn't so sure of was whether it would work. A tramp he might look, but Harry Hunter had the air of a man capable of fighting his own corner, of a man not easily intimidated.

11

What were you thinking of? Cycling at your age!

Sister Edith Harrison gritted her teeth and kept her admonitions of her own stupidity inside, though her bottom lip curled each time the cycle bumped over an uneven surface.

On the plus side, the day was dry or her uniform would have been muddied from splashing through puddles.

So what had she been thinking of? Sister Gwen Peebles and her aching hip of course. What else could it be?

The man who'd asked for directions. He'd been built like a haystack, like a giant of old who could sweep a whole village off their feet in his mighty arms, let alone a forty-something woman.

Ma Skittings had prophesied that she would meet a tall, dark stranger.

On casually mentioning him in the post office where she'd stopped to purchase two stamps, the postmistress said that his name was Harry Hunter.

Sister Harrison had lingered to hear more.

'If my memory serves me right, his mother was a domestic servant up at Orchard Manor. As for the father,' said the postmistress, becoming taller as she drew in her chin, for all the world like a marionette being jerked up by its strings. 'Dirty old goat. Couldn't keep his hands off the servants. It was an embarrassment to her ladyship, I can tell you that for nothing. No wonder she went marching with the likes of women for votes. The likes of him were enough to make anyone a suffragette!'

It was not entirely fresh news. Rumour had it that his lordship had been a bit of an old goat. Even her own mother had told her that. In, fact she could hear the familiar voice ringing like a cracked bell in her head.

The subject switched to Ma Skittings, her healing ointments and her standing in as fortune teller at the May Day fair.

'She might be good with creams and ointments, but she ain't no gypsy. Only gypsies are good with the crystal ball.'

Someone else disagreed.

'Ma Skittings knows one or two things about the future,' the speaker whispered low, as though afraid anyone hearing might question her honesty – or her sanity. 'There's always been rumours about her being a witch and doing witchy things.'

'Witchy things?' The postmistress drew in her chin and focused her eyes on the speaker. 'What do you mean by that?'

'Well,' said the rotund little woman who seemed diminished under the spellbinding gaze of the postmistress. 'Keeping a cat.'

The postmistress pointed out that she kept bees, not a cat.

'And flying around on a broomstick,' the speaker argued.

Sister Harrison nearly choked.

'She's a herbalist, but that doesn't make her a witch. Anyway, can you really see Ma Skittings riding a broom.'

Still laughing, she'd left the post office with a picture in her mind of the overweight Ma Skittings astride a broomstick and flying through the sky.

Nonsense of course. She'd chuckled a bit before regaining her usual upright composure.

Taking over Gwen's round for the day should be quite an experience. The district nurse had told her about the woman who had only dropped in at the clinic for tea and biscuits. After she'd gone, it was found that she'd stolen a whole plateful, no doubt taken away in her coat pocket. She had to be very hungry to do that – after all it was only a handful of digestives and malts.

Anyway, here she was out and about on a reasonably fine day. She wasn't one to gather cobwebs, but breathing in God's fresh air was energising.

As she cycled along, she told herself a few honest truths, such as there was no way she was ever going to meet a sweetheart inside the hospital all day.

Social events were few and far between and the only thing waiting for her at home were her cats and a blue macaw. The latter could talk, but its language was questionable. Mr McCawber, as he was called, had been left there by a sailor who had lodged with them for a while. For a time, she'd walked out with him but stopped when a letter had arrived from his wife in Newcastle. He wasn't available. Yet another possible Romeo had turned out to be already spoken for.

Concentrate, Edith Harrison. That's what she told herself as she brought her bike to a standstill so she could gather her breath before cycling on.

Gwen had provided her with the list of patients in need of having dressings changed or just a general check-up. She took the opportunity to check the list before cycling on.

A bit of a mix of expectant mothers, children and the elderly. The terminally ill were also visited, those for whom nothing could be done. None of them paid for this service. The wages for the district nurse visiting the poor were met by Lady Araminta Compton-Dixon, a stalwart benefactress of those who needed it.

With keen-eyed interest, Sister Harrison ran down the list Gwen had given her and recognised the name of the woman who'd stolen the biscuits – June Newman.

Up until six months ago Tommy and his mother had been happy living in their little cottage overlooking the river before Frank had moved in.

'Not the boy's father, of course, but you know how it is. Some women can't live without a man in the house.'

Edith knew what Gwen was saying, but then unless a woman had a proper profession, she was dependent on a man to put a meal on the table and a roof over their heads. Not that it always panned out that way. Some men wanted it all without having to pay a price.

On her way to Lower Foxford, she'd called in at the chemist and tried not to blush when Mr March had smiled, asked her what she wanted, and touched her fingers when handing across the required items.

Mr March was still a contender for her affection, but she couldn't see it going anywhere whilst his sister was around. Dorothy March was a bit of a harpy, the elder sister to whom the late mother had handed the reins of control.

At least she didn't have to cycle past the smithy where Toby Sledge would down tools when he saw her. No matter how much he might be enamoured of her, she just couldn't countenance him as a Romeo to her Juliet. Another possible liaison bit the dust. Neither man set her heart on fire. Perhaps that was why the results of having her fortune told had left such an unexpected impression.

The cottages of Fisherman's Row faced the still green waters of the canal and, judging by the paperwork, were a regular call for Sister Gwen Peebles. Many of those living here had turned up at the soup kitchen. Due to the ongoing situation – widespread poverty whether the men were on strike or not – a hot meal would be offered at the Methodist Hall two days per week.

The services of a district nurse based at Orchard Cottage Hospital were free, as was the soup kitchen. Doctor Brakespeare and her staff were of the same accord, agreeing that its presence would make a big impact on the people hereabout.

After leaning her bicycle against the garden wall without getting stung by the rampant growth of nettles, Sister Harrison eyed one of the cottages more keenly than the others.

She wondered whether June Newman would recognise her from the clinic. She doubted it. The uniform was noticed first before the face above the starched white collar.

It was easy to see that the cottage could do with a little updating but was no better or worse than any other on the rank. Without needing to go round the back, she knew a zinc bath hung from a nail in the wall outside the back door and the privy was at the bottom of the garden.

Inside the cottage, June saw her coming and immediately told Tommy to get out of sight.

'Or she'll be fussing over you, and Frank will be here soon. Don't want him to know we had a visitor, do we? And he don't hold with charity.'

Tommy scarpered out of the back door as the district nurse entered the front.

To June's mind, she seemed to fill the room, not that she was that much taller or wider than she was herself. It was just her crisp uniform, her air of authority, the fact that her eyes were everywhere.

After she'd introduced herself and explained that she was taking over from Gwen for the day, Edith remarked on the front garden.

'Proper cottage garden. Nice mix of flowers and vegetables.' The fact that there were nettles growing on the other side of the wall was neither here nor there.

Peas, beans and cabbages thrived amongst the lupins, bluebells, and summer roses. Blooming was the best way to describe it. June, however, looked bedraggled and wilted like a flower at the end of the summer.

'So where is your son?' Edith asked, referring to the notes and Gwen's comments about the boy's bad chest.

'I didn't ask you to come,' June said, initially with an air of defiance.

Sister Harrison's eyebrows rose. If Mrs Newman thought being defensive was going to put her off, she was very mistaken. 'Your son is not in the best of health.'

June's retort was equally resolute. 'He's not going into hospital. I can't afford it.'

'Nobody said he needed to go into hospital. I'm here to make sure that he doesn't. There's no charge, but then you already know that.'

'My Frank don't allow me to 'ave charity.'

'Well, there's a brave man, risking offending her ladyship. She'd be down here like a shot if I tell her that was the case. Could he cope with that?'

Lady Araminta Compton-Dixon was known to be the source of many philanthropic projects in the town. Overbearing men could receive the sharp edge of her tongue if they upset her. Few indeed could get the better of her.

Her comment about her ladyship paying a visit seemed to make June think again. She folded her arms, her expression one of resignation.

'Tommy's out with the dog. He's out with that perishin' dog all the time. Scruffy little thing it is and getting old. It's a wonder them tiny little legs can run at all.'

An attempt to laugh was strained. Edith fancied she kept looking at the clock sitting lopsided on the mantelpiece. Its face was cracked, and it seemed to be missing one leg.

Edith looked pointedly to the small square window overlooking the front garden and canal. Dust motes floated in sunlight that struggled to reach the darker corners of the single ground floor room of the cottage. She could see no sign of the boy.

'Not much for me to do here, then.'

Only two more calls after this and Edith could return to the hospital.

'I suppose I could go for a walk. I heard there's a stranger living on a boat along the towpath. I might go along and introduce myself.'

The curiosity she held for the bearded man and his conversation with the vicar gnawed at her mind.

'You won't find Tommy there.'

The defiance had returned. Again, Sister Harrison was not in the least bit intimidated.

'I can give it a try. Can't miss a small boy with a dog. Anyway, I could do with a bit of fresh air. It's not often I escape from the hospital. I'll see myself out.'

Even before she'd left, June's gaze slid back to the wonky clock as though she was counting the minutes away. *Relieved*, thought Sister Harrison, *that I'll be gone before her man gets home*. She'd heard that Frank Steele was something of a bully and couldn't really blame June for wanting her gone.

The fresh air felt good, but her feeling of pity for June Newman was not easily banished. June was hardly the first abused women she had met, far from it. She felt the same about all of them, women who had need of a man, women who had been let down, women who hoped for so much more than they ended up with. Where was all that romance she'd read about in novels?

Grasping the handlebars of the bicycle, she pushed away, heading further along the canal, her balance improving with each push of the pedals.

In the distance, a goods train rattled and clanked along the railway line.

Before she got there, she saw the boy with the dog. To her surprise, he was alighting from a narrowboat, the only one moored there.

Behind Tommy was the bearded man who had asked her directions. All that hair and creased clothes. Almost a tramp. Goodness, what a terrible example to give a young boy. That was what she thought at first until it struck her that there was something imposing about his height and aura of power.

Her heart raced. His presence had tickled her heart outside the door of the soup kitchen. Now she couldn't help asking herself if this was indeed the tall, dark stranger Ma Skittings had seen in the crystal ball.

Dismounting but still wheeling the bike forward, Edith kept her staunch gaze focused on the boy. Although the man might not be aware, she was keeping him in the corner of her eye.

'Tommy. I'm Sister Harrison. I called in on your mother expecting to see you there. You know I need to listen to your chest, don't you?'

Tommy blinked and took a few steps backwards, the side of the boat being at his back.

For a moment, she thought he was about to run away until realising that the weight of the dog he was cradling in his arms would impede his speed.

'Right,' said Edith in her no-nonsense manner as she leaned the bike against the side of the boat. 'Let's have a listen to your chest, shall we?'

She felt the eyes of the man on her as she began unbuckling her bag, which was affixed to the rear of the bike behind the saddle.

In an instant, she had a stethoscope around her neck.

'Put that dog down, please. I can't listen to your chest with him snuggled against it.'

The boy's face clouded with defiance. 'No. I ain't doing it. Leave me alone.'

'The dog can't walk very well. That's why he's here.'

The man's voice was deep and seemed to reverberate on the air before fading.

When Edith met his piercing eyes, her heart skipped a beat. Those eyes and that voice made her almost forget the forest of hair on head and chin.

One movement, a cross between a stride and a leap, and the man was off the boat. His strong, brown fists braced at his waist.

'The dog's ill. He brought the dog here for me to take a look.'

Not one to be intimidated by anyone, Edith curbed her unease as she ran a professional eye over the boy. His clothes looked as though they'd been patched a hundred times, and his eyes were big as starfish in his thin face. Not enough food. The dog didn't look much better.

Edith recovered quickly and fixed her daunting gaze on the bearded man. 'Are you a vet?'

The man shifted slightly as though her question had taken him off balance. 'My work was with animals. Yes.'

A vet at some time, though not now. A vet during the Great War? So many animals – notably horses and mules – had died back then. It had been the army vet's job to keep them going.

She would not be intimidated. She had a job to do and do it she would.

'You are qualified with animals, and I am qualified to serve human beings. I trust we understand each other.'

The man paused before giving a curt nod before addressing the boy.

'Tommy. It's a grand idea for this lady to take a look at your chest. She's here in yer best interests. Pass the dog to me whilst she does it.'

Obediently, Tommy did as requested. The dog whined as he handed it over but quietened once it was cushioned against the profusion of chin hair, a broad hand stroking its pulsating body.

Edith prepared to flick at fleas as she opened the boy's shirt. He wouldn't be the first patient hereabouts to be infested. It was a pleasant surprise to find that his clothes, though shabby, were clean. So was his body.

She ordered the boy to cough, aware that the man was watching every move. Such scrutiny surprised her, taking her back to when she'd been in training, long before she'd qualified, long before she'd taken charge at the Orchard Cottage Hospital.

She had him cough once, twice, three and eventually four times. Once she'd heard as much as she was likely to hear, she returned the stethoscope to her bag, trying not to appear nervous, not to respond to being watched so closely.

She concentrated on the boy. 'As far as I can tell, your chest sounds better. The fresh air at this time of year is good for you.'

She didn't add that his problem might worsen once winter returned or they had a wet autumn. Cross that bridge when they came to it, a sentiment that she would not put into words.

Being a qualified senior sister, she had never been averse to getting down to the heart of things. Her attention turned from the boy to the man standing behind him, still stroking the dog.

Before she could open her mouth, he said, 'I've no need of medical attention.'

Unfazed that he'd read her mind, she responded, 'Constitution of an ox, I take it.'

'You could say that.'

'Then you're one of the lucky ones. There's few who fought in the Great War who are in robust health.'

Whatever he might have been going to say stalled, but eventually he said, 'As if that's any of your business.' His tone was sharp, his eyes unblinking.

Edith shrugged. 'In case you haven't noticed, it *is* my business. I qualified in the King Edward the Seventh hospital in Bristol.' She controlled the urge to sigh or dare to be tearful. She just wanted him to know that she'd been involved in patching broken men back together. 'We had so many injured and not enough beds. We resorted to pitching tents on the green slope opposite the hospital. Fifteen-hour days were nothing.' Her eyes glazed over as the memories came flooding back. Everything she said was true. It was well known that soldiers relived their experiences in dreams. What was less known was that those tending their wounds, rebuilding faces, amputating limbs and soothing the dying also relived their experiences. The memories of that time were still with her.

For a moment, there was something like an electrical charge in the air, a silent period of apprehension when sound – in the form of speech – would not be welcome.

Judging the time was right, she said, 'I've always felt terribly sorry for the poor animals used in the war. It must have been horrendous.'

'It was,' he said softly.

The not knowing what to say next hovered there until Edith exclaimed, 'I've got cats. Three of them, in fact.'

Her mother had bequeathed them to her. She'd always thought she hated them, but now, living alone, she found she did not.

Tommy's lips curled in a snarl. 'I don't like cats.'

'And a parrot. I also have a parrot.'

Tommy had not been impressed by the mention of cats, but he showed immediate interest at mention of a parrot. 'Can he talk?'

'To a point, though I never allow him to speak in polite company.'

'What colour?' he asked, face bright with enthusiasm.

'Blue. His name's Mr McCawber.'

The boy looked surprised. 'Why?'

The tall man had made himself comfortable on the coach roof of the boat. 'Because he's a macaw. They come from South America. Is that right, Sister...?'

'Harrison. Sister Edith Harrison.'

There. She'd told him her full name and surprised herself.

The stranger's comment about the parrot was correct and she told him so.

'Do you know anything about parrots, Mr...?'

She waited for him to fill the gap.

'Call me Ben, or Harry. I don't mind either.'

It was difficult to finger what had changed, but his surroundings and some of the people he'd encountered were softening that harsh burden he carried inside.

'Well, Mr Ben...' A comment that was also a question waiting to be answered.

'Tyler. Ben Tyler.'

The name would suffice for now.

There was something close to understanding and even companionship between them when he passed the dog back to the boy.

'Take Patch home now, Tommy. He'll be wanting his supper and a sleep.'

Dog cradled in his arms, Tommy bounded off.

He'd only gone a few yards before Edith expressed that she too should be heading to her next calls.

On a whim and even though he'd stated that he had no need of her ministrations, she suggested that if he ever had need of medical assistance, he need only call at the hospital. 'Or have me drop in on you.'

'Are you fine on boats, Sister?'

'I've never been to sea but am sure I can cope with something floating on flat water. There's not a wave in sight.'

There was a smile on his face as he helped Edith with the bicycle, holding it upright whilst she swung her leg over and got her foot fixed on the offside pedal. As he did so, she couldn't help noticing his hands. He might have been a vet at one time, but his hands were those that betrayed traces of hard manual labour. Strong hands. Hands baked brown by wind and weather.

'Will the lad get better?' he asked quietly.

Edith's eyes met his. 'With good food and looking after.'

He frowned. 'I'm not sure he's getting that. His mother's a widow?'

A grimace accompanied Edith's curt nod. 'So she says, but she doesn't live alone.'

He nodded thoughtfully, his eyes clouding over. 'A freeloader taking advantage of a woman alone in the world.'

'Have you met him?'

His hair ruffled in the wind when he shook his head. 'No. But I can guess at the type from what young Tommy has told me.'

She dared ask him if he'd be staying here for a while in Lower Foxford.

He replied that he would. A smile suddenly lit his face.

'I've come into a legacy. So I might be here a fair while.'

'How very nice.'

'It might be.' A frown creased his rugged brow. 'Let's see how it goes.'

Edith was about to push off with her foot but paused. It was impulsive, not like her at all, but she asked him if he cared to look at her cats some time.

'They're getting on a bit. I do worry how much longer they'll last. They're in need of a good vet.'

He seemed to think about it.

She offered to pay.

He smiled. 'I'm a charity. I do it for love.'

'Surely you deserve something?'

'A cup of tea for my troubles? Even cake?'

'You're making fun of me, Mr Tyler, but at your own cost not mine.'

'I did not mean to make you blush.'

'Me? Blush? At least you can see my face, whereas I cannot see yours. All that hair…' Her response had been quite stormy. His comment about her blushing had caught her off balance.

'I'm a man of mystery.'

'I concede that you are. At least for now, but at some point, you'll have to expose the features beneath all that hair. If you dare!'

There. She'd had a dig at him, but there was no way of knowing whether he was blushing.

She knew he was watching her ride off. She did not know what he was thinking, that exposing his features was not an option. Once his hair was trimmed, his face bare, his true self would be exposed, and he didn't want that to happen. Not yet.

12

June Newman grabbed her son before he had time to step over the threshold with Patch, the black and white terrier, nestled in his arms.

It broke her heart to tell him that he couldn't bring the dog in, but she had no choice.

'You know Frank don't allow it,' she whispered whilst tousling his tight curls. 'And another thing, don't tell him that the district nurse called. You know how he is about interfering old busybodies.'

June felt guilty on seeing Tommy's wide eyes and the faltering of his bottom lip.

'Here. Take these scraps for his supper. Give it to 'im now before Frank comes 'ome.'

Furtively but firmly, she pushed the muslin-wrapped scraps into Tommy's pocket.

'Go on,' she whispered. 'Get on up there to the sty before Frank gets 'ere.'

They both looked towards the front of the house, straining their ears for the sound of Frank's Douglas motorcycle tearing along the towpath.

Her heart was already in her mouth. Why was she living like this? Why couldn't she stand up to Frank and tell him never to darken her door again?

She recalled her darling boy asking her why she'd let Frank move in seeing as she'd always declared how much she'd loved his father.

Explaining to a nine-year-old boy that she was lonely was easy enough. Getting him to understand was a different matter.

'But you've got me,' he'd uttered plaintively.

'It's not the same. I need somebody my own age – somebody to talk to and laugh with. Besides,' she added in a brighter tone of voice, 'he brings 'ome some nice things for us now and again, don't he?'

Nice things. No questions asked. Tins of meat, mostly, or chunks of raw chocolate straight from the docks. Any food had been welcome. Still was, and besides, Frank hadn't hit her back then. Hiding the bruises had become a part of normality, but she knew from the look in Tommy's eyes that he was aware of the razor-thin line between normality and violence.

She watched him take the dog out back to the old pigsty at the end of the garden. Its roof of corrugated tin kept out most of the rain and he'd made a bed for the animal from two old sacks stuffed with straw, to which he'd added a stained pillow. It was a far cry from the days when Patch had lived indoors, his bed next to the stove, but it was the best the boy could do.

Frank didn't allow his mother to buy dog food.

'I don't go to work to feed mongrels.'

Tommy had protested, 'He's a terrier, not a mongrel.' The outburst had earned him a clip round the ear.

Frank's grin had been vicious, his sweaty face slammed into that of the boy, tobacco bile running from the corner of his mouth, the stink of green farmhouse cider on his breath. He'd snarled, 'I weren't meaning the dog.'

The insult had hurt, just as Frank knew it would. Tommy was the result of a romance between his mother and a merchant seaman. It had happened in Bristol, but June had refused to give up her child. In an effort to play down her shame, she'd left the seaport, worked in posh houses in a steady journey east and finally landed in Norton Dene.

It made her go soft inside when Tommy asked her to tell him what his father was like, which was quite often. How he looked. How he spoke.

'He was honey brown – a bit lighter than a conker, but just as shiny. And he could sing and play the piano. He was so entertaining! Such fun! Everybody used to get up and dance when he played that piano and sang.'

Before Frank, she'd never tired of talking about him, her face shining with treasured memories. Her face never shone nowadays, except with sweat when she was cooking or doing the laundry.

Sister Harrison had suggested bringing Tommy to the hospital.

'I'm going to suggest that Doctor Brakespeare takes a look at his chest. She's a very good doctor. I'm sure Tommy would benefit from an examination by her. No charge.'

June sighed and closed her eyes. *Please God, I lost my Joe. Sailed away without a word. I don't want to lose Tommy too.*

* * *

'Those cottages are damp. There are black patches on the walls inside and layers of moss on the stone on the outside. Time they were pulled down and everyone moved into healthier places.'

Doctor Frances Brakespeare finished perusing the report Sister Harrison had created on her day as district nurse. She frowned at her own memory of a visit to that terrace. The cottages were constructed of rough stone back in the days when the canal was built. The navvies digging the canal had also been tasked with building their own housing after they'd complained about living outside in tents. An ancestor of Lady Compton-Dixon had grudgingly obliged, providing rough stones for the ad hoc buildings, enough wood for small square windows, rough planks for doors. Everything had been done as cheaply as possible, including the inner walls dividing rooms which were made of pine panelling. Soundproofing was non-existent, cooking and heating by the grace of a growly old range in the downstairs room. The pine-panelled walls, gamely wallpapered by those who lived there, divided the upper floor into two bedrooms. A single toilet pan occupied a brick-built outhouse that vaguely resembled a sentry box – though less skilfully put together. At least they didn't have to share. Frances had come across six cottages all sharing a single toilet.

Sister Harrison had known Doctor Brakespeare long enough to work out where her mind was going. She voiced what was in her mind. 'Has the health of the people in those cottages ever come up at the monthly meeting of hospital governors?'

Attending those meetings was purely the doctor's prerogative, though Sister Harrison could guess at some of the subjects discussed.

Frances's hands were clasped against her mouth, her eyes narrowed and fixed on the opposite wall as if there were a picture there. 'I'm unsure whether they're still in the ownership of the family, but I will enquire. Gwen visits there on a regular basis, though not nearly enough. As for me...' Throwing her hands away from her mouth, she expressed a deep sigh. 'I think I would like to visit those we have mentioned on our list. Have any of them attended the mother and baby clinic – or, dare I say it, sought advice on family planning?'

'Mrs Newman, the boy with the bad chest's mother, does call in on a regular basis, though it seems to be so she can have a cup of tea and filch some of our biscuits to take home with her. Thankfully, the soup kitchen will go some way to keeping her body and soul together. And help us maintain our biscuit supply,' Sister Harrison added with a playful grimace.

Frances raised her eyebrows. 'Poor woman. She must be pretty desperate to do that. But no family planning or pregnancy?'

Sister Harrison shook her head emphatically. 'No.'

'Well, that's hardly surprising. Can she read and write?'

'I have no reason to believe to the contrary.'

Slamming her hands down on her desk, Frances got to her feet. 'Are you free tomorrow? You or Gwen? I don't mind which.'

Sister Harrison thought she knew what was coming.

'You fancy making a visit, Doctor?'

'I do.'

Sister Harrison sniffed. 'We only have one bicycle.'

Frances had already made up her mind. 'Lucky that I have a car. I never did fancy riding a tandem.'

13

It wasn't like Gregory to be undecided about anything, and Harry Hunter was right about his duty to keep secret anything told in strict confidence.

All the same, his loyalty was divided. Should he tell her ladyship about what was coming her way?

He imagined her shocked expression. Decision made, he went out into the hallway and the telephone, a wooden and Bakelite contraption hanging on the wall next to a round-faced barometer.

The earpiece was in his hand, one finger poised to dial, when he noticed that the barometer needle was heading from fair to stormy. He'd never been one to believe in omens – not of the supernatural kind – but the dropping pressure stayed his dialling finger.

Betraying a confidence and bringing shock to an elderly lady were both likely to cause consternation.

Her ladyship should be warned, but in person, not via the telephone. However, he would warn her that he would drop in, perhaps using the excuse that he was coming on parish business, or even regarding the hospital. He wasn't sure what. Never mind. He dialled.

He recognised the voice of Minette, a new addition to the household.

After wishing her good morning, he asked if he could drop in. 'If her ladyship isn't too busy.'

'I'll just check.'

In his mind, he rehearsed what he was going to say. It wouldn't be easy. He wasn't sure how much she knew about her late husband's personal life. Business, yes. She'd taken the reins of running the estate and everything else left her with shrewd competence – better perhaps than her husband. As for personal matters...

The maid came back and explained that he would be welcome to visit but had to take her ladyship as found.

'She's out in the stables with Clive.'

'Clive?'

'Yes. Mr Sledge is coming to trim his hooves. Clive is a bit nervous, so her ladyship is out there ready to calm him down.'

Clive, the last of the estate's hunters, one her ladyship couldn't bear to part with.

'Ah! Yes. I'll be about thirty minutes.'

He set down the phone and took a deep breath. If Frances had been around, he would have asked her how he should approach what he had to say. But she was already at the hospital and wasn't likely to be back until this evening. He could pop in, of course, and chance she might have a minute or two...

No. He shook his head. Best get it over with.

Gird up your loins, Gregory Sampson. You'll think of the right words when you get there – without breaking a confidence.

* * *

Climbing the lane up to the main road and the estate beyond that, Harry kept his head down, walking close to the drystone walls enclosing fields of grazing animals. Sometimes he stopped and on seeing him the horses, cows or sheep wandered over expectantly. That's how things were with animals. They seemed to sense his kindness, actively seeking to be with him.

He passed a group of children heading down the hill, one of whom he recognised.

Tommy had dark skin and curly hair. He waved, then ran across the lane.

''Ello, Mr Ben.'

Tommy's companions remained in a close-knit group, staring and mute on the other side of the lane. They weren't interested in the dog. They only had eyes for the man who looked as though he'd never had a haircut or taken a shave in his life. A bath neither for that matter. The latter appealed greatly to boys who preferred to keep their grubby knees and dirty faces rather than be scrubbed clean in a bath.

'Mr Ben lives on a boat,' Tommy shouted over his shoulder.

After looking awestruck, his mates tittered amongst themselves, exchanged whispered comments, their eyes never leaving the bearded man.

The boy straightened and twisting from the waist, looked back at him as he ran sideways across the road to rejoin his friends.

One of his companions was brave enough to make comment.

'You don't look like your name's Ben. Lion, that's what I think your name should be 'cause you've got the mane of a lion.'

''Ow would you know? You've never seen a lion!' shouted one of the others.

'I did. I seen it in a book.'

They ran off, looking as though they were chasing each other.

Smiling to himself, Harry ambled on. Brambles spilled over from the verge at the edge of the lane, snatching at his trousers.

Talbot trotted along at his side, stopping every so often to look longingly in the direction the children had gone.

'Aye, and you'd be off playing with them if I gave you half the chance.'

The dog nuzzled his leg as if seeking his forgiveness.

'Well, you're not going. I'm calling on a lady, so I am, and you're coming with me whether you like it or not – and whether she likes it or not.' He'd already decided that if she refused the dog entry, he would be off back to the boat and away on his travels. If that occurred, she would be none the wiser of why he was there and what he had to say.

After two miles or so of walking, the slate roof of Orchard Manor Hall loomed up ahead above a red-brick wall and wrought-iron gates.

The house was clearly visible through the ornate ironwork at the end of a sweeping drive. One tug of the iron bell pull to one side of the gate and somebody would appear and give him entry.

He eyed the bell pull, noting the ornate ironwork leaves at its base. More like daggers, he thought and asked himself for the third time that day what he was letting himself in for.

He felt the dog poke at his leg with his shiny black nose but stood firm as though he hadn't noticed. Riddled with doubt, he began pacing up and down until there was danger of him wearing a deep furrow in the ground.

Talbot sat down, his eyes following his master's pacing until hearing footsteps crunching on gravel.

The small woman who dragged open the gate had a pert look about her, bright eyes and hair as fluffy as a dandelion head.

She frowned as she looked him up and down. 'I was expecting the blacksmith.'

'I'm sorry to disappoint you.'

Her frown deepened. 'What's your business here and why didn't you push the gate open for yourself? Why drag me all the way down here from the stables?'

'The gates were closed. I thought it only polite to ring the bell.'

'Sledge unavailable, is he? Nursing a hangover I wouldn't be surprised. Never mind. Come on in.'

She looked about to question him further when a black sedan approached the gates from the direction of the house. It was driven by a chauffeur. The passenger in the back seat looked straight ahead as though he hadn't seen him standing there.

He eyed the car's progress, thinking the passenger aloof. What did he expect? Anyone connected with this family was bound to have a superior air. They couldn't help themselves.

His expression must have betrayed what he was thinking.

'My son. He's not arrogant, just blind. The war, of course. Isn't it always?'

'Yes.'

There was something in him that held back from acknowledging just how many such men existed. Men who had gone to war in the fullness of youth and returned broken and old before their time.

After all, if he was her son, then he was his half-brother. His chest tightened at the thought of it.

Shaking himself back to the here and now, he found himself looking into a pair of intense eyes set in strong features. The blizzard of white hair stuck out like a halo around her head. It looked as though an effort had been made to control it with a series of pearl-edged combs and clips – items more associated with an evening dress than what looked like a man's checked shirt over faded green corduroys tucked into a pair of oversized wellington boots. Shorter than him and quite wide, she looked as though somebody had lifted her up and planted her into the over-large boots.

He felt her eyes scrutinising him, weighing him up as to who he was and what was his business. Rather than asking him outright.

And then she did.

'My word. That head of hair and beard are going to cause a stir in the village, my boy. Pompous lot some of them. Especially that lot at the golf club.' She cocked her head to one side as a thought came to her. 'You don't look like a golf player.'

'I'm not.'

She rested her meaty fists on her hips and chuckled. 'That's a bloody shame. I would have joined myself just to see their smug expressions turn shell-shocked. Well, never mind all that.'

She scurried quickly ahead of him, her like a Jack Russell, him like a long striding deerhound.

The horse was standing on three legs, one fetlock bent, the tip of the hoof delicately in contact with the floor.

He slid his hand down from the animal's rump to the swollen fetlock. 'A touch of laminitis. I would suggest a less rich diet, and certainly no turning out to grass. It's too rich for some at this time of year.'

'Right!' She smacked her hands together in the manner of someone satisfied with a job well done. 'Tell Sledge to send me his bill. And tell him you seem like a good addition to the smithy. Someone to rely on when he's suffering from too many pints at the Jolly Boatman.' A sudden thought seemed to come to her. 'He did hint that he would be taking on someone but didn't say when. How long have you been working for him?'

The brightness of her enquiring eyes held him. This, he decided, was the right time to declare himself.

'I don't work for anyone. Only myself.'

Dark eyebrows, a stark contrast to her pillow of frosty hair, rose in surprise. 'Well, I'm grateful for your advice, but who the devil are you?'

He'd imagined this moment so many times. Imagined her shock when he insisted that the ashes in the biscuit tin should be buried in the family crypt.

Before this moment, he'd relished the thought but imagining it and actually doing it were two different things. It took more courage – no, not courage –

coldness, no trace of emotion. *Just fix your mind on the memory of your mother and how this family's actions led to her death.*

Everything warm was buried before he said, 'Your ladyship. I've come to ask you something on behalf of an old army friend. His name was Harry Hunter.'

Her merry expression vanished. Her complexion, rosy cheeks and all, turned ashen. She stared silently at him, not looking as crestfallen as he'd expected – or hoped.

When she finally found her voice, it was not with acrimony but showing a resigned acceptance. 'We need to talk.'

'I don't want to be wasting your time, so if you don't mind, I'll get to the point and be on my way.'

A sudden sadness came to her face. 'I've plenty of time to waste. One's faculties fade as one gets older and the social life goes with it. I have fewer visitors nowadays – unless it's to do with horses, but they mainly come for the horses, not me. I think tea is in order. Plus cake. It's that time of the morning.'

She turned so swiftly, she almost left her gumboots behind, her short legs turning before the boots did.

'Damned boots. I couldn't find mine. Had to borrow a pair belonging to my son.'

'What about my dog?'

'I assumed he was coming with us. Don't mind dogs in this part of the house, and he looks like a good 'un. Nice conformation, though I prefer a Labrador or a lurcher. Still, I pride myself on knowing quality when I see it. Looks to be getting on a bit. How old is he?'

'I don't know. He was a stray and a bit grey around the muzzle, so I think he's about eight.'

'I would guess that too. Good for his age – as big dogs go. Shame they don't last as long as little yappers. Small dogs make up for their size with noise. No matter. Now come along. We've given each other the once-over on the outside and I think we both like what we see. Now let's see if you and I really can judge a book by its cover. Round here,' she said, swerving to the left off the driveway and onto a red-bricked path bordered with fancy red tiles. 'Tradesmen's entrance, I'm afraid. I've been mucking out the stables. I've got help but like to give a hand. The horses are used to me. Think I'm their mother – or at least I like to think they do. Silly old mare that I am.' She giggled at her own joke. 'My housekeeper Minette huffs and puffs a bit if I go in stinking of horse shit – sorry – manure. Slip of the tongue. I'm used to using expletives in front of the stable lad but make the effort to curb my language once I'm inside the house. Minette doesn't like it. I'm every inch the lady indoors or in society. Outside, I please my bloody self.'

He followed her through a wide back door and along a flagstoned passageway, where she stepped out of her boots, kicking them beneath what looked like an old church pew. From there, she trod onwards in knitted seamen's socks that, like the boots, seemed far too big for her, the toes flopping like flippers.

The room they entered had a homely rather than a stately atmosphere. The furniture was old but handsome, the faded upholstery worn in places and the Turkish rugs had holes. Hunting portraits in gilt frames hung alongside bigger portraits of poker-faced people from some years past against a background of heavily embossed Victorian wallpaper that might have been a riot of rich colouring in its day but was now faded.

She rang the bell twice. 'Twice tells Minette that I have company. Tea for two.'

He took the seat she offered him.

'As you can see, this is not the most salubrious part of the house. Worn out by the years – just like me.' She looked around at the old-fashioned decor, the stuffed gamebirds in glass cases, a collection of lacklustre butterflies in a glass dome. 'The fact is, this part of the house is lacklustre. It's comfortable with being scruffy – just as I am – when I can be.' The diminutive woman in the overlarge socks pointed a wrinkled finger at a winged armchair and the roundel of black fur sitting on it. 'Throw that cat off the chair and take a seat.'

At first, the cat seemed loath to move until Talbot came out from behind his master's bulk. Hissing, it showed its needle-fine fangs before jumping from the chair and hightailing it out of the room.

Lady Compton-Dixon made herself comfortable in an armchair opposite the one in which the cat had been sleeping. Once grand, it was in a bad state, its horsehair stuffing and the webbing that was supposed to support the horsehair falling. Time had shaped it to the curve of her bottom.

'Whoops!' Her legs went up in the air as her backside sank downwards into the chair's innards.

He sprang to her assistance, his strong arms pulling her upwards until she was balanced on what bit of the chair was still functional, her chuckling all the time until she was out of the hole.

'So wonderful to have a pair of strong arms come to one's aid... was never used to that. Hasty Compton-Dixon's arms were usually to be found assisting another woman – mostly into bed. But then, you already know how he was. Hasty was my husband's nickname. He was hasty taking a fence out hunting, and just as hasty chasing young women.'

Due to her being of minimal height, her feet hovered some way off the floor.

Patting the chair arms with what might be interpreted as affection, she said, 'I really should get these old chairs repaired. I'll get one of the staff to find someone to sort them out. You seem very knowledgeable about horses, Sergeant Major.'

'I should be asking you how you know that I'm a sergeant major, but I think I know the answer.'

'The vicar came dashing out here earlier. He didn't linger. Out of courtesy, I suppose he gave me a brief outline of who you were and why you were here.' Her look was steadfast. 'There's the land of course, but it's more than that, I think. Would you like to elaborate?'

He fell to silence as he assimilated his thoughts, one of which was that he would never trust a man of the cloth ever again. He reminded himself that the Reverend Gregory Sampson was a vicar, not a priest. Only Roman Catholics heard confessions.

'How much did he tell you?'

'A bit. That your name was Ben Tyler and that you'd been a friend of Harry Hunter, illegitimate son of my late husband.'

He nodded. 'My best friend died in the war.'

There. He wasn't really lying. The two of them had been friends. It was just a case of their names being interchangeable.

She nodded. 'I'm sad to hear that.' She frowned. 'My son, Devlin, seldom talks about the war. He used to have nightmares, so I don't push him to relate his experiences.'

Harry's voice was hollow. 'Do you know there were times you couldn't move forwards without falling into a rotting corpse. The worse were the horses, their carcasses big enough to fall into.'

She eyed him silently before saying, 'That must have been dreadful for anyone who likes horses as much as you. I like horses too.'

'Reliable. Loyal,' he said and nodded thoughtfully before adding, 'I like animals more than humans.'

'I feel very much the same.'

She sat back in her chair and her look turned businesslike over the clasped hands in her lap.

A deeper silence descended. In times past, Araminta would have steeled herself to hearing about Harry, her late husband's son from one of his many liaisons. Not nowadays. Jealousy was for the young. Forbearance had come with age.

She decided it was time for her to take charge of the meeting.

'All these years and suddenly you turn up now with this unusual demand.' Her jaw stiffened. 'Is there any particular reason you've left it so long?'

It was hard to read the look she gave, causing him to study the hands resting on his knees as he considered an answer.

'I was in a dark place after the war,' he said at last. 'The war was supposed to be over, but it never left my head. Until recently. Thanks to Talbot.' His gaze went to the dog.

Araminta glanced at the animal. 'Talbot. A very noble name.'

'You've heard of it?'

'A war dog originating in Normandy. That's where the name hails from.'

'It does.'

With a crash of heavy wood against a stout wall, the door suddenly flew open hitting the wall fiercely. When it rebounded, a tall woman with bad-tempered features gave it a back kick whilst balancing a heavy tray with both hands.

'Ah!' Lady Compton-Dixon said. 'Now here comes Minette with our tea and cake.' She pointed to a low table. 'Put it there, Minette, then you can go. We'll help ourselves.'

Minette poured out a litany of the refreshment offerings. 'The sandwiches are fish paste, and the cake is supposed to be fruit cake, though you won't find too much fruit in it. You'll have to make do. It's all that's available.'

'If you say so. I thought somebody was making a coconut cake. I'm sure I smelled it cooking.'

'There is one.'

'When will the coconut cake be ready?' her ladyship asked enthusiastically.

Minette stopped at the door, her pasty, pimpled face held at a jaunty angle. 'It'll be ready when it's ready.'

Then she was gone.

Her ladyship shook her head. 'She's a sauce box that one. I'd dismiss her if I could, but beggars can't be choosers. Before the war, we had our pick of domestic servants. Since then...' She shrugged. 'The pool is diminishing.' She nodded at the teapot. 'Do you mind pouring?'

'Sure I will.'

'I think your dog likes the smell of the sandwiches. Have one yourself and give him one. I'm not going to eat any. I hate fish paste sandwiches. I'm sure Minette makes them purely to spite me.'

He gave Talbot a sandwich but didn't take one for himself. His mouth was too dry and his guts tight with apprehension.

He felt her eyes studying him. After taking a sip of tea, she said, 'You don't have much to say.'

'No.'

'You're not alone. It's been reported that a lot of the men find it difficult to talk about it. War changes them.'

'Your son was the man I saw in the back of the car when I arrived, I'm sorry.'

'We're all sorry, though my son copes. He has a wife and a child. He is loved.'

Her statement stirred in him an immediate pang of jealousy. Here he was, forty years old with only a dog for company. Did she have any idea how it hurt to measure up her son's contentment against his own loneliness?

As though reading his mind, she asked if he had a wife or family somewhere. He answered that he did not.

'Do you not long for hearth and family?'

'I'm not the sort who needs the earth beneath his feet and a roof above his head.'

He made no mention of not needing a wife, yet of late the loneliness that was part of his everyday existence had gripped him as never before.

Araminta eyed him speculatively. She considered herself a good judge of people.

'Now this business about burying Harry's remains in the family crypt. Why?'

Harry's eyelids flickered. What other reason could there be but revenge?

He took a slurp of tea to whet his whistle.

'Where better for the son of the household but with family?'

He felt the intensity of her eyes and saw the disbelief clouding their brightness.

That same intensity persisted as she eyed him over the rim of her teacup.

'So why do I not believe you?'

Before coming here, he'd expected to be shown into the presence of a refined woman of the upper class, one who never got her hands dirty. One whose prime function in life was to socialise with others of the same class. Finding her mucking out the stables had taken him by surprise.

His gaze strayed to the window. It was lofty and the glass was set into gothic stone arches.

'Beautiful windows. A beautiful house. Stables, even a church in the grounds.'

'Get to the point and tell me what it is you want from me.'

He placed his cup and saucer on the table. His head dropped forward, it was difficult to see his eyes, surrounded as they were by a forest of hair. 'A shell exploded on top of the barn where he was, my best friend. A lot of horses died in the same fire. It set the building alight.'

Palms made a rasping sound as he rubbed them together and revisited the memory.

'It was a fluke. Sheer bad luck. We managed to get a few horses out, but not all. Nor the tired man in there, having a kip in the straw.'

He gulped as he recalled the grim remains, his tears as he'd shovelled a handful of ashes into the sack and then into the biscuit tin.

Araminta said nothing but waited for him to continue.

'Harry wanted to be buried back here. His ashes, that is.'

Initially, her expression was warm, but it didn't last. Her eyebrows rose as the remarkable truth dawned.

'Are you telling me that you've been carrying his remains around all this time – in a biscuit tin?'

He nodded. 'I know what you're thinking. 'Tis a wonder I didn't spill the contents or lost the whole lot – tin and all. But I didn't. And who in their right mind would steal a battered old biscuit tin?'

'Harry.'

She said the one word. He waited for her to continue, to say that Harry Hunter had no right to be laid to rest in the family tomb.

When he finally met her indomitable gaze, it was hard to read her expression. There was shock, there was also an undeniable hurt that had lasted for years.

It suddenly came to him that his mother was not the only one who had been hurt. He also became aware that the woman sitting in front of him was not the selfish, high-society lady he had envisaged. He felt her hurt but also the warmth that glowed in her face.

Her look was very direct, her voice soft. 'Now tell me the truth.'

A moment of shock that she had seen through him was followed by a torrent of truth pouring from his mouth. Much as he'd wanted to hurt this woman and her family for his mother's death, he couldn't do it. The pent-up hatred of all these years that had smouldered inside was burnt out. He'd found himself liking her.

Silent, for he didn't think there was anything worthwhile to say after everything he'd said, he stood up.

Her ladyship wriggled about in her worn-out chair into which she was wedged like a cork in a bottle. 'This chair is so difficult to get out of. I think I might christen it the Slough of Despond – shades of John Bunyan.' She held out her hand. 'Can you give me a good tug, Sergeant Major?'

He took her hand. It was light as a sparrow in his and soft, so very soft.

Once he'd set her on her feet, he stood before her, unsure whether she had understood the torrent of explanation. If she had, then she had taken it very well indeed.

She gestured for him to go ahead of her, out of the room and into the passageway that led to the back door.

'Harry Hunter.' She said the name softly and shook her head. 'I remember your mother.'

Harry stared at her, wanting to ask what she was like but afraid to ask.

'She was sylph-like with a merry laugh. Innocent in her outlook and loving.' Her expression darkened. 'All the fault lies with Hasty – my husband. Not with her.' She sighed. 'We were separated at the time, my husband and I.

The suffragette movement took up a lot of my time. In a way, I blame myself for what happened, having her married off like that.' She shook her head. 'It would have been better if I'd taken her with me to London and got her involved in the cause. She was my maid, you see. But it was early days, before the war, and we were only just finding our feet, the smell of change still no more than a puff of smoke in the air. If only…' she said again, shaking her head.

Araminta pursed her lips. No jealousy inside, but there was anger. Harry Hunter was her late husband's son, but he was hardly the only one.

'I trust you to keep this matter between us until I've spoken with my son. Will you do that?'

He said that he would.

Hat in hand, he paused at the back door and turned to face her. 'I have plans for the land I inherited.'

'I'm glad to hear it.'

'I won't be selling.'

'You may do with it as you wish.'

He frowned. 'I will do so, no matter Mr Weaver and his offer.'

Araminta frowned. 'Mr Weaver? Who is he?'

'I thought he was representing your interests.'

She eyed him quizzically, a slight crease between her brows. 'Weaver? I don't believe I know a Mr Weaver.'

'I thought you had sent him. He came to see me at my boat.'

Looking totally perplexed, she frowned. 'What did he want?'

He didn't need an answer. He could tell from her eyes that Weaver was nothing to do with her. So who was he acting for?

'No matter.'

Araminta was not fooled. She was a woman who knew how conniving men could be. Her look was direct and her voice strong. 'Don't treat me as a weak and feeble woman, Harry. Tell me what this is about. Did he offer to buy the land?'

'He told me he was acting as an agent for an interested party.'

She shook her head. 'Not me.' She thought about it. 'I'll make enquiries.'

Deep in thought, he stood, running the brim of his hat through his hands, round and round.

'So will I,' he said grimly. If the man had been stood next to him at this moment in time, he would have gripped his scrawny neck and shook the details from him. But he wasn't, and besides, he'd told him he was only an agent.

* * *

'I'm feeling old,' murmured Araminta to herself once Harry had left.

Him turning up had unnerved her, though, goodness, it shouldn't have done. Sometimes when in Norton Dene, she glimpsed similarities in the features of people passing by. None had made a claim directly on the estate and only Harry Hunter had followed up his affinity to the family. He wasn't to know that her husband had told her – that Harry's mother had been the love of his life. At the time of his declaration, the knowledge had been like a knife piercing her heart. But now? Much time had passed. The raw emotional reaction was gone, a dull ache where there had been an open wound.

She went upstairs to her bedroom, where Minette had laid out her day dress. Her hand brushing the delicate lace and cool silk, she smiled at the difference between the dress and her current attire. Needs must. Clothes did not make a lady. It was what she was inside that really mattered, but at this moment she felt undecided as to how she felt. Her husband was dead, but the past had caught up with her and she wasn't quite sure how to deal with it.

14

Doctor Frances Brakespeare and Sister Edith Harrison were in the car travelling to Lower Foxford. Frances often likened the little car to a box on wheels. It was not spacious and took only four passengers, including the driver, at a squeeze.

Frances apologised when the top of Sister Harrison's head hit the roof of the car for what must be the third time. 'Sorry, Sister Harrison. Are you all right?'

'My mother told me I've always had a hard head.'

Frances fancied she was disinclined to criticise. It was the umpteenth time the top of her head had slammed against the ceiling, thanks to the car wheels dipping in and out of a pothole. The gravel towpath was prone to flood water taking away the gravel used to fill in the holes. The car bounced its way along, its wire spoked wheels spinning when a hole proved too big to get out of. A bit of declutching, a few choice words and they were on their way, the wheels sending up showers of stones when it finally got traction.

On arrival at Fisherman's Row, Frances stood and looked at the terrace of canal-side cottages. Paint peeled from the window frames, which didn't look as though they fitted very well.

She sighed. 'Hardly a home fit for heroes. Are they as bad inside as they are outside?' Her comment related to the promise by authority that servicemen returning from war would have a decent place to live. Some did, mainly on the burgeoning council estates built around established cities. The rest had to make do with homes that were far from ideal.

Sister Harrison replied that they were worse than they looked. 'Loose plaster on ceilings and walls, damp flagstones underfoot, privy at the end of the garden.'

'No wonder Tommy Newman has a bad chest.'

The garden gate put their teeth on edge as Frances's gloved hand pushed it open. Terracotta tiles that formed the garden path were slippery with moss.

Edith advised her to watch her step. 'These steps are especially bad after rain or when the canal overflows.'

Mrs Newman tugged her cardigan around her when she answered the door. Shrunk and discoloured from a long history of washing, the buttons barely met the buttonholes, the material strained over her sagging breasts.

She looked surprised to see them and seemed reluctant to invite them in.

'Mrs Newman, I'm Doctor Brakespeare. Is your son here?'

'I didn't ask you to come,' she said defiantly.

Despite the availability of modern medicine, the establishment of district nurses, and a parish scheme for the poorest of society, interference – snooping – was resented by some of the residents. 'Sister Harrison was concerned when she recently examined your son and asked if I could attend just in case there was something she'd missed.'

Sister Harrison missing anything was not very likely.

The defiance remained. 'He don't need no doctor.'

'Mrs Newman, have you any idea how many children never get to see their tenth birthday?'

The woman's head jerked up, eyes round as saucers.

Frances shook her head. 'It doesn't matter. Not to you. All that matters to you is that Tommy gets to see his tenth, eleventh, twelfth and many more birthdays after that. Is that not right, Mrs Newman?'

June Newman's face turned more ashen than it was already. Frances sensed capitulation. She was proved right when June said, 'He's up in the pigsty with Patch.'

Frances suggested Sister Harrison take care of the other scheduled visits while she climbed to the disused pigsty to see Tommy.

A series of steps led up through the sloping garden to the brick-built pigsty at the very top.

The door was low, pig or child size. Frances bent from the waist and, keeping her medicine bag at her side, entered.

'Hello, Tommy. No need to be afraid. I'm Doctor Brakespeare. Your mother said I could come up and see you. You don't mind, do you?'

Tommy's head jerked round. At the sight of her, he backed away and shouted, 'You ain't putting that thing over me chest. That woman already did it.'

'That was Sister Harrison. She's a nurse. I'm a doctor. She thought it best I take a look. Do you mind that, Tommy?'

Although her voice was soft and gentle, Tommy was having none of it. 'I ain't doing it.' His little jaw jutted defiantly, and his small hands were formed clenched fists at his sides.

Frances eyed the rise and fall of the dog's ribcage and heard its laboured breathing. An idea came to her.

'What's your dog's name?'

He glanced from her to the dog and back again.

'Patch.'

His look remained hostile, and he pronounced the name in a surly style.

Frances conceded that she would have to tread carefully. 'He looks ill.'

Tommy nodded. 'He... won't... wake up.' He uttered the words in a broken fashion, each one interspersed with sobs that would not be held back.

She glanced from boy to dog and back again. There was no point in suggesting the boy take the dog to the vet. The likes of him didn't have that kind of money.

'How long has he been ill?'

'A few days. Frank kicked him.'

Although horrified, Frances kept her voice even, though it was hard not to show a reaction. She must continue in a calm frame of mind, though already she had assessed the kind of man Frank was and what he was to the boy. She asked, 'Is Frank your stepfather?'

Tommy shrugged. 'S'pose so. Not me dad, he'll never be that! My dad was a sailor and came from Africa.' Pride burned in the boy's eyes, dark grey in a complexion of light brown.

His tears mixed with a series of splutters that might have come from his chest but equally might not. She could only discern that by examining him. But he'd refused to be examined. Still, she'd thought of a way around that.

Smiling a warm, calm smile, she gave his shoulder a squeeze. 'Right, Tommy. How about I examine you first and check your chest is better, and then I take a look at your dog.'

The wary look was replaced by one that verged on hope.

Wiping his snotty face on his sleeve, Tommy nodded, eyes flickering as he studied her face as if seeking some ulterior motive.

Frances thanked her intuition. She asked him to unbutton his shirt. She also gave him her handkerchief so he could more ably wipe his running nose – tears as much as snot.

All the while she examined him, the boy's eyes stayed fixed on his dog. Frances concluded that his chest was improved, but, goodness, as Sister Harrison had pointed out, the cottage he lived in was substandard and no good for even a healthy child. She determined to look into it.

'You can do your shirt up now, Tommy.'

He didn't bother to rebutton his shirt, but merely pulled on his jumper, his attention fixed on the far-from-well little dog.

'Patch,' Tommy whispered, bending down so that his mouth was close to a doggy ear. 'The doctor's going to look at you. Don't be frightened. All right? Don't be frightened.'

The dog did not react to the caress of the boy's fingers or his gentle voice.

Frances took her stethoscope and dabbed it twice on the little dog's ribcage. Not that she needed to do that. She could tell by looking at him that the dog was in a very bad way and likely to die. But how to tell Tommy that? How to tell anyone who was as devoted to an animal as they were to a parent or child?

Tears tipped from the corner of his eyes and made trails in his dirty face.

Quietly, she took off the stethoscope and placed it back in her bag.

As she did this, she contemplated how best to proceed. 'Perhaps we could take him to Mr Skinner, the vet. He would know what was for the best...'

'No!' Tommy's eyes were full of fire. The trust he'd shown her had turned back to hostility.

'Tommy, it would be best...'

'No it wouldn't.' Tommy threw himself over his dog's body, totally obscuring it from view. 'I know what he'd do. Give 'im the needle, that's what!' His head drooped over the dog and the tears came.

Frances sighed. 'All I can say is to keep him warm and comfortable. I'm sorry I can't do any more.'

'You're not a dog doctor! I'm taking 'im to Mr Ben again. He knows what to do.'

'Mr Ben?'

'He lives on a boat called *Talbot* and 'is dog's called Talbot too.'

Frances recalled the man on the boat Gregory had told her something about, the man who had admitted that his name was not Ben Tyler, but Harry Hunter, half-brother to Devlin Compton-Dixon. It was a secret she was sworn to keep.

She'd remarked to Gregory that it must have come as quite a shock when her ladyship knew the full details.

'Not as shocked as I thought she would be.'

Stalwart, thought Frances, was the best word to describe Araminta.

Tommy picked the dog up, cradling him protectively in his arms. 'Don't you worry, Patch. I'll take you to Mr Ben. He'll know what to do.'

For once in her professional life, Frances felt lost for words. It was rare indeed for a patient to have no faith in her advice, but here was a little boy doing just that. No matter what she said or did, he would not listen to her but to the bearded man, the loner who, it seemed, had more regard for animals than for humans.

'I hope he can help Patch get better,' she said to him before bending down to move backwards out of the low doorway.

The boy didn't answer but buried his face in the dog's panting body.

Frances retreated, making her way back down the sloping path to the cottage, the boy's mother and a more human problem, that of a woman who had put her faith in a man and found him wanting.

* * *

Sister Harrison had finished visiting the other patients and was waiting for her in the car.

Frances leaned into the back seat for the starting handle.

'So how did you get on?'

Sister Harrison's face was turned away. She was watching as a man got off a motorbike and leaned it against the garden wall. 'Look.'

Frances looked to where she was looking.

June Newman was standing at the front door. Her face paled as the motorcyclist glowered at Frances and Edith before striding off up the garden path, pushing June inside, slamming the door behind them.

'I take it that's the stepfather.'

'His name's Frank Steele. I know of him,' growled Sister Harrison.

'A bully from what the boy's just told me. He kicked the dog. I don't think the poor thing will last much longer.'

'He doesn't only strike out at the dog.'

'I'm guessing he also strikes the boy's mother.'

'Yes. She's too scared to give him his marching orders. I can't say I blame her. He's a nasty piece of work. If I was a man, I would...'

'So would I,' returned Frances, 'but it's her choice. All we can do is pick up the pieces and bathe the bruises.'

Frances asked the senior nursing sister how the rest of her charges were faring.

'As well as can be expected.'

'Those cottages should be pulled down.'

Sister Harrison agreed with her. She'd finished her visit in record time. Her eyes and her thoughts wandered along the towpath.

Frances recounted what Tommy Newman had said. 'He insisted he was taking the dog to our interesting stranger who lives on the boat. His real name is Harry Hunter.'

'Is it indeed.' Sister Harrison was intrigued and found herself wondering if from the very first she'd seen through that gruff exterior. There were some who had thought him little more than a tramp, a penniless vagabond. However, it seemed he was much more than that.

'Before you ask how I know, her ladyship informed Gregory of his visit, although Gregory was already party to the secret.'

Sister Harrison sifted the details she'd known before against what she knew now.

'Why the subterfuge? It seems very strange.'

'You're right. I thought the same thing. All I can put it down to is his state of mind, upset by war.'

'I feel for him.'

Frances nodded. 'It's as though that war reaches out with long tentacles, the tips still invading men's minds.'

'We need to make ourselves known to this man. Offer our services should he need them.' She didn't admit that he'd already refused her services. 'Anyway, I could do with a bit of fresh air. How about you, Doctor?'

'Then let's do so.'

'Yes, Doctor.'

Sister Harrison had a spring in her step as they sojourned the towpath, like a young girl impatient to get to her beau. Frances was in no doubt that the heart of her most senior nursing sister had been stolen by the man from the boat.

The funny thing was that Frances felt complicit in accompanying Sister Harrison on this venture. It was, she thought, not without amusement, as if they were a pair of schoolgirls with something naughty in mind.

There was no sign of life when they got to the boat. The cabin door was closed, and it had an unwelcome look about it.

They peered at the field opposite the boat. The land was marshy, too wet for ladylike heels.

'He's usually over there,' said Sister Harrison, nodding her head in the direction of the tumbledown shelter in the far corner. 'And look at all these hutches and suchlike. Birds in some, animals in others.'

'Gregory told me that Harry Hunter looked after the army horses and mules during the war. No wonder Tommy believes he would know how to treat his dog.'

'That would make sense,' said Sister Harrison in an authoritative manner.

The small laugh that escaped her throat sounded a little forlorn, but her eyes were bright and fierce with expectation.

Frances recognised all the signs of a woman who had fallen in love. *What fools we women are*, she thought. *We fall in love so easily, without knowing whether our feelings will be reciprocated.*

She mentioned Gregory saying that he'd been left this piece of land and that he was going to establish an animal sanctuary.

'I think it's a splendid idea,' declared Sister Harrison.

What with the glow in her eyes and the tone of her voice, Frances knew that anything this man did would meet with her approval.

There was no sign of anyone. The field was empty and knocking on the side of the boat brought no response.

'Time to be going back,' she said, backing away from the muddy entrance to the field and back onto the towpath. 'We've a hospital to tend to.'

* * *

Harry had seen the two women from inside the ramshackle hut at the far end of the field. He blinked in their direction for a moment whilst deciding whether he would acknowledge them or continue with what he was doing.

The animals came first, though he had been impressed by Sister Harrison, so clean in her crisply starched uniform. Nurses in the field hospitals had looked like that. No matter how terrible the conditions, they had somehow managed to keep up appearances. To men in pain and caked in mud, their bright cleanliness had made them seem like angels rescuing condemned men from the jaws of hell.

He had not expected to meet their like ever again, but here she was and he couldn't stop thinking about her.

15

Keen to get in on the act with the big boys, Clifford Fletcher had made friends with a local bank manager who also happened to play golf. He'd gone out of his way to cultivate what was basically a business relationship pretending to be friendship. Thank God for the golf course! And the nineteenth hole. Oiling one's target with a few drinks was a must in the world of making money.

The bank manager had wanted reassurances that a loan could be engineered as long as Clifford could put in a decent sum. Could that be done?

Yes. Of course it could. He'd raise the rents on the cottages he owned and perhaps sell the boathouse. Whether his tenants could afford a rent rise or not was neither here nor there. They'd find it from somewhere, increase their working hours perhaps? Sell something that they didn't really need.

The newspaper headlines were hinting at a slowdown in the economy, a lack of manufacturing jobs and a looming depression. Clifford didn't believe any of that. The British Empire was a force to be reckoned with. All those colonies supplying raw material and ripe for exploitation. He gave no credence to the grumblings of the labouring classes. They had no choice but to accept their lot – the rich man at his castle, the poor man at his gate. That was the way things were ordained.

The friendly acts over a game of golf and a few drinks proved worthwhile. On hearing about raising the rents, there was no reason why the venture could not go ahead. Clifford was confident. As it was he was proved to be correct.

'Yes,' said his bank manager, nodding affably as though he were just about to pull the necessary out of his wallet there and then. 'I'm investigating all avenues as regards finance. Government housebuilding is booming, and I can't see it diminishing any time soon – as long as they can get the land of course.'

'And that is just what I am offering,' said Clifford as he took a swing at the ball.

* * *

Back behind the bar of the Jolly Boatman, he helped himself to a double Scotch and tipped it back in one.

The finance was in place to purchase the piece of land he wanted. Weaver had failed to persuade the bloke on the boat to sign on the dotted line. A eureka moment flashed behind his eyes. Why not use the same method he used to snare the bank manager with the tramp, the bloke who'd been lucky enough to inherit a piece of land that was in the right place and was the right size to accommodate a whole estate of houses. That field was the key to the ones surrounding it because it offered access to what were at present land-locked fields.

In his mind's eye, he could see house after house stretching all the way to the horizon. What a sight!

But first, get the tramp to agree to sell it to him. Make it worth his while. Be friendly. Offer him free drinks at the Jolly Boatman perhaps?

First off to persuade him. Meet him face to face.

His wife, Nellie, caught him pouring himself another double, was about to snatch it from him when he swigged it back, got to his feet and announced that he was taking the dog for a walk.

Her eyebrows rose. Walking the dog had always been a chore he willingly passed on to anyone and everyone. 'What brought that on?'

'I want to give that bloke on the boat the chance to think again about that field.'

'You're gonna make him an offer he can't refuse?'

'Eventually I will, but for now I'm going to make him my friend.'

'I'm sure he'll be pleased,' she said somewhat sarcastically.

Clifford reached for the tidy tweed jacket hanging on the back of the chair.

Scrutinising it closely, he decided it was too posh looking to wear when making friends with a tramp.

'A means to an end,' he said while taking off his cufflinks and rolling up his shirtsleeves to just above the elbow. He also removed the bones from his collar and the tie from around his neck.

Nellie couldn't work a smile, but she did manage a sneer. 'You've got a bee in your bonnet about that bloody field. Is it really that special?'

Clifford's eyes glittered as he swiped the residue of booze from his lips. 'Yes, my love.' He pinched her cheek, a playful act, though it left a red mark. 'Homes fit for heroes will be built on that field. There's an act of parliament and a need for available land – land not too far from built-up areas so they can all run in together. New houses making a new town. And yours truly will be in on it. It'll make us our fortune.'

'So you're going to make him your friend.'

His wife cocked an eyebrow. Clifford thought he could befriend anybody, that everybody liked him.

'That is my intention.'

He sounded full of himself.

The dog looked surprised when the leash was clipped onto his collar.

'Don't drag him,' she said as he pulled the dog towards the door.

Clifford gave the dog a stronger tug so it had no option but to get up on all four legs. 'What's wrong with the bloody thing. Doesn't it like going for walks?'

He dragged it out through the door.

'Yes, he does like going for walks,' she murmured, 'just not with you.'

* * *

Days living on the boat away from humankind passed seamlessly, one day rolling imperceptibly into another. Harry Hunter valued solitude. Few people plodded the towpath unless they had good reason to be there. Being a canal rather than a river, it wasn't known to have many fish, so fishermen were few and far between.

A full twenty-four hours after he'd seen the women standing between his boat and the gate to the field, a distraught Tommy Newman arrived and interrupted the tasks for the day. At present he was setting out orange and cardboard boxes which he used to house injured animals. The cardboard box that had once contained tinned peaches housed a baby hedgehog he'd found all alone in a brown paper carrier bag stuffed under a hedge. He'd no idea what had happened to its mother, just that the little chap had taken refuge in the carrier bag and was hungry. He'd been trying to drip milk into its mouth with the aid of a piece of cloth soaked in milk, when Tommy had arrived, calling from the riverbank asking for help.

'Mr Ben! Mr Ben! Help me. Please help me.'

He didn't need to see tears to know that Tommy's heart was breaking.

The smell of small animals was left behind as the fresh air of the riverbank hit him.

Just as he'd expected, Tommy was standing there sniffling like mad in a bid to stop the tears. But still they came.

'The doctor couldn't do anything. She only knows how to cure people, not dogs!'

Although it amused Harry that Tommy could be so condemning, he held back the smile that threatened and stepped down off the boat. 'Give me him here. Let's see what we can do.'

His own dog, Talbot, followed him and looked up as he took Patch from the boy. The eyes of man and dog met with mutual sadness. He knew his dog well, and his dog knew him too so well that words were not always needed.

'He's very sick,' he said to the boy. 'You say the doctor couldn't help?'

Tommy shook his head. 'She said to take 'im to Mr Skinner. Skinner would put 'im to sleep. I don't want 'im put to sleep.'

Harry ran his hands over the dog's quaking body and surmised that putting the dog down would likely be the vet's advice.

'I can't promise,' he said as, with the dog in his arms, he got back onto the boat. The boy looked so panic-stricken that he couldn't help but add, 'Leave him with me. I'll do my best.'

The boy stood there looking unsure whether to go or stay. On seeing Clifford Fletcher accompanied by a dog, he took off.

Normally he would have stopped and petted the dog. He liked all dogs. People frightened him – or at least some did.

The man with the dog gave him no regard but, with bottom lip curled in contempt, headed towards the only boat moored here, its chimney stack puffing a plume of white smoke.

Clifford was on a mission to befriend the owner of the field he wanted to buy, a piece of land that could net him a fortune. He'd arrived just a bit later than he would have preferred and caught a glimpse of the top of the man's head disappearing out of sight.

Coming back another time was not an option. Taking the dog for a walk would be a one-off. *Strike while the iron's hot, Clifford. Strike while the iron's hot.*

Taking his own advice, he rapped on the side of the boat. 'Anyone there?'

Down below, Harry was laying a scrap of flannelette in an orange box where Tommy's dog lay barely clinging on to life. He'd also put in a stone hot-water bottle, then covered the dog with an old woollen pullover.

The interruption was a nuisance. He carried on with what he was doing in the hope that whoever it was would go away. Perhaps it was Mr Weaver? The thought of sending him off with a flea in his ear was too attractive to dismiss.

Bending his head, he ducked beneath the narrow opening between cabin and cockpit and stretched to his full height.

Talbot was lying halfway along the roof, growling deep in his throat. Harry had read somewhere that God had given humans reason so they could work things out for themselves. But he'd given animals instinct, the ability to discern whether to trust or distrust.

'Good day to you. My name's Clifford Fletcher.' Joviality rang in his voice though not a jot of insincerity.

Harry made no sign of knowing the name and, despite the feigned amiability, decided he didn't like the man. He grunted something in return that was almost a greeting, though barely discernible.

The smile on the ruddy face faltered when he got no clear response.

'I've been wanting to meet you. Heard a lot about you.'

Harry didn't press him for details. Just looked and waited.

Clifford, thinking the other man's silence meant he was the one in charge of this interchange, carried on in his bumptious manner. 'I wanted to make your acquaintance. You're a topic of conversation in the town, and in my pub. I own the Jolly Boatman, in case you didn't know.'

Harry still said nothing.

The man looked disarmed but not defeated.

Sensing his lack of response was making the other man nervous, Harry stayed silent.

'Travelled far, have you?'

Again a grunted response.

'I do admire an adventurer. Once an adventurer, always an adventurer. Where to next, if you don't mind me asking?'

Harry shrugged.

Irritated, but trying not to show it, Clifford went on, 'It's nice around here, don't you think?'

Harry gave no sign of having heard. He kept his eyes on the stranger. Was this who Weaver represented? He suspected as much.

'You must pop into the pub. The Jolly Boatman.'

He'd already said that, but seemed bent on ensuring that this traveller, this tramp, could find him.

He jerked his head to where tall brick chimneys showed like sentry boxes above the trees. 'The first drink is free. A welcome gesture, if you like.'

Harry was instantly on guard. A pub was a lethal mixture of people and jollity. He wouldn't be going there, certainly not alone. He dared to think that the nurse whose acquaintance he'd made might accompany him.

For now, not committed to anything, he turned his back.

'Can I expect you to call in?'

Clifford Fletcher didn't exactly sound desperate, but Harry sensed there was a reason for his attempt to entice him to the pub. There was also the look of him, that of a man who thought highly of himself.

He threw Clifford a blank look before slamming the overhead cover and washboard door behind him, shutting out whatever Clifford was saying.

Gathering his thoughts, Harry sank onto one of the narrow seats that doubled up as a bed. The cabin seemed stuffy after being up top. It had its own smell of glowing coals and diverse animal smells. A cosy smell, accompanied by the sound of snuffling creatures who needed his help.

Rain began pattering on the roof. It was a soothing sound, one that made the little cabin seem even more cosy.

He fingered the side of the orange box as he looked down at the boy's dog, Patch. What could he do? The dog was old and had two broken ribs thanks to the kicking he'd received. If he ever got his hands on Tommy's stepfather, he'd give him a kicking.

16

Teatime at Orchard Manor. Devlin was taking tea with his wife and his mother. Araminta had informed him of the visit of Harry Hunter, his half-brother.

At first, all three had sat there silently, eyeing the coconut and jam covering of the cakes, the spongy whiteness of the sandwiches.

Recognising that mother and son would prefer to discuss what was in effect a family matter dating from before her time, Lucy, Devlin's wife, used the excuse that, thanks to her condition, five months pregnant, she needed a lie-down.

Once the door closed behind her and after some thought, Devlin found his voice.

'I'd like to meet this man.'

Devlin had long known that his father had been generous with his favours, a charming man who used that charm to his physical advantage. Women fell for him and he could not resist responding.

Araminta nervously entwined her fingers. 'I thought it was all done and dusted. I presumed he'd died in the war. It seems I was wrong.'

'You never mentioned much about him.'

His mother's lips set in a bitter line. 'Your father died and to some extent the past died with him.'

'What about Harry's mother? What happened to her?'

His mother played with a loose thread on her cuff. 'Your father provided for her, though it didn't turn out as planned. Her name was Emily Hunter.'

'He gave her a settlement?'

Eyes averted, Araminta nodded. After all these years, she was being forced to face the reality of her late husband's infidelity. 'Your father thought he was acting for the best. Having a child out of wedlock was more shameful then than it is now. So he settled an allowance on her and found her a husband.' She looked up then, courage suddenly appearing in her eyes. 'It wasn't that uncommon, finding a willing man to accept a fallen woman complete with an allowance. In fact, I know of someone else who...' She waved her hand dismissively. 'That's neither here nor there.' Doctor Brakespeare had also been born into similar circumstances, though her mother had fared better than Emily Hunter. It was her business, separate to this one.

She carried on explaining how it had been for Emily Hunter.

'So Emily Hunter became Mrs Emily Skittings.'

'Skittings!' Devlin's eyebrows arched with surprise. 'You mean... he was Ma Skittings' brother?'

Araminta nodded. 'And nothing like his sister. He was a brute, too free and easy with his fists. One day she was sent sprawling. Her head hit a cupboard.' She shook her head. 'That was it.'

'Was this man, Skittings, prosecuted for the crime?'

His mother seemed to think about it before shaking her head. 'He ate something bad for him and died shortly afterwards. Harry disappeared. We heard that at only a few years after he was twelve years old, he joined the army. Lied about his age, I suppose, one of the early ones before the war happened and boys lying about their age became a flood.'

Devlin rubbed at the bridge of his nose. His eyesight had been destroyed in the war, but a vivid imagination had given him an inner sight. He could imagine his mother's face from the picture in his mind retained from his youth.

'Describe him more fully, Mother. I want to know what he looks like.'

She sighed and for a moment he thought she would not comply. After another sigh, she began, 'His hair is overlong and he has a full beard.'

'Very big?'

'Yes.'

'And a fine head of hair?'

'Correct. He looks like a lion.'

'Not a man to go bald then,' he said with some amusement as he rubbed hair that was thinning and receding from his forehead.

His laughter faded. He was not unduly worried that his hair was thinning. He was middle-aged and getting older. He was still alive and although he had to cope with blindness, he had a good life. There were many casualties still in pain from the war that was supposed to end all wars – though, somehow, he didn't feel that it would. Humanity was self-destructive; that was the way it seemed to him. They would find an excuse to kill again.

He shuffled his thoughts back to the here and now, the pleasant room where sunshine through the large windows fell on his shoulders.

'He sounds like a man who went off the rails after all he'd experienced. Slaughter changes men's character. I've heard that some cannot face returning to their former life because they are no longer that person.'

'I want to meet him.' His voice was forthright, demanding even.

Hidden from his sightless eyes, his mother tossed her head and tried not to recall how much she'd loved her husband and her anguish each time he'd strayed.

'I will ask him to check Captain. He prescribed a bland diet for the old boy, but it wouldn't hurt to have him check that all is well.'

Her thoughts were back before the war when she'd burned with the fire of women's suffrage. She knew now that her attitude had made her insufferable to her husband. She had no longer been the girl he'd married, the one who'd conformed to what a dutiful wife should be. Perhaps others were responsible for changing her, Izzy Brakespeare, Doctor Brakespeare's guardian. Or perhaps the firebrand she'd become had always been there, waiting for someone or something to bring the flame into being.

Whatever, a divide had opened between her and her husband, although she had been warned before marriage that he had a roving eye.

'Love is blind,' she whispered.

Devlin heard her. *Yes*, he thought. *It was*. Though his blindness had brought him the love of his life.

'I look forward to meeting him. Let me know what you arrange.'

17

Yesterday's wind and rain had left the air fresh and streams of water coming down the lane from the main road fanned out across the path before falling into the river.

The man who had brought the message from her ladyship asking him to check on her horse had offered to take Harry to the manor house in the car.

He'd refused.

'Not until I'm ready.'

The car had left. He'd taken his time doing the chores he had to do until he was ready at his own convenience.

His legs were strong. He got to the manor house at a reasonable time.

Know your place, he thought as he made his way around the back to the stables.

The stables surrounded a central courtyard. They were built of red brick, had an arched entrance big enough to take a coach and horses and now cars. A clocktower sat like a sentry on the slate-tiled roof overlooking the yard.

The stable lad who took him to the horse named Captain had a curious look on his face.

'There's nothing wrong with 'im. Reckon they got you up yer on a wild goose chase.'

Harry suggested that he be the judge of that.

He ran his hand down each of the animal's legs. There was no sign of laminitis. He hadn't expected there to be, so long as his advice had been followed.

The stable lad informed him that her ladyship wished to have a word before he left.

Scratching his head, he left the stables and went out into the yard. The lad escorted him, keeping three steps behind.

Her ladyship was waiting at the back door.

He glared at her. *Why was she wasting his time?*

'There's nothing wrong with the horse. Do you want to tell me the real reason?'

She fixed her perceptive gaze on him, convincing him that there was another reason she had asked him here.

Their looks held. There was a slight smile on her face, a controlled expression on his that gave nothing much away.

'My son wants to meet you.' Her eyelids flickered. 'Please don't dwell too much on the war. Devlin still has nightmares, you see.'

Harry bent his head, his broad hands flexing and unflexing over the handle of the spade standing upright beside him in its bed of manure.

'We all do. Even those men who came back and look whole, uninjured, are no longer whole.'

She took a deep breath, eyes half closed as she thought through what she intended saying.

'A shell exploded close to where Devlin was. He lost his sight and walks with a stick.'

Harry looked to where a rambling rose was bursting with buds, clambering up a stout brick wall as though seeking to escape.

She felt more so than heard what was in his head. Like Devlin, the sounds and sights of battle were still there. It was all part of the aftermath of a war that had begun with patriotic fervour and somehow had ended the same way, as though the victory achieved had not come at such a high price.

She studied him cautiously. The silence was going on too long. She kept it simple.

'Follow me. I will take you to meet my son.'

They went through the shabby room filled with dogs and a Persian cat that lay curled up on the chair. They attempted to follow but she ordered him shut the door.

'We don't want them following us. They're not allowed into the parlour.'

Feeling slightly unnerved, he shoved his hands into his pockets and thought carefully about what he was going to say and how to say it. He felt an innate trepidation. Lady Compton-Dixon had not turned out to be the superior lady of leisure he'd envisaged. What would his half-brother be like?

There was a world of difference between the back of the house and the front. The rooms were not opulent as palace rooms might be, but they did have grandeur.

A maid stood back against the wall as they passed from the corridor into a hallway where light flooded like liquid from a glass dome at the full height of the ceiling.

Her ladyship ordered the maid to bring tea to her son's apartments.

'For obvious reasons, my son's living quarters are on the ground floor. They've been enlarged since he acquired a wife and child.'

The maid hadn't moved, her startled gaze fixed on Harry.

'Stop being a goose, Mildred, and do as I say.'

Araminta chuckled as the maid finally left.

'Your appearance has impact.'

She wanted to ask him whether he owned a shaving razor, but decided it was none of her business. He was hiding. That was the conclusion she'd come to.

The warmth of the room, by virtue of the sun shining through the windows, hit him.

Devlin was standing by the fireplace leaning on a stick. Harry noted the alert expression on his half-brother's face as he turned. He guessed that other senses made up for that of eyesight.

'Mr Hunter. Harry.' Devlin stretched out his hand to be shaken.

Harry noted the slight trembling as he took it, a sign that men who had served noticed when others did not.

'Pleased to meet you. Sorry to drag you in here, but I so wanted to make your acquaintance. There's so much we have in common – besides having the same father, that is.'

The maid bustled in with the tea things balanced on a large silver tray.

It surprised Harry when Lady Araminta made moves to leave but paused at the door. 'Gentlemen, I leave you with tea and your memories.' She threw a warning expression at Harry.

Devlin requested he might like to pour the tea.

'Makes sense. I would only spill it,' Devlin said laughingly.

'That's fine.'

'Sugar and milk for me.'

Harry took in the details of Devlin's scarred face before pouring tea, adding sugar and milk. He passed the cup and saucer over.

If Devlin had been able to see, he would have seen his half-brother staring at him, searching the fair features, the shape of his jaw, the high forehead and the broad shoulders. There were more familiar features than unfamiliar. He was only glad that Devlin could not see his astonished expression.

Not for one instant did he consider how he should address her ladyship's son. Thankfully, Devlin took the lead.

'First, let us discard with formality. Call me Devlin. And I will call you Harry. If that is all right with you?'

It was difficult to stop his hands shaking and he just about managed to stop his voice from doing the same. 'I'm fine with that.'

'Can you take my cup and saucer and place it on this small table to my left?'

He noticed how accurately Devlin reached for it once he'd placed it there, as though by sound alone he knew its exact position.

Tea forgotten, totally immersed in this moment, Harry sat down where it seemed most convenient.

'Where do we begin, Harry. I've heard about your background, and the war. I'm betting my mother ordered you not to mention the war.' He gave a light laugh. 'She's more protective of me than my wife, almost as though I'm still nine years old. But there, she has good intentions. She believes in doing things right.'

Harry looked down at the way his hands dwarfed the fragile bone china teacup and saucer. The crockery was a bit like how he'd envisaged her ladyship. Finding her in the stable yard that first time had shattered his deep-held beliefs.

'She seems quite a woman.'

'And not at all how you expected her to be.'

Harry had to reply that it was true. He'd expected a delicate woman dressed in lavender silk, not someone attired like an aged yard manager. 'I have to admit, she did surprise me.'

'She told me you were a wrangler, taking care of the army horses. Quite a task. A lot of us owe our lives to their untiring strength.'

'Like mates. You become closer to some of your mates than others.'

Devlin remained silent. Though his eyes could not see, he so wanted to talk about the war to someone who had been there, someone who shared his blood.

'What do you look like?'

Harry got where he was coming from. Like him he was curious. However, he was reluctant to answer in detail.

'I'm tall, broad and my eyes are a bluish green, so I've been told. My hair used to be lighter than it is now. A muddy brown, I suppose, though the grey is taking over.'

Early, so he'd been told. Caused by extreme terror.

'Do you have a sense of humour? I'm presuming you do. I do, and I recall my father had a sense of humour. My mother does too, but that's irrelevant under the circumstances. And are you musical? My father was, though sadly I am not.'

Harry curled his callused fingertips into the palms of his hands. That's what playing an instrument did, especially a stringed instrument like the violin.

There was more small talk, dates, memories of what the trenches had been like, what France had been like. The wine. The cheese. The women.

They also talked about mates. Harry spoke of Ben, his best friend. 'We were dead close.'

'My mother said you still have his ashes.'

Inclined to nod at first before reminding himself that Devlin couldn't see his nod.

'I do.'

'You pretended that he was you and that you wanted his ashes interred in the family crypt. An odd way of exacting revenge for the circumstances of your birth, if you don't mind me saying.'

'Yes. That was the plan.' A plan that now made him feel guilty. 'I'm sorry.'

Silence came when the biggest question hovered between them.

'You want to know what happened. My experiences,' Harry surmised.

'Yes.'

The silence again, like a shroud between them, a shroud that encompassed so many bodies, so many young men.

'Chaos all round. Shells and bullets whizzing all around us. The order to keep going forward.' He expressed a low chuckle, a derisory chuckle, certainly not one of amusement. He went on to describe a bloodbath that seemed to go on all day. 'Eventually there was respite – at least for us. Out of breath and worn out, we made it back to a ruined barn on the other side of a small copse of trees where we kept the horses. It was cold, so we lit a fire. We shouldn't have really. Straw and hay were stored there. But we were exhausted.'

Harry bit his bottom lip as he collected his thoughts. Went on to tell about hearing someone outside, going out there alone to investigate.

'A shell hit it. The whole thing blew up. Stones everywhere. There was a fire. The horses were screaming.'

Harry shook his head. He hadn't meant to repeat that same scenario ever again, but it kept flooding out.

'I was the only one who survived. There was nothing left but ash.'

'Take your time, old chap.'

The tea helped. Once that was gone, he cleared his throat and in a wavering voice told Devlin of waiting for a whole day until the ashes were no longer smouldering. Of how he had scooped the still warm ashes of his best friend into a sack. How once he'd got back to the trench, he had transferred those ashes into a biscuit tin.

For Devlin's part, it felt as though his eyes were on fire and his throat had closed. He could see it behind his eyelids, hear the exploding shell, the screams of animals and soldiers.

He related as much of his own experience as he remembered.

'I was knocked out. I came round in the hospital unable to see but do remember the smell of it: festering wounds, carbolic soap. The greatest relief was when a nurse leaned over me. She smelled so clean.'

'Angel of mercy,' Harry whispered.

'Yes. An angel of mercy.' Devlin paused. 'I'm sorry about what happened to your mother, married off to that brute, Jack Skittings.'

Harry's head jerked up. He thought he knew everything there was to know, but did Devlin know something he did not? He decided it was worth pursuing.

'Skittings. Is he still alive?'

'I wouldn't know. The only person who would know that is his sister, Ma Skittings. She still lives in the town, though, according to my mother, Jack Skittings died from a stomach condition after eating something that disagreed with him.'

18

It was a fine Sunday morning, sunny outside the church, the shade inside relieved by the red, blues, yellow and green falling onto the nave from the arched windows.

The Reverend Gregory Sampson shook the hands of his congregation. One eagle-eyed soul remarked that a few stones had come loose above the church porch.

'I could fix that for you in no time.'

Of course he could; Ted Baker was a builder.

Gregory remarked that the winter rain was to blame, plus the heat of the summer before. Occurring one after the other made the mortar crumble.

A small notebook and pencil appeared as if by magic. 'I'll make a note of that.'

The smell of Sunday roasts was drifting from nearby houses. Church, a Sunday roast and a stroll in one's Sunday best; that was the norm for most people on the day of rest.

Frances had loitered in the cool shade of the church while Gregory did his duty. She watched him shake hands and make comment that was personal to whoever he was addressing.

He asked Miss Matthews, the pharmacist's sister, how her roses were doing. He asked after the rheumatic knees of Mrs Cambridge, an elderly widow. He also enquired of Ma Skittings whether her bees would produce a good crop of honey this year.

Frances looked on, full of affection and admiration for this man she had agreed to marry. Gregory was one of the few people she'd ever met whose memory enabled him to engage in this way. He might not have a clue about the growing of roses or the keeping of bees, but he made it sound as though he did.

After instructing her son, his wife and baby to go ahead of her to the car, her ladyship, Araminta Compton-Dixon, asked to have a word with him.

'It's a private matter,' she said, once it was just the two of them – although Frances still lingered close by. 'Someone is after the field my late husband left to Mr Hunter. I'd like to know who it is and what I can do to deter him. Have you heard anything?'

Gregory shifted his stance a little so that he was facing the inner sanctum of the church, his back to the warm glow of a sunlit Sunday. 'I've heard nothing; though, of course, I will inform you if I do.'

Araminta's look was steadfast, her expression as rigid as if it had been sculpted from a whole ice block. 'I hold my late husband responsible for a lot of cruel things, not least his treatment of me. But I will not allow anyone to upset his atonement for one of his indiscretions. He left that field to Harry Hunter. I believe he's quite capable of looking after himself, but if needed, he has my full unqualified support.'

The sins of the fathers, thought Gregory. Only, in this instance, Sir Compton-Dixon had shown his regret through the giving of the gift of land in his will.

* * *

After church, Ma Skittings was checking last year's stock of honey. She kept it in a meat safe, a metal contraption with perforated doors, designed to be left in a cool place. The meat safe was kept in shadow at the rear of the cottage next to a water butt.

With almost childish delight, she watched a glistening royal blue damsel fly flitter around the entrance to the water butt before flying off. 'Delightful.'

Shutting the door on her sweet and copious harvest, she turned, meaning to obtain the cool pleasance of her cottage kitchen. Instead, she found herself up against a solid structure that at first seemed like a wall. She swiftly realised it was a man.

Taken aback, she gasped and looked up at him. His beard and hair were streaked with grey but remarkable for all that. His deep-set eyes were a bluish green. The look in them was hard to read. Alarm? Hate? She saw the iron-clad look of determination – but determination to do what?

'You're Ma Skittings.'

He didn't ask her whether she was. He knew she was and had addressed her accordingly.

She returned what wasn't so much a compliment as a challenge.

'I've been expecting you.'

She didn't need to ask his name. She knew. Not because the vicar had told her, or anyone else for that matter. She just knew.

Giving the back door a push with her meaty hand, she invited him in.

As expected, it was cool inside, the small square windows preventing the increasing heat of early summer from entering.

She didn't invite him to sit down but did ask if he would like a cool drink.

'I've some blackberry wine, last year's vintage. Or water infused with mint.'

He shook his head.

She sensed his pent-up anger.

'You said you were expecting me.'

'Once I heard your name mentioned.'

He didn't ask who had told her. It didn't matter.

'I wanted to know about the man who killed my mother.'

There was something about the way Ma Skittings looked at him that raked at his inside, as though she was gathering up fallen leaves – or his thoughts. His very history.

She nodded slowly, eyes downcast. 'My brother. He was no good. Left outside the front door by the gypsies – or the little folk, according to my mother. It was neither. He was just a bad lot. Always had been.'

'Can you confirm that he is dead? I find it a tall tale to swallow.'

When she smiled, her eyes were unblinking.

'What have you been told?'

'That he died after eating something that had disagreed with him.'

'Don't you believe that?' The look on her face was unfathomable, almost mischievous.

Odd as it seemed, it felt as if he'd been backed into a corner. Did he believe it or did he not?

'Is it true?'

Ma Skittings didn't answer straight away, but looked around the kitchen, the bunches of herbs hanging from beams, the jars with odd-looking contents sitting in an ordered battalion on shelves set into alcoves.

'My brother made my life a misery. He made my mother's life a misery and he made Emilia's life a misery. And then he killed her. Enough was enough.'

She crossed the room and stood close to the shelves, her finger marking each one as though she was counting them.

'None of them have labels,' she said to him. 'I've memorised the contents of every single one. I know what I need when I need it. Is that enough for you,' she said, suddenly turning round and taking him by surprise.

Her eyes met his. He knew what he was reading in them. There was no need for anything else to be said. Justice had been done, though not in the more orthodox manner. It was enough for him.

19

Monday had a different feel to it than Sunday. The day of rest was over. The working week had begun, for Harry one day was very much like another. For him it meant inspecting the injured and sick creatures in his care. Even before he had examined them, he knew which ones had recovered. He could tell just by the sounds they made, or even the atmosphere, the smell in the air.

Patch lay in his bed beneath the scrap of blanket. His pink tongue protruded from his mouth. His eyes were closed.

Harry pulled the scrap of blanket around him. Wild creatures who did not survive he buried in the soft mud among the whispering reeds. Patch was a different matter. He belonged to Tommy, and it was up to Tommy to decide on the burial arrangements – when the time came, and he was sure the time would indeed come very soon.

He hoped young Tommy would be brave but knew there were likely to be tears.

Resigned to what would happen, he went up top with a mug of tea, sat on the boat roof with Talbot beside him and waited for him to come.

* * *

On that same morning, Tommy had eaten his piece of fried bread with little appetite. Not eating had attracted the wrath of Frank Steele who was waiting to be fed even though he had no intention of making an honest day's living. He'd make his money tonight, trapping wild animals whose pelts he would sell to furriers, the meat to anyone with a shilling to spare – though there weren't so many of those at present. Sometimes he had to settle for tenpence or even sixpence.

Regardless of his lack of enthusiasm for turning an honest shilling, he still expected a workman's breakfast. Not for him a slice of stale bread fried in lard. Two eggs sizzled in the pan alongside a rasher of bacon.

The air was blue with the smoke and smell of the generous breakfast. If it didn't come soon, the air would turn blue with angry words.

June knew it wouldn't be long before that happened. She was doing her best, but the best was never good enough for Frank.

'Come on, woman! If you don't scoop them eggs out shortly, they'll be frilled all around the edges. You knows I don't like 'em like that.'

'But if you want your bacon crisp...'

'Of course I wants me bacon crisp, you stupid cow. But I don't like me eggs brown 'round the edges.'

June had regretted cooking eggs and bacon at the same time.

'Nearly ready, Frank. Just putting the fried bread in the pan.' She kept her voice upbeat.

In a last-minute desperate attempt to keep the eggs warm, she put a pan of water onto the gas and a plate on the top, a saucepan lid on that. With a bit of luck, the water would boil quickly enough to warm the plate, which in turn would keep the eggs warm.

Face red from the heat of the gas stove, she scooped the eggs out of the pan and placed them on the plate. She added a large lump of lard to the pan, along with a doorstep of bread. The bacon rashers were crisping nicely and hopefully the addition of the lard wouldn't turn them soggy.

'Pour me another cup of tea.'

One eye on the frying pan, June jumped to it, even though the teapot was on the table next to him.

She felt his eyes on her, his gloating expression. Last night, he had used her like a dog might a bitch. He'd hurt her, pulling on her hair as he thrust again and again, ignoring her cries that he was hurting her, threatening to hurt her more if she didn't stop her whining.

It was becoming obvious that he liked hurting her, not just physically, but mentally. So far, she'd managed to keep a distance between him and her son, but it didn't stop him threatening to do cruel things. The worst would be to part mother from son. It was something he indulged in on a regular basis.

'I was reading in the paper that you can offer up orphans and bastard kids for resettlement in Australia. I'm thinking you should offer up the kid. There's no future for 'im here. Out there he might make 'is way in the world.'

This was a threat she had not heard before. She almost dropped the teapot.

'Frank, you can't mean it. I couldn't do that.'

Frank's gloating expression intensified and there was pleasure in his eyes at the torment he was causing. 'Well, the boy's got to live somewhere.'

'But he lives here. With me. With us!'

'It's up to me who lives 'ere. I'm the one who pays the rent.'

It wasn't entirely true, but arguing would only make things worse.

'I could chuck you out if I wanted, so mind what you say, woman. Mind what you say or it'll be the worse for you and that sooty-faced scrap. The best thing would be to send the boy to Australia. They don't mind having mongrels live there. They take all sorts.'

'That's terrible to call him that. He's not a dog.'

Frank's eyes glittered at the pain he was causing, and he wasn't finished yet.

'He's a mongrel. A black man's kid. How could you have spread your legs for 'im, eh? A bitch on heat! That's what you were.'

This was too much. For this once, June dared to argue.

'I was not! I loved his father and he loved me,' she said, the tears of fear and pain running down her face.

She was hit sideways by the strength of the blow. Never had she seen Frank looking shocked as well as angry.

And then it came to her. He had hit her because she'd said that she'd actually loved Joe, Tommy's father. It was very likely the worst thing she could have said.

Smoke suddenly billowed from the frying pan behind her. Responding swiftly, she grabbed the handle and cried out because she had used her bare hand instead of a cloth.

Tending to everything as quickly as she could, she just about saved the eggs and swiftly fried another piece of bread. The bacon she turned out onto the plate was brittle and broke when Frank stabbed his fork into it. She was close enough for him to punch her in the ribs.

'I like it crisp, not burned, you silly cow!'

Tommy curled up in the corner, trying desperately to make himself as small as possible.

On finishing his breakfast, Frank flung down his cutlery so hard it almost broke the plate. 'Burnt bloody offerings,' he muttered and lit a cigarette, sighing with satisfaction as a plume of smoke rose into the air.

If he'd noticed she'd burnt her hand, he made no mention of it. Either, she thought, he hadn't noticed or didn't care.

Persuading herself that he did care for her had become a habit that was hard to break, but it was breaking now. His treatment of her son, his plan to have him shipped off to Australia, had impacted on her. Far more than a burnt hand.

June's hands trembled as she got to her feet. Her nose was bleeding. Such was her habit, that she blamed herself, of course. The bacon had been too crisp.

He didn't offer to do anything to staunch the bleeding. He never did and never blamed himself for hitting her. It was always her fault. She cringed when he scraped a sliver of tobacco leaf from the corner of his mouth and looked at her with nothing but contempt in his eyes.

'Wash yer bloody face. You ain't fit to be seen.'

She held a cloth under the cold tap. It did help to ease her bruised nose and in time would stop the blood.

Out of the corner of her eye, she saw Tommy make a run for it.

Frank saw too. 'Oi. Where do you think you're going.'

June already knew that the boy's dog was very ill and expected the worse, though she wouldn't mention that to Frank – just in case. If the dog was dead, Frank would throw him in the river or even in the dustbin and to do that would break Tommy's heart. If she dared say he was close to death, he would finish the job off and not in a compassionate way. He enjoyed inflicting pain; she'd learned that the hard way.

Thankfully, Tommy had left the dog with the stranger on the narrowboat.

She sighed with relief when Frank went out the back door whistling. The fact that he had a newspaper tucked beneath his arm meant he'd be out in the privy for some time.

June turned on the kitchen tap, bent over the sink and covered the dirty dishes in the sink with hot water from the kettle. By adding cold water, the spots of blood from her injury were dispersed and ran with her tears down the drain. More cold water to ease her burnt hand.

She stared at her hand. There would likely be a scar though not a big one. The biggest scar was the hurt she carried inside, but along with it was a determination to protect her son no matter what.

20

Tommy had skedaddled as soon as he could, wishing he was big enough and strong enough to land a few blows on Frank Steele's flabby face. But he wasn't, not yet. In time he would stand between Frank and his mother, but that time was yet to come.

On seeing Tommy running along the towpath, Harry tamped out the tobacco from the pipe he'd been smoking and tossed the dregs from his mug into the canal.

Standing on the towpath, he waited for Tommy to get to him, not saying anything, just waiting.

Perhaps it was something about his stance that relayed a message to Tommy without a word being said. His running steps slowed, and a knowing look came to his face. By the time Harry reached him, his feet were dragging.

When Harry shook his head, for a moment his hair hid his eyes.

'Come aboard,' he said softly.

There were few luxuries on board, but the heat from a coal-fired range – a small affair used for both cooking and heating in the cramped conditions – staved off the early-morning chill. Despite that, the boy still shivered.

As he looked down on the dog, he half-filled an enamel mug with tea and handed it to the boy. Tommy glanced at it before his hooded eyes went back to the sick dog.

'He's not very well is he, Mr Ben?' Tommy had not yet got used to using his real name. Not that it mattered much. It was something special between them. All that mattered to Tommy was his beloved dog. 'Is he going to die?' asked Tommy, laying the tea aside, his voice no more than a whisper.

Harry kept a steady voice and unwavering eyes as he skirted around the truth. 'Might. Might not. He'll go when he's ready and not before.'

'How do you know when it's the right time?'

'Not me. Him. He'll choose his time. Be grateful that you've given the animal the best years of his life.'

Not so easily fobbed off, Tommy asked the same question again. 'But is he going to die?'

'Of course he is,' was the gruff response, given in a bid to hide his own heartfelt emotions. 'Though I can't tell you when he's going to die, or when I'm going to die or even when you're going to die. It's a mystery, so it is. A mystery.'

Taking a sugar lump from the bowl, he pushed it between the dog's flews. At first, Patch licked and then hesitantly sucked the whole thing in.

'That'll give him a bit of energy,' he said. 'Help him survive a bit longer.'

Suddenly Tommy looked hopeful. 'Thanks, Mr Ben.'

'Harry,' he said. 'You can call me Harry.'

'Thanks, Mr Harry.'

'Just Harry.'

He felt Patch's chest and the pounding of the little heart against the fragile ribs; almost as though it was trying to break free. Even without the pulsating frame, he could see the ribcage moving in an abnormal fashion. More than one rib was broken, the jagged end possibly pressing on the dog's lungs, if not his heart. If the blow had been strong enough, there was a chance that the chest bone had snapped.

He stroked the dog gently and was concerned to see that the animal seemed unaware of his presence. In his estimation, the dog's last serious attempt at living had been the sugar lump.

It wouldn't be long.

'Shouldn't you be in school?'

'I don't want to go. I've got to stick around for Patch.'

'Ah! I'd forgotten. I've had a busy day.'

His mind was still busy. Although she hadn't said it outright, what Ma Skittings had said was enough to tell him that her brother had died of food poisoning. That row of jars on her kitchen shelves confirmed the heavy hint she'd given him. Ma Skittings had dealt with her brother as she saw fit.

Although the dog was on its last legs, it was best he was with the boy. It was, he thought, like being in hospital, away from your relatives and mates.

Tommy had a good heart. Still, he had to give him the option. 'I think you know he's dying, don't you, Tommy.'

Tommy nodded sadly.

'Do you want to leave him here?'

'No. I'll take him home.'

'He can't walk there, mind you.'

'I know that.' Tommy's little voice was flecked with anger.

'Your wish is my command. If you can get yourself off over the side, I'll hand him to you. Can you do that?'

The boy rubbed at the dirty wetness of his tear-streaked cheeks.

Once Tommy had clambered over the side of the boat and was back on the stony path, Harry gently handed the dog over the side of the boat.

'Keep him comfortable. That's all you can do. If you need me tomorrow, come and fetch me.'

He watched the boy walk away, the skin-and-bone terrier cradled in equally skinny arms. He knew nothing much about Tommy but guessed the boy didn't have much of a home life and that the dog was his only comfort.

He clutched at his chest. A cough threatened. He knew what it was. Blood smearing the back of his hands or spat into a scrap of cotton that served as a handkerchief. He'd thought he was over it, but apparently not.

The fresh air did him good, though he knew he should see a doctor – but what for? TB was what it was. His experiences in the trenches hadn't helped. Back then, he and his comrades had endured a poor diet, poor hygiene and constant infections passed from man to man. Trench foot had been another problem. Gangrene for the wounded. Some survived. Some didn't.

When he turned to climb back on the boat, the world turned too. Like the one and only time he'd been to the fair and got sick on the merry-go-round. That's how it was.

He was vaguely aware of a few people walking along the towpath, his blurred vision failing to take notice of who they were or how smartly they were dressed.

Dizziness was a swarm of bees circling his head, playing with his vision.

Weakness was a sinking feeling travelling from his mind, through his muscles and down to his knees.

Weakness was something he abhorred, but in this instance was stronger than him.

He dropped to the ground, unaware of the hard ground beneath him, the stones that scratched at his face. He knew nothing except that Talbot was barking. It was difficult to tell when he stopped but stop he did. No barking but the faint sound of concern, the unmistakeable sound of human voices.

He was vaguely aware of a female voice insisting on calling an ambulance to take him to the hospital straight away.

The voice was gentle yet firm and she smelled crisp and clean.

Not that he could respond.

Oblivion called. He wondered if this was the day he would die, but he wasn't afraid. He'd faced death before.

21

It was on the Wednesday following Harry's admission into hospital that Frances and Sister Harrison stood looking down him. Professional expressions covered their concern. Falling to pieces when faced with grave illness was never an option.

'I won't tell you how to proceed, Sister Harrison. Thank goodness we had the isolation room available.'

They were both wearing masks as a protective measure. As yet, Frances wasn't convinced they were faced with tuberculosis, but it paid to be cautious. Blood spots spat by someone suffering this awful disease were known to be highly contagious. Her inclination was that he'd incurred a weakness in his lungs whilst serving in the trenches. He was hardly the first she'd come across but knew there was little she could do, except advise good food and fresh air. He was certainly getting a large dose of the latter living on the boat.

Sister Harrison was unusually quiet. 'It strikes me that he's a man who needs to look after himself better.'

'You could be right.'

'He might feel a bit better if he didn't have all that hair growing around his face.'

The senior sister was eyeing the man in a certain way. Over time, Frances had gained some skill in reading what was on her mind.

However, the poor man had the right to make his own decision about whether he was shaved or not. Frances felt obliged to mention this fact.

'Sister Harrison. Can I suggest you wait until he comes round and ask his permission before you shave his face and cut his hair?'

'It's sound advice.'

Frances sighed. There was something almost motherly in the way Sister Harrison was eyeing the sleeping man. 'It may be, but it's his decision.'

There were times when Sister Harrison had to be reminded that her word might be law for the nurses in her charge – even for patients – but she frowned at the prospect of shaving an unconscious man without his permission.

'Wait until he comes round. Is that clear, Sister Harrison?'

'Of course, Doctor.'

Sister Harrison took the man's temperature yet again. Doctor Brakespeare wouldn't know it, but she sorely wanted to see the features hidden by all that hair.

What a turn-up, her a dutiful woman, still a spinster, but one who delighted in reading trashy romances. Yet they weren't trashy. Not to her. They took her away from the daily grind and into worlds she had no hope of ever experiencing.

Her addiction to romantic fiction was well known. Not so her belief in the supernatural, fortune tellers, the force of the full moon in a cloudless sky, a black cat crossing her path. She believed it all.

And this man. What if he was the romantic dream envisaged? All she needed to do was to see his face without all that hair. Was that such a big wish?

And it might help him breathe better. And her see what lay beneath.

* * *

Gregory was in her office when Frances got back there.

'Hope you don't mind. Sister Peebles showed me in.'

'And brought us tea,' said Frances, nodding at the tea tray set at the very centre of her desk.

She sighed as she took the weight off her feet.

'Let me.'

He took the pot and poured, added milk. No sugar. Not for her. She'd never had a sweet tooth.

They sipped silently, each contemplating their own thoughts.

After taking a sip of tea, she tried to read the look on Gregory's face. There was reticence. There were also lines furrowing his brow.

He asked her whether Harry would recover.

She nodded as she replaced her cup in the saucer. 'Yes. I believe he will. His main problem is that he hasn't been taking care of himself properly for a long time. I think I'm right in saying that boats are damp contraptions – hardly a cosy fireplace for an invalid.'

'I don't think he would like to hear you referring to him as an invalid.'

'I'm afraid it's what he is – at least at the present time.'

She noticed Gregory's frown lines deepen.

'Something about him worries you.'

His sigh was swallowed at the same time as a mouthful of tea.

'I knew so many men. Their faces become a blur. Meeting up with him takes me back there.' He shrugged. 'Never mind. It's water under the bridge, but I'm intrigued.'

Frances's smile was in her eyes as well as on her lips when she said, 'Not so intrigued as Sister Harrison. I do believe she's in love with him.'

Gregory's corn-ripe eyebrows rose. 'Really?'

'You may recall that Ma Skittings, in gypsy fortune-telling mode, told her there was a romance on the horizon.'

'A tall dark stranger?' He looked highly amused. 'Isn't that what they all say?'

'Don't laugh. She believes in strange things, though you wouldn't think so to look at her.'

'But surely she knows it wasn't a real gypsy fortune teller, that it was Ma Skittings filling in?'

Her smile faded. 'Sometimes we want to believe in the impossible, but she did know. She just chose to ignore it in order to preserve hope.'

Their respite was short-lived. A junior nurse came to advise them that Mr Hunter had regained consciousness.

Once she'd left the office, Gregory wound his arms around Frances and looked down into her face. A lovely face, though creased with more lines thanks to the advent of the years. He kissed her forehead. 'I never thought that Sister Harrison and I had anything in common. I was wrong.'

Frances's grey eyes fixed on his, her chin drawing in with amused surprise. 'And what might that be?'

'Hope,' he said softly. 'Just hope.'

Feeling slightly unnerved, she unbound herself from his arms. 'I have accepted your proposal.'

'Not publicly.'

'No. Not yet.'

A crease appeared between his eyebrows. 'That's what worries me. I will be on edge until we name the fateful day.'

She threw back her head and laughed. 'Fateful! A word that smacks of doom and gloom.'

'I didn't mean it to sound that way.'

She smiled. 'We will get there, Gregory. Our fate is sealed.'

'With a kiss?'

She nodded. 'With a kiss.'

Her lips tingled in the aftermath of that kiss and she was sure she smiled all the way to the ward.

When she got there, the smile slipped from her face on learning that Harry Hunter had already left.

Sister Harrison looked mortified. 'He waited until nobody was on the ward and fled.' Her dismay was obvious. 'He should have waited for you to examine him before he left.'

Frances knew she was right. There was only one thing they could do.

'If the mountain won't come to Mohammed, then Mohammed will have to go to the mountain.'

Sister Harrison looked confused.

'I won't impose myself on him. That's for you to do.'

Sister Harrison looked surprised. 'Me?'

'He needs a nurse to call in on him on a regular basis. Sister Peebles can't take on any more patients, so it will have to be you.'

22

It had been two days since he'd left the hospital, two days when he'd pretended not to hear the banging on the hull and the female voice declaring that she was there to help him. Amazing, he thought, how female fists could land as powerful a blow as those of men.

He ignored it for now. Hospitals and administering angels disguised as nurses tended to bring back old memories. He needed to rest. He needed to consider everything that had occurred to him. Sleep came easily.

On the third day, Talbot pawing at his arm, whining and licking his face, woke him earlier than normal.

Waking up was a slow process, but once he'd rubbed at his eyes and got his feet on the floor, his first act was to look at the time on the old clockwork time-piece he kept in a cupboard. It was still dark, though breaking towards dawn.

The dog was acting strangely, scratching at the door and whining, not responding to his command to keep quiet, to be patient.

A slight bump brought him fully awake. He leapt into his boots, sprang up the three wooden steps too quickly, forgetting the overhead portion of the door was closed and banging his head on the way up.

He swore when Talbot tried to get up the narrow companionway at the same time as him.

The trees bordering the riverside path and the reed beds were further away than they had been the night before. The boat was moving out into the river and even in the dim light he could see both the bow and stern mooring lines drifting on the surface of the water.

More swearing. A deep growl in his throat.

The lines had either been cut or untied. He guessed the latter. Somebody was responsible, but this was no time to rage and no time to vent his anger. He glanced only briefly at the shore but saw no one. He hadn't thought he would. The culprit – and it was certainly done by human hands – was gone.

Having few clothes made him careful with how he treated them. He stripped off and without a second thought dived into the water. The dog jumped in too.

The cold water took his breath away, but at least he did not fall into a paroxysm of coughing.

The boat was heading to the middle of the canal. Further on, the canal gave way to the river.

Taking a line between his teeth, the hemp wet and coarse on his tongue, he swam towards the bank. The dog, clever creature as it was, clamped its jaws over the length of mooring line hanging from the front of the boat.

He'd guessed right that the lines had been loosened, not cut. There was enough to tie it into the round mooring rings set into concrete and stone at regular intervals.

As he closed to the bank, his feet sank into the soft mud as he regained his legs. The water finally at waist level, he began to thread the line through the mooring ring, tying it off in a double clove hitch instead of the usual bowline, which even when wet was easy to undo.

There was now enough daylight to more easily see what he was doing and also to note Talbot's whereabouts.

Mooring lines over his shoulder, he heaved the boat to the shore. Every sinew strained. His muscles spasmed. He took great gasps of air that brought on coughing. He stood for a moment until the coughing bout ended. Once it did, he heaved again on the mooring line and finally, with enormous effort, secured it around the mooring ring set into the stone of the ancient quay.

Breathing laboured, he braced himself against the slime-covered stones at his back and surveyed the position of his boat. Retying the lines had been easy, but hauling in all that weight was not an easy task for a man by himself.

Taking great gulps of air, he psyched himself up for the task. A good portion of a narrowboat was beneath the surface. The displacement of water would work against him rather than for him, unlike a boat that floated on the surface and had no depth to it.

Using the boat's engine would work if he could loop the mooring line around the ring then thread it all the way back to the boat, where he could wind it around a winch and use the engine to pull it in. The trouble was he wasn't sure he had enough length of line to do that.

Studying the distance of the boat from the land, he calculated he needed at least another third of the length he assessed he presently had.

There were no boats close by and not any likely to have what he wanted. One look at the bow then at the stern clarified what he was going to have to do.

The line at the front of the boat was the one the dog had brought ashore. It was this one that he undid, tied around his waist and swam back out to the chunky bow of his boat.

Heaving himself up on board, he untied that rope from its fixing and made his way to the stern, where he tied a bowline using both ropes, dived back into the water and went back to where the stern line was still tied to a metal mooring ring.

Splicing the two with the knot in his hand, he now had a length of line he could work with that would reach the shore. Another swim out to the boat taking the line with him should do the trick.

Swimming backwards and forwards from the boat was arduous work, but at last he had a continuous loop between himself and the shore. Tailing the line off around the winch, he now had enough to begin winding the winch. It was a big weight to shift, but slowly and surely the stern of the boat turned towards the shore, where his dog was waiting. His tail began to wag slowly, then more quickly the closer he came. Eventually, the stern of the boat bumped against the bank, allowing him to tie off half the length of the line. Once that was secured, he went up front to reconnect the line to the bow of the boat. From there, it was now only a short distance to the shore.

As daylight finally dawned, the boat was nestled back against the bank in its previous position before the lines had been released.

He stood on the coach roof of the boat, looking around for any sign of the culprit. This kind of thing had happened to him in the past and was usually down to the pranks of kids or drunks waddling back along the towpath from the pub. This time, he'd heard nothing and seen nothing, unlike the others who had whooped and yelled at their devilment. The silence heralded something else, something more dangerous and of serious intent.

He added extra mooring lines to both the bow and stern of his boat. If another attempt was made at sabotage, they'd take double the time and perhaps this time he'd hear them.

So who were the culprits? He wasn't one to let sleeping dogs lie or have his fists resting against his side. He intended to find out who was responsible. Even the tightening in his chest wouldn't stop him from doing that.

His first stop was one of the elderly fishermen. The old man tapped his pipe against his teeth and looked at him with one eye closed as though it would aid his concentration.

'You have to nip that in the bud.'

'I intend to.'

'Can't help you with a name. Could be anybody.'

Harry put two and two together. First the visit from the bowler-hatted Mr Weaver. Then from Clifford Fletcher and his invitation to visit the pub, to talk things over.

The two were linked, and that was where he would go. Once he'd caught his breath, that was. Once he was well enough to do so.

Money hadn't worked. Was intimidation Fletcher's next step? It was very likely, though he wouldn't be the one getting his hands dirty. He'd pay someone for that.

The pub didn't open until seven that evening. There was time for him to get out of his wet clothes, to sleep, to regain the strength he needed.

23

'Mr Hunter. Are you in? It's the district nurse.'

There was determination in the way Sister Harrison banged on the hull. She would not be ignored again.

No response.

She waited.

'I'm not going away until I see that you're all right. Even if I have to camp out here all day and all night!'

Shaking the sleep from his eyes, Harry swung his legs from the narrow bed and onto the floor.

'Can a man not have any peace?'

He doubted whether she'd heard him, and anyway, she deserved to be seen.

The dog went up top first. Harry followed.

The breeze blew his hair across his face. The sun was warm on the top of his head.

There was a stern look on the strong features, yet he discerned compassion in her eyes.

'You disappoint me, Mr Hunter, leaving the hospital without permission.'

He blinked. 'I didn't know I needed permission.'

'You should have at least waited to be examined and be cleared by me or the doctor before you left.' She shook her head and tutted. 'It was very remiss of you.'

'You make me feel like a child being told off for playing truant.'

'That's exactly what you are. A truant. Foolishly so. It was for your own good.'

Good grief. This woman made him feel genuinely guilty!

He made an attempt to make amends. 'An examination? What for?'

'To check if you're on your way out of this world or here for a few years to come.'

Despite her formidable stance, he couldn't help being amused.

Well, she was confronting him with a problem, so he would confront her with one.

Let's see how gutsy she is, he thought.

'If it's that important, you'd better come aboard.'

He could tell by her initial expression that she hadn't considered having to clamber aboard.

But if he thought he was going to put her off, he didn't know Sister Edith Harrison.

The saddlebag containing the tools of her trade – ointment, iodine and an array of hypodermic needles – was swiftly unbuckled, the bag handed to him in as brusque a manner.

So fierce was her action, that he was forced to take a step back, hugging the bag to his chest.

Deciding there was only so much room in his cabin for her crisp appearance and brusque manner, he ordered Talbot up onto the cabin roof.

'Let me help you.'

She didn't hesitate but placed her hand in his. His palm was big and callused, his grip like iron. A thrill shot through her as he assisted her to board, so swiftly it was as though she was a youthful sylph not a middle-aged woman carrying a little more weight than she should.

Down into the cabin. He regretted not having had time to make his bed but resigned to her accepting that this was the real him. Harry Hunter. Who'd never lived with a woman, never had felt the urge to present himself to one in a good light.

'First, I need to listen to your chest.'

She busied herself getting the stethoscope from her bag, not looking at him until it was in place around her neck.

When she finally looked at him, it was difficult to stop her heart from racing.

Rather than just open his shirt, he'd taken it off and was naked to the waist. She could smell the fresh perspiration of masculine flesh, the pungency of the water he'd washed in.

The chest piece in one hand, her ears plugged with the earpieces, she tried not to tremble as her fingers brushed his chest.

He was lithe but muscular, a smattering of hair forming a 'y' shape down to the waistband of his trousers – which were too loose-waisted. From what she could see, it was only his hips holding them up.

Thump, thump, thump.

His heartbeat was regular. It kept thumping when she no longer needed to know that it was healthy.

Now for his lungs.

It would have been logical to ask him to turn round so she could do that. Instead, she brushed closely against him as she squeezed past and felt the heat of his body.

She held her breath as her eyes followed the route of his spine down to his waistband.

After taking a breath herself, she asked him to breathe in.

Stroking his back was but a brush of the fingers away. It was hard to concentrate on the job in hand but concentrate she must.

There it was. A faint gurgle of fluid. If he had TB, which was very likely, it was in its infancy.

All the years of being a professional nurse could be frittered away if she carried out what she wanted to do – throw her arms around him and say that she would stand by him no matter what.

'If you would like to put your shirt back on, please.'

Even to her own ears, her voice seemed to shake. Given half the chance, she would have offered to do the buttons up for him.

The cabin was so miniscule, she had to step back when he turned to face her. In doing so, she dropped the stethoscope. He caught it at the same time as she did, their hands entangled.

'Thank you.'

He let his hands fall to his sides.

'I have to thank you for caring.'

Her mouth felt dry and just for once she couldn't get out what she wanted to say.

What was it she wanted to say?

The fact was they were standing so close together that the cabin seemed even more claustrophobic. Was that his heart she could hear or her own?

'That's my job,' she said once she'd clutched the words. 'You do have a problem. You know that, don't you? Your lungs...'

'Mustard gas, foul conditions and lousy food. The reasons,' he said when her expression seemed not to show she'd understood what he'd said. 'Opening my eyes in a field hospital and seeing a nurse was like going to heaven. Not that I've ever been there,' he said with a grin. 'Not sure I ever will.'

'Doctor Brakespeare is a very good doctor.'

'I don't doubt it.'

'Well, that's something.'

'Why should I doubt it?'

'A woman doctor. Some men cannot countenance her being any good. But she is. She too was in France. She intends seeing you tomorrow.'

'Does she now.'

'I take it you'll be here all day.'

'I didn't say her visit would be welcome.'

'Don't be so ungrateful. She's coming for your benefit, as did I today.'

'One woman one day and one the next. Let's kill two birds with one stone and have the pair of you tomorrow – shall we?'

She smiled. 'If you like.'

'Sister, can I know your name?'

'Sister Harrison.'

'No. Your real name. Your first name. Your Christian name.'

She didn't hesitate. 'Edith. My name's Edith.' Not a sign of a simper. She said it loudly and boldly.

'Well, Edith, I have a little business to tend to at the Jolly Boatman, a preliminary visit to get the lay of the land so to speak, though I fear the company there will not be to my liking. I prefer to choose my own.'

'And your point is?'

'Edith, I would like you to be that company. No obligation of course. Shall we say seven thirty at the door?'

'Seven thirty. Yes. Thank you, Mr Hunter.'

'Harry. My name's Harry.'

She repeated his name. 'Harry.' Now he knew her first name and she knew his. She couldn't help feeling privileged.

24

Sister Edith Harrison was a stickler for punctuality in others and in herself. This evening had proved an exception. Following her visit to Harry Hunter, she'd got cold feet about meeting him at the Jolly Boatman.

After a great deal of soul-searching, asking herself in fact if she felt sluttish accepting his invitation, she'd finally thrown caution to the wind. Blow what everyone else thought. She was going to keep her assignation with him and was only a little late.

Her hand hovered over the polished brass knob of the glass-paned double doors before telling herself that she'd come this far so might as well go the whole way.

A good push, a determined set of her head and the door grated open over the flagstone floor of the public bar.

At sight of her, conversation cascaded into a rumble and then ceased. On recognising who she was, there followed a touching of forelock, a polite nod of welcome, even a few 'Good evening, Sister.'

Not one person dared ask her what she was doing there, knowing full well they would get short shrift if they did.

Not used to seeing her out of uniform, her attire seemed to come as something of a surprise. Her uniform had been discarded in favour of a green checked dress with a frilly peplum. This was a dress never seen in the Baptist church she attended because the neckline dived far enough down her chest, exposing an inch of décolletage. She patted the area a little self-consciously and tried not to relate it to the experience of standing in Harry Hunter's cabin with him stripped to the waist.

Head held high, she weaved her way through tables and polite remarks towards the bar, a dark oak affair where pewter tankards hung from hooks and brass beer pumps shone like the candles on an altar.

The air smelled of dark beer and old leather thanks to an ancient horse collar hanging at one end of the bar next to the inglenook fireplace. There were scratches on the flagstones thanks to Mrs Abbot's old carpet sweeper that she also tended to use on any floor surface regardless of the harm done.

Mrs Abbot was one of her regular patients. Varicose veins climbed the woman's legs like vines and hung like grapes from her inner thighs.

Although she knew it was likely a worthless task, she looked for her, received nods of welcome from some of the customers and puzzled glances from others. Sister Edith Harrison did not have the reputation of a woman who entered pubs by herself. What was she doing here? They were mostly thinking that, more so when her gaze raked over flat-capped or trilby-hatted men in cheap suits, a tie gripping their throat, a waistcoat straining over their chest.

If they'd asked, she might have told an outright lie, that she'd come to see Mrs Abbot and her plump grapelike veins. The truth of who she had come to see was none of their business.

Where was he? Had he changed his mind?

Two men standing at the bar had refrained from the task of sipping from the pint tankards clasped in their callused grip. Drunken demands from a group of three women sitting at a table in front of the inglenook brought them back to their senses.

'Where's our drinks?'

The moment the women's glassy eyes fixed on her, their heads came together like the witches in *Macbeth*. The most wrinkled of the three, her hat the shape of a squashed cake, sucked in her toothless gums. Whispers were conveyed behind grubby hands and twiglike fingers.

When she stopped and glared, eyes were lowered, and thin lips were clamped tight.

'Sister Harrison.'

Her head jerked round. He was here, his hair and beard as wild as ever, one arm resting on the bar, a foot on the brass foot rail.

He smiled. At least she thought he did.

One day, I will cut all that hair off and have you looking like a gentleman. In her mind, she was saying it to him; in reality, she wouldn't dare.

'Sister Harrison. Will you allow me to buy you a drink?'

She tried not to look around her, to eye the curious gazes and try to guess what people were thinking of her.

Suspecting she was more respectful than any of the other customers, the barmaid asked her what she would like to drink.

'A small sherry, please.'

'I thought you weren't coming,' Harry said as he handed over half a crown and waited for the change.

'I got held up at the hospital.'

An outright lie, but she didn't want to admit that she'd had cold feet.

She cast a glance over the clientele. Which of them looked menacing? Which of them had an axe to grind?

It was hard to tell exactly. Deep inside she tried to convince herself that Harry might have invited her for personal reasons. She hoped so.

'Thank you for inviting me. I don't get out often.' She leaned in closer and whispered, 'This business you've come here to do, dare I ask if it has anything to do with Clifford Fletcher?'

'He wants my field. I've said that I am unwilling to sell, but he's not a man to take no for an answer. I feel a tussle coming on so need to get the measure of the man. He invited me here. I need to meet him although am loath to indulge in his company.' He smiled. 'Hence bringing company that I am keen on.'

She blushed when he smiled at her and she saw the knowing look in his eyes. Was he making fun, surmising that she was sweet on him?

His voice thrilled her. It sounded as though it were coming from somewhere dark and deeply hidden, like a subterranean cavern where voices echo against granite walls of stone.

Her professional side, the senior sister whose word was law to patients and made junior nurses tremble, just about managed to overcome her romantic nature. Fearing rejection, she would not admit to that.

Back into professional mode. 'It was quite foolish of you to leave until you were entirely better.'

Any other man who knew her – or didn't for that matter – would have given in to the dominating streak that drove her. But not Harry.

His hairy eyebrows kissed above his nose; his brow was furrowed. She dismissed the urge to reach out and smooth it away.

'Then I'm a fool, Edith, my dear.'

If her cheeks were warm before, they were now on fire, so much so that she blurted, 'My dear?'

'Do you mind me calling you that? Do you mind me calling you Edith? I haven't heard anyone else calling you by name. Your name.'

It would be easy to blame the sherry for her flaming cheeks. But it wasn't.

She managed to say, 'Consider yourself privileged. And you're not a fool. You can call me Edith or my dear. I like both of them.'

'So do I.'

If her cheeks got any hotter, she might catch on fire. Change the subject. That should subdue the effect.

'I was sorry to hear that Tommy's dog isn't likely to survive, though I can't say I'm surprised.'

Harry fondled his glass, his look dark and deep. 'Frank Steele kicked the dog in the ribs.'

'He's done his wife some harm too. He treats her worse than a dog. I wish he would clear off and never come back.'

It wasn't often she spoke of anyone with such bitter hatred but made an exception for Frank Steele.

Harry grinned and there was gentle mockery in what he said next. 'I wouldn't come back if you ordered me gone. Wouldn't dare.'

She knew he was only joking and couldn't help but chuckle.

'Will you find Tommy another dog? I mean, when it finally happens?'

'I rescued a stray the other day. She's heavy with pups, though I don't think they're due just yet. Tommy might not be ready to have a new dog. Time is on our side.'

She liked the fact that he'd said 'our' rather than 'my'. She was included. It made her spirits soar.

'You must have travelled all over this country in your boat.'

'Yes.'

She fancied his eyes were looking beyond her, studying the men supping pints, who, for the most part, seemed to keep their gaze averted.

It took courage to say what she said next.

'You've never thought of settling down, or are there still places you want to see?'

'Far horizons,' he murmured. 'There are always far horizons, another hill to go beyond.'

Her spirits that had been soaring plummeted. She'd so wanted him to say that the time had come to settle down. Unless...

'You never married?' Her fingernails made a ticking noise on the side of her glass. 'Never thought about getting married.'

He turned his gaze from surveying the customers and swept back to her.

'I've never married.'

'Never met the right woman, I suppose.' She said it brightly, coquettishly, a smile fixed to her lips like glue.

The question wasn't entirely unexpected and was one he'd been asked before.

He knew that it had taken a lot of courage to voice. Personal things usually did.

'Hope springs eternal,' he said.

Her heart leaped.

What would a heroine in a romantic novel do? she wondered. A Jane Austen character might remain aloof, a couldn't care less attitude – until she could gauge what sort of man he was – and whether such man was of interest.

A slight movement on his upper lip convinced her that he *was* smiling through all that hair – though only at a minor level. However small it was, it gave her pleasure.

She decided to veer away from the marriage question.

'You were right in saying that I don't allow people to call me Edith. I like to keep myself to myself.'

'Well, there you are. It's not only men who are islands. Women are too. That's only my opinion, mark you.'

There was a question mark in the way she raised her eyebrows. 'Indeed.'

Amazingly, his eyes continued to look at her whilst at the same time scrutinising the men leaning on the bar, the ones huddled in groups, muttering amongst themselves.

Harry's smile was for her whilst his searching gaze sought those most likely to be in the pay of Clifford Fletcher.

He still seethed with the damage that could have been done if the dog hadn't awoken him. So far he'd kept it to himself, but for once in his life he needed someone to listen, someone to share his concern.

He said, 'Someone slipped the lines on my boat.'

She was unfamiliar with the term. 'Slipped?'

'Untied the lines fixing me to the bank. Clifford Fletcher wishes to make it clear that he wants me gone, though only once I've sold him the field.'

She showed no surprise and felt none. Clifford Fletcher had a reputation for being ruthless. On the other hand, she couldn't imagine him wandering the towpath and doing things that took a modicum of agility. He was rotund and gasped when he overexerted himself. There was a definite advantage to knowing people's medical history, who was healthy and who was most definitely not.

'I wouldn't think it was him who untied the lines.'

Harry shook his head. 'He hired someone to do it. Someone who knows the canal and the fields around it. A lowlife who would stoop to anything as long as he's paid well.'

Edith whispered the name of the man most likely. 'Frank Steele.'

Harry nodded slowly, his expression remaining alert.

Although the conversation in the bar remained no more than a background noise to them, she guessed the two of them were a topic of conversation. She could well imagine what people were saying, played it over in her mind. What the devil is Sister Harrison doing in the company of a man who looked as though he slept rough, hadn't had a wash in ages (though, of course, they had no proof of that). A tramp! A scruffy man compared to a woman of pristine habits who issued orders with the same force of tone as an army sergeant major. If she wanted the attention of a red-blooded man, there were plenty in town and around the Jolly Boatman who would be more than happy to be her beau.

A small dog tucked beneath the stool of an elderly pipe smoker edged out to look at them. Somehow sensing a change in atmosphere, it looked up and wagged its stump of a tail. Deciding Sister Harrison was not a threat, it laid his head on his paws and closed his eyes.

The door to the private accommodation behind the bar opened. Clifford Fletcher appeared wearing a cashmere sweater and a red-cheeked, self-assured expression. His gaze locked with that of Harry. If he noticed her at all –

a woman who had given him an injection in his posterior for a disease best not mentioned to his wife – he gave no sign.

He looked at Harry as though he had his measure. 'Mr Hunter. Can I buy you a drink?'

Harry declined.

Water off a duck's back, thought Edith.

Looking like an overlord peering down his nose at a serf, he poured himself a whisky and leaned his forearms on the bar, his face greased with arrogance.

'Have you thought any more of my offer?'

Set in fatty pits, his eyes narrowed over the rim of his glass as he slugged back a good measure. He looked confident, assured that Harry had succumbed and was here to accept whatever Clifford wanted to offer.

Harry leaned forward in the same manner, his nose only inches from Clifford's, his broad arms and elbows taking up more of the bar. 'That's what I came to see you about.'

Clifford beamed. 'Aha! I thought you would come around. I'm sure we can agree a fair price…'

'I don't think so. The land is priceless.'

Clifford sneered as though he'd misheard. Contempt and disbelief mingled on his pudding-shaped face. 'I'm sorry. Can you repeat that?'

'That piece of land is priceless. It's the fulfilment of a dream.'

Clifford's expression hardened. 'A dream? Did the war turn your head?'

'No. What did it do for you, make you a lot of money? On the bodies of the dead?'

Not recognising he was facing an intractable force, Clifford continued to ooze contempt in his manner and his voice.

'If you're trying to shame me, it won't work. Should never have gone to war in my opinion. Serbia! Going to war over a place few of us could point out on a map.'

Edith glanced around the bar. Conversation had all but ceased. Faces were painted with alarm and hostility.

'That piece of land brought me home. In all aspects. Away from turmoil to perfect peace.'

Clifford scowled, the corners of his mouth spearing into the age lines in his jowls.

Totally dismissive of what had been said, he kept going, kept pushing to hear what he wanted to hear. 'You can't take forever thinking about it. Time's running out.'

'For all of us,' said Harry. 'Stay away from my boat. Stay away from my land. You're not welcome there. Now, if you don't mind, Edith and I have personal business to discuss.'

To Sister Harrison's surprise, he took hold of her elbow with one hand and his drink with the other. She just about managed to grab hers.

He guided her to a corner table as far from the bar as it was possible to be.

Personal business, thought Edith. *What can he mean?* On reflection and not without some disappointment, she decided his action had more to do with breaking off the conversation with Clifford than truly having personal business with her, although she lived in hope.

'I'm guessing that your conversation with Mr Fletcher is at an end.'

'But not my business. He's not used to being refused. By hook or by crook, he'll continue to push for that land – and push me off.'

'Off? You mean push you overboard.'

He grinned. 'It's a possibility.'

His eyes lowered as he took a sip from his glass. Then they were looking into hers again.

She drew in her chin and gave him the sort of look a matron had once given her when she was a student nurse.

'I know him, but only as a patient. Pushy and arrogant.'

This time, his smile was broad enough to cut through the hair that surrounded his mouth. His lips were generous, his teeth white.

'And he didn't get the better of the kind of woman you are, not of Sister Edith Harrison.' Amusement rippled through his voice.

'What do you mean?'

'I'm not implying that you're a bit of a battleaxe.' He laughed. 'I've met some in my time. But you, you pretend to be hardline but beneath it all...? You do your duty, but there's a good heart beneath that starched uniform. And you're not a confirmed spinster. I'm guessing you've had your chances, but the right man is still to make an appearance.'

'I'm not sure what you mean.'

'You asked me if I had ever met the right woman, now I'm asking you if you've never met the right man.'

The blushes were coming thick and fast. She'd always considered herself above such a thing, but Harry Hunter had hit the mark. There had been other men in the past – not least a past manager of the quarry who had turned out to be very unreliable.

A suitable response did not come easily.

A noisy interruption gave her enough time to compose herself, when in the process of tottering to their feet, the three sour-faced women – the *Macbeth* witches – had sent a chair crashing backwards.

Their loud voices were aimed at two men leaning at the far end of the bar who were head-to-head with Clifford.

'Come on you lot. Ernie? Drink up.'

'William, me 'andsome old man. Time to go.'

One man was dragged bodily from the bar by a woman with arms as thick as Wiltshire hams. The other two drained their glasses of the last drop of beer. Their cowed obedience attracted the amusement of their peers sprawled in chairs, pipes in hand, eyes glassy from too much beer.

Calls of derision followed them.

One call went out, 'Under starter's orders then, Ernie?'

Expletives flew back from wet and surly lips, along with a sarcastic comment.

'Thought you two used to be heroes. Now yer only henpecked.'

Guffaws of laughter rang amongst the tough-looking men with their rolled-up sleeves and fob watches hanging from a chain in their waistcoat.

'Oh come on, Bill. 'Ave another.'

'I can't. You know 'ow it is.'

'I'm buying,' said his colleague.

One of the two men about to leave wiped his lips with the back of his hand, not too pleased that they'd dried so quickly.

'Fred Barnett putting his hand in his pocket and buying me a drink! Did you hear that, Ernie? Well seeing as that don't 'appen too often, I think I'll stay.'

There were catcalls and ribald laughter.

Clifford, the ringmaster in the circus, the law behind the bar, persuaded them to ignore the women and stay, glowering at the wives as though their rights over their men were second fiddle to his.

'Tell them to get on home and get your supper on the go. And warm the bed, if that's what you want! Love, honour and obey. That's what they promised when they married you.'

The women gave up, and although the banter continued it was more muted.

Whilst Clifford Fletcher berated the men, his eyes slid in the direction of the corner table.

Harry's sharp eyes travelled swiftly to the recently gathered group sensing a plan was unfolding. Whispers and hostile glances brought him to a decision.

He got to his feet. 'I think it's time we left.'

Edith followed suit. She saw Clifford's beady eyes regarding them over the rim of his glass before he tipped the contents down his throat.

An odd silence descended as they made for the door. Edith felt unnerved. The three drunks that should have left with their wives were still there. At first, they seemed to be hanging onto every word uttered by the man on the other side of the bar, but it had stopped as they passed. One of Harry's big hands tugged the door open.

'Edith. Let me take your elbow. The path along here is stony.'

'I can find my own way home.'

'I don't doubt it.'

'Please. I will be all right. And it's raining again.'

'I don't mind a drop of water.'

'You'll get soaked. Your boat is in the other direction.'

'I know that, but my mother trained me to be a gentleman where ladies are concerned.'

She gave in and let him lead her. Of course she wanted him to take her home.

Within minutes, as though having mercy on their predicament, the rain stopped, the clouds scurried away replaced by a thousand stars like sequins in the sky. She'd read about nights like this in the novels she so loved. This was the first time she'd experienced one first-hand.

'I've got my bike.'

They stopped where she'd left it.

'Ah,' he exclaimed.

Was that a hint of disappointment she heard in his voice? She certainly hoped so.

'I'll walk you to the road. You might need a hand in pushing it uphill.'

'I can go straight along the canal. It's flat all the way.'

She could have bit off her tongue for offering him an alternative, one she didn't want him to take.

She had to admit that it was a bit of a climb to go uphill, and anyway, she did want him beside her for a little longer.

'Mr Fletcher seems to be something of a thorn in your side.'

'It's that piece of land. He wants it badly.'

'But he won't get it.'

Her voice was soft and her sympathy was genuine.

'He will not.'

A bat flew out of the brooding mass of trees hanging over the towpath.

Edith's eyes followed it and from there to a star. Was it true that you could wish upon a star? How delicious that would be!

She made a wish. *Please let him be the tall dark stranger I've always dreamed of.*

'Clifford Fletcher will do anything for money. He's always had an eye for the main chance.'

Harry made a sound of agreement. Not a word, more of a grunt.

'No doubt he stands to make a packet from it in some way. But I have my own plans. An animal sanctuary. That's what I want.'

His steps slowed, and although it was dark, a sudden strip of moonlight helped her see the expression on his face.

'Back in the war, I took care of horses and mules.' His look hardened. 'So many of them were maimed or killed, if not during the war, then after.' He stopped. Throwing his head back, he looked up at the stars. 'It might sound foolish, but I'm totally committed to starting an animal hospital. I won't make much money, but that's not what it's about. It's paying back in a small way what those animals did for me and the men that lived and died in those trenches. That is what I want to do.'

Edith was rarely a woman to be stunned to silence, but she was silent now. Although Harry might have a rough exterior, his plans proved he had a soft heart.

'I think that's very commendable. I can only imagine what horses and suchlike went through in the war. Poor creatures. Hundreds of them.'

'Thousands. Like men, their nerves were shattered – along with their bodies.'

With her hands gripping the handlebars, Edith took a deep breath.

He took the bicycle from her and insisted on walking her up to the main road.

'It's dark and the batteries in that bicycle lamp might not last all the way to the top of the lane.'

'Thank you.'

From experience, she knew that her bicycle lamp would very likely last out, but she wasn't going to argue. Harry Hunter's mother had truly made him a gentleman.

* * *

Back in the bar of the Jolly Boatman, Clifford had made his way into the back room, following the arrival of Frank Steele.

Frank licked his lips as Clifford poured himself a whisky, a strong hint that he'd like one too.

Clifford ignored him. After all, there was only a smidgeon left in the bottle.

'He's built a load of ramshackle sheds in the field. Hutches and suchlike for dogs, cats and all manner of vermin! Shouldn't be allowed.'

'Made of scrap bits of wood from what I've seen. Fit only for putting on the fire.' Frank emphasised the point. 'Would go up in a minute all that stuff.'

Catching his drift, a slow smile crept across Clifford's face.

'Kindling,' he said. 'That's all it is. Let's drink to that.'

25

It was a pleasant drive to Lower Foxford. Few people had cars and although coal lorries and delivery vans had put in an appearance, the milkman, baker and die-hard coalmen still used a horse and cart.

'Lovely day,' Frances remarked.

Sister Harrison agreed with her.

Frances peered ahead out of the car windscreen, then upwards as something caught her eye. The swan was a white dart flying not far above roof level. Something caused it to swoop lower. Its sudden dive towards the road was followed by a flash. It had hit the telegraph pole.

People spilled from houses or stood looking skywards instead of serving or purchasing groceries from the horse-drawn carts. Frightened by the sudden flash, one horse reared up onto its hind legs, sending cabbages and potatoes rolling along the road. Keen hands grabbed what they could, leaving the cart owner looking exasperated.

Those who had seen what had happened from behind garden fences came spilling out onto the road.

A crowd quickly gathered, so many that they blocked the turning into the narrow lane leading to Lower Foxford. Frances had no option but to stop and thrust her head out of the open window.

'Did I see what I thought I saw?'

A man with rolled-up shirtsleeves explained. 'A swan flew into the telegraph wires. The lines are still live, but I'm not sure that he is.'

Frances voiced her intention to take a look.

'Be careful,' someone said as she knelt beside the stricken bird. 'They be bad-tempered creatures at the best of times.'

'Looks dead,' said someone.

'It's alive,' said Frances on finding the pulse of the creature.

'No it isn't,' said a superior-looking lady in a pork pie hat with a net veil.

'The doctor knows best,' said Sister Harrison, who had followed Frances.

'Sorry, I'm sure,' said the woman on recognising the forthright figure of Sister Edith Harrison – and of Doctor Frances Brakespeare.

Reminding Frances that they had a home visit to make and trying not to sound too impatient, Sister Harrison suggested that they take the bird to Harry Hunter.

'He's sure to know what to do with it.'

There was pleading in Sister Harrison's eyes, an uncharacteristic wheeling in her usually forthright tone.

Glances of consternation and outright amusement ran from one bystander to another. A few had heard of the wild man living on a boat opposite the old flood field and the information was passed on from one to another.

An elderly man rested his hands on his knees so that his face was level with that of the doctor. 'And how are you going to get him there, might I ask?'

'In my car.'

'If the bird's got a chance to live, we should give him that.'

Somebody commented that it might make a mess on the fine leather upholstery.

The vegetable man offered two empty potato sacks. 'I've plenty of empty ones. My old horse reared and tipped loads of potatoes into the road. I'm not likely to see them again,' he added, fetching an accusing glance around customers who had scattered with their gathered bounty of King Edward potatoes.

The swan's wings fluttered weakly as, with great care, the potato man rolled it onto one of the potato sacks. Once the other sack was folded over, the swan was cocooned safely in a giant pocket of tartan blanket.

'Now all we have to do is get it in the back seat of the car. Can someone hold the creature's neck?'

'Lady, we can do that for you.'

Another man also offered.

Between them, she and Sister Harrison manoeuvred the bird onto the back seat.

'My, but you're a strong woman,' remarked the lady in the pork pie hat.

'I try to be.'

Without being prompted, Sister Harrison sat next to the swan in the back seat.

'Will you be all right?' Frances asked.

'Is there any reason why I shouldn't be?'

As had been pointed out earlier, swans could be temperamental.

Checking through the rear window, Frances saw that the crowd had failed to disperse. No doubt they were discussing the incident.

'Do you think this will be the talk of the neighbourhood for days to come?'

'I guarantee it. Let's face it, nothing terribly exciting happens much around here.' She burst out laughing. 'An incident that will live in history – at least it will around here.'

Frances thought it might be possible that the swan would be somewhat recovered by the time they got down to the towpath. On opening the back door of the car, it would likely fly away without Harry Hunter taking a hand in dealing with the bird. She sensed Sister Harrison hoped otherwise if she was to have another meeting with the man who lived on the narrowboat.

As she drove, Frances glanced into the rear-view mirror. Sister Harrison's face was flushed.

'Everything all right?' she asked.

'Yes. The poor creature is still unconscious.'

Frances fancied that her flushed complexion and the excited sparkle in Sister Harrison's eyes had not much to do with the swan.

The car bounced its way along the towpath, coming to a stop with the boat on one side and the field on the other.

Harry was sitting on the roof, a violin tucked into his chin. The last notes of whatever he was playing died when he saw them.

Violin and bow clamped tightly beneath his arm, he slid down off the roof. His dog, which had been lying next to him, followed suit. She noticed it was limping a bit, though like its owner it had an air of determination.

Frances left the car door open behind her as she explained the problem. 'I have an injured swan. It flew into the telegraph lines.'

He looked from her to Sister Harrison's flushed face peering out of the rear window.

'I'm not sure it's come round yet. Sister Harrison has it wrapped in hessian sacks in case it makes a mess.'

'They do that sometimes.' Not a hint of a smile nor sign of amusement.

She wasn't sure if he meant them making a mess or flying into the telegraph lines.

He moved to the back of the car and looked in. She saw Sister Harrison nod at him before asking if it would live.

'If I have my way, he will,' he replied and sounded as though he meant it. He looked in to assess the situation, turned and left, returning with a wheelbarrow that squealed like a trapped rat as he brought it closer and set it in place.

Tugging the car door ajar, he instructed Sister Harrison to hold onto the swan's long neck whilst he gathered it up into his arms.

The bird's beak opened and shut. No noise was emitted. The legs paddled for a while. He uttered some soothing words before lowering it into the wheelbarrow. The body was loaded first, black webbed feet hanging over the end of the wheelbarrow between the handles. Once he was satisfied with the positioning, he gently bent the long neck so that its heavy head was resting on its chest.

'Will he be all right like that?' Frances asked him.

'He will be if I'm careful. A quick jolt over a stone, his head falls over the side, and his neck could be broken. Could you walk at the side of the wheelbarrow and support its neck.' He addressed Sister Harrison.

Many considered Sister Harrison dutiful but full of her own self-importance. Frances had kept her own counsel, though on seeing her following Harry's instructions, one hand gently but firmly placed on the swan's neck, she realised that sick or injured patients were the most important thing in her life – even if they were of the avian variety!

His strides longer than theirs, they hurried to keep up as he led the way into the field.

'Close the gate behind you.'

Frances was last in, so it was her who obeyed the clipped order.

Sister Harrison kept pace with him, supporting the swan's neck when she thought a bump in the field might dislodge it.

'You referred to this bird as male. How do you know that it is?'

'The male – the cob – has a bigger lump above its beak.'

'I see.'

Frances smiled to herself. Sister Edith Harrison was smitten. Look at the way she stayed close to the man.

How long before Sister Harrison persuaded him to have a shave and a haircut. He might not know it, but she could be very persuasive. *Give it time*, she decided.

She watched as he undid the gate to a pen, its palisade fencing thick with moss and of varying lengths.

She heard him instruct Sister Harrison to go inside and stand in front of the swan that was already there. It amused her, though didn't surprise her, to see his instructions carried out to the letter.

Cradling the creature in his strong arms, he stepped into the enclosure.

The swan already there stretched its neck, beady eyes curious but wary. It hissed as he placed the unconscious swan on a clean bed of straw inside the wooden hutch.

'Female and male,' said Harry. 'They'll get on. Let's leave them to it.'

With that, he reopened the gate, ushered Sister Harrison out, then shut it behind him.

It was the most Frances had heard him speak. Not only that, but the Irish accent she'd detected seemed to have lessened – if not disappeared.

'Will it live?' asked Frances.

'Oh, I'm certain it will,' said Sister Harrison.

Frances was inclined to ask her how she might know. Her experience was nursing humans not animals or birds. She held her tongue.

Harry directed his answer at Sister Harrison. 'I think he will but there's no telling.'

'Is there anything I can do?' Sister Harrison's voice verged on pleading, the pleading of a worshipper, not a beggar. *I want to help you in any way I can.*

Those were the unsaid words Frances imagined were waiting to be spoken.

Sister Harrison was all smiles. 'Do you need money for looking after him?'

'Thank you, Edith. Every penny is appreciated. Money goes in there.'

He pointed to a box nailed onto the gate, a painted figure attached to it.

Frances noticed the faint hint of an Irish brogue had returned. She wondered whether Sister Harrison had noticed but doubted it.

'That's novel. Perfectly wonderful,' she trilled, sounding like a well-mannered young lady admiring a gentleman's uniform, his horse or his aptitude for dancing.

Frances took a few steps towards the gate so she could see it better. 'I agree with Sister Harrison. It is quite novel. Where did you get it?'

There was something purposeful about the way he turned his head from the wind. Strands of long straggly hair hid his face, even the intense look in his eyes.

'France.'

There was no need for him to explain further, but he did.

'A farmhouse destroyed by shells. It was all that was left.'

'It looks like a child's toy.'

He shrugged and began to take steps back to the towpath and his boat. The dog loped along beside him.

Frances waited for him to tell her more, but he didn't. At the gate, she drew out a few coins that up until then had been rolling around at the bottom of her pocket. Copper mostly.

When the gate was closed behind them, she turned her attention to the wooden figure nailed to the top bar of the gate. The idea was that when coins were fed into a slot, the figure brought a small hammer down onto an anvil.

One after another she fed pennies into it, both she and Sister Harrison laughing each time the hammer hit the anvil.

Harry stared back into the field, his eyes alighting on each hutch and pen in turn.

Sister Harrison, in an obvious effort to keep his attention, asked him what it was like living on a narrowboat.

Frances stood some way off, though within hearing distance. She heard him say that sometimes it was dangerous.

'I'm surprised. I thought it would be so peaceful.' Sister Harrison had been hanging onto every word.

The grass shivered like waves on the sea when the wind began to rise, whistling through the trees and sending snakes of hair blowing around Harry's face.

Sister Harrison was exuberant when she conveyed her belief that his animal sanctuary would be well received by everyone. That he'd become an accepted member of the community in no time.

'As you are very well aware, Edith, there are some in the community who want me gone.'

It was Frances who showed surprise on hearing him refer to Sister Harrison by her Christian name, Edith. Nobody but nobody was allowed to do that without the sister's permission.

After a polite interval, Sister Harrison stated that she would be around tomorrow or the day after to examine his lungs.

'No excuses. Or you can start counting your days, and what would the animals do then?'

There are those moments when something shifts unseen. That's what Frances felt now, a shifting with the two figures standing in front of her. One of them was under threat, the other had every intention of standing with him whether he liked it or not, though not necessarily because of his health.

26

There was a red sky that night. It was still there the next morning.

Harry had tied extra lines to the shore just in case whoever had cast his boat adrift tried it again.

The lines, like the red sky, were still there in the morning.

He looked up and down the towpath. Not one human being. No animals either, just a few cawing jackdaws high up in the elm trees.

His first job was to inspect the swans. A smile appeared beneath his thick facial hair when he thought of Edith Harrison. He'd known a matron back in his service days just like her. The memory made him smile until he recalled that she'd died in the Spanish flu epidemic. What would his life be like if she'd lived? He pushed the thought away. The dice had been thrown, and the cards had landed unfavourably. That was life.

He liked women of Edith's character, women who refused to be treated as a lesser sex than men. Doctor Brakespeare seemed of the same ilk, but she didn't attract him as Edith did. Even her name. He'd guessed that few people were allowed to call her by her first name. He felt privileged as he reminded himself that she was calling in to examine his chest.

His great joy that morning which outshone everything in importance was to see the neck of the male swan entwined around that of the pen. It made him smile. 'You're fine now then.'

The severe injury of the female's leg by fishing twine was still healing. She had to stay where she was at least for the time being.

He explained this to the cob and believed it understood. 'She has to stay, but you can go.'

The male swan expressed instant interest on seeing the gap suddenly appearing in the rickety gate and didn't hesitate.

'Not you, girl,' he said, putting his hand across the opening so the pen could not follow her new love interest.

He reckoned they'd hitch up as a breeding pair if he let her follow the cob, but her leg was still weak. On trying to get to the gate, she favoured one leg, flopping to one side or the other. It made him think of Edith. How odd that after all this time a woman had turned his head. At some point he would look at her ailing cat. All he had to do was pluck up the courage.

Fixing the gate shut, he turned to watch the young swan scything through the air, stretching its neck as though by that alone to reach the morning sky.

'Avoid the telegraph wires,' he muttered in a muted warning and couldn't help but smile.

His smile disappeared at the prospect of his second task of the day, which was far from joyful.

He'd found a fox in a metal trap, one that should not have been where he'd found it. There was no proof, but he had his suspicions that Frank Steele, acting on the orders of Clifford Fletcher, had had something to do with it. The fox had died of its injuries. The metal trap had been thrown into the canal.

Half an hour later, he grimly patted the last of the earth onto the grave, wishing he could get his hands around the neck of the man responsible.

There would be another burial shortly. He could just about cope with that. How Tommy would fare was another matter. He estimated it would have happened last night and that he would hear the grim news today.

Having not yet breakfasted, he ate a piece of buttered toast and made a strong brew in a small brown pot. The first cup of tea had gone down well, and he had every intention of pouring another when he heard Tommy calling.

'Mr Harry. Mr Harry.'

Despite telling Tommy that he didn't need to call him Mr, the boy couldn't seem to help himself, but at least he had learned to call him Harry rather than Ben. His own fault, of course. Carrying a thirst for revenge had gone too far. When he thought about it now, the idea of upsetting the family seemed stupid.

Tommy's plaintive voice peeled like a rusty bell above the pitter-patter of the rain that had just started. So much for the red sky the night before. It was the red sky this morning that had heralded the rain.

Bending down, he rubbed between Talbot's ears. 'Cometh the day,' he whispered, 'The one that comes to us all.'

Talbot was looking up at him as though he understood. Ears flattened, head carried low, the dog followed him up top.

Tommy's wet hair was plastered to his head and rain was dripping from his eyebrows and the end of his nose. He was wearing what he always wore, a shabby pullover, a shirt with cuffs that flapped around his wrists. Raindrops dripped from his nose and chin and his socks were crumpled around his ankles. What looked like a wet hairy cushion lay in his arms.

'Patch is dead and me Mum won't let me bury him in the garden. Said it's for growing carrots and spuds, not for planting dogs, and anyway, Frank won't like it.'

The boy's arms shook; proof that he'd carried the dog unaided all the way from home to here.

With slow deliberation, Harry climbed over the side of the boat and held out his arms. 'Let me.'

'No. I can manage,' he snapped, his grip tightening around the limp body.

''Course you can.'

Man and boy stood silently for a moment. He ached inside in time with the boy's shaking shoulders but said nothing until his sobs had subsided.

'So what next?'

Tommy sniffed and wiped his nose on his sleeve. 'Frank won't have me burying him in the garden. And I don't want him chucked in the dustbin or in the river. I want him buried somewhere peaceful.'

Harry let his eyes wander around the field, the far corners and the nearer places where rabbits lived in burrows.

'Do you want to pick somewhere for me to dig a place for him? Or do you want to choose one yourself? We can bury him any spot in the field you fancy.'

Tommy nodded, raised his arm and pointed a trembling finger to a spot just a couple of feet from where he'd just buried the dead fox.

'A good choice. Close to another canine I buried there. They can all play in heaven together.'

The fact that he'd buried a fox rather than a dog was neither here nor there.

Tears squeezed from Tommy's eyes and snot trickled from his nostrils.

'Right,' said Harry. 'Stay here.'

He went back to where he'd left the spade sticking upright.

Patch was not a big dog, so it wasn't long before the grave was big enough to take his lifeless body.

Eventually, he was patting the mud down on top. Throughout it all, Tommy stood perfectly still and silent.

He didn't ask if Tommy wanted to say a prayer, guessing he would have said so if he'd wanted to. Instead, they stood there a moment in silence, the birds providing a morning chorus.

At last, Harry judged it time to move on.

'A good workman takes care of his tools. I'll clean this off before we go.'

Once the spade was cleaned and placed back in the tool shed, he suggested they have breakfast even though he'd not long eaten.

Tommy shook his head. 'I'm not hungry.'

Of course you're not, thought Harry, eyeing and pitying the dejected youngster. *'Tis too soon.*

'Let's take a stroll then, shall we? I'll walk home with you. How would that be?'

'Yes.'

The boy wiped his eyes with both hands. Something in his demeanour seemed to change. There was a look of determination in the set of his jaw and a darkness in his eyes that Harry recalled seeing in those of soldiers about to avenge the death of beloved comrades.

Glancing over his shoulder, he saw that Talbot was following them. He was in two minds to tell the dog to stay behind but thought better of it. The dog's presence might help ease young Tommy's pain.

'I'll walk you back to Fishermen's Row. That's where you live, isn't it?'

The boy looked up at him. 'Yes.'

'With your mother?'

'And Frank.'

'Not your father.'

Tommy shook his head. 'My dad was killed at sea.'

'Ah!'

He realised the boy would never have known his father. He wasn't alone in that. He hadn't known his, but that was another matter.

'Did you fight in the war?' Tommy suddenly asked.

Harry grunted a response.

'That means you're brave. And tough.'

He considered what that statement actually meant. Tough because he'd killed or tough because he'd seen all that slaughter and survived? Or was it because he was big and looked frightening?

'There's tough and there's tough.'

He glanced at the boy and felt for him. There were a number of coloured children in Bristol, a city that had been a seaport for centuries. Sailors from all over the world had visited. Lonely women had found solace in the arms of those men.

The boy looked down at his scuffed shoes for quite a few minutes, as though something serious had occupied his mind. He suddenly looked up and said, 'I knew you were tough.'

When they got to the cottage where Tommy lived, Harry ordered Talbot to sit and stay outside the front gate. The dog obeyed immediately, ears erect, tilting his head to one side so as not to miss any further instructions.

He pushed the gate open and let Tommy go first. He'd expected the boy to be dragging his feet, instead he sensed nervousness and even excited apprehension.

Instead of going through the front door as Harry had assumed, Tommy took the side path to the back of the house and Harry followed.

'Patch used to sleep up there in the pigsty,' said Tommy, pointing to a small rectangular brick building at the end of the garden.

The garden looked as though it might have been quite productive at one time, but weeds were fast strangling the vegetables that might once have provided a decent meal.

June Newman was feeding wet laundry into a cast-iron mangle, her hair damp from steam so that wisps of it stuck to her face. The sight of him made her gasp.

He saw her, nodded in her direction.

In response, she raised a hand to her face, knowing he must have seen the bruise beneath one eye and dried blood beneath her nose.

If she could have read his mind, she would know that, yes, he had seen her battered face. But he'd also seen the iron trap hanging from the privy wall. He clenched his jaw, a bitter taste in his mouth.

A fox fur fetched a good price. A very high one for the creature so desperate to escape that it would attempt to chew off its own leg.

'Tommy, you're supposed to be in school. What are you doing home?'

'Mr Harry – Harry – buried Patch for me.'

Harry explained. 'He was a bit upset, so I offered to walk back with him. Nice to meet you, Mrs Newman.'

A voice came from the other side of the privy door. 'Who the bloody hell is that out there? Is that you, you shitty little mongrel. Bunked off school, 'ave ya? Just wait till I get out you'll get the rough end of my belt...'

There was the sound of a chain clanging followed by flushing water before the door swung open. At sight of a stranger, and a big one at that, Frank Steele froze. He considered himself a hard man though if he'd been able to look at himself from the outside he would – or might – observe that he was hardly in fighting form. His tattooed arms were hefty but not muscular. His braces hanging at his side were barely holding his trousers up around his flabby middle. The whites of his eyes were tinged with yellow – like rotten eggs. He put on his bully boy face, cigarette hanging from the corner of his mouth.

'You're that bloke from on the canal. What do you want yur?' Frank was big enough, but beer and fags had had their toll on his body.

Despite his chest problem, Harry thought himself fitter than the man facing him.

Face greasy with sweat and remains of this morning's breakfast, Frank turned to June. 'I suppose this is your bloody fancy man, is it?'

June visibly wilted. 'No! Of course not.'

'Lying cow!' His trousers slid as he aimed a blow at her head. Harry was quick on his feet, quicker still with the hand that caught Frank's wrist.

'No need for that.'

'Let go of me, mister, or it'll be the worse for you.'

Frank's chin was black with two days' growth of stubble and his eyes peered out from fatty slits. In his youth, that face might have been firm and handsome. It was now flabby.

Harry noted the clenched fists, the sloppy mouth and the hardness in the small, sunken pupils. He had seen brave men. He'd seen cowardly men and also bullies. He recognised Frank as one of the latter.

Tommy's mother trembled like a reed in the wind, her eyes darting in terror from one man to the other. 'Please, mister. It's best if you go. There'll only be trouble if you stay.'

Harry heard a whispered 'stay' and he knew it wasn't from inside his head. Tommy was looking up at him, his eyes bright with pleading.

He knew what Tommy was asking of him. *Stay and save us from this monster.* He told himself it was none of his business.

'If you want me to go, I will.'

Frank had puffed himself up, arms held slightly apart from his body. Fists clenched. 'Yeah. Go!'

'Please. Please. Me and Tommy'll be all right.' June's voice quivered with fear.

Up until now, the bleary-eyed Frank had not focused his temper on Tommy, but he was the kind that recognised an easy target when he saw it. His expression clouded, his bushy eyebrows almost meeting above his cider-ravaged nose. 'You!' he shouted, pointing a nicotine-stained finger to within an inch of Tommy's face. 'What the bloody 'ell are you doing 'ere, you no good scraggy mongrel?'

Tommy staggered backwards against the house wall, then made a sideways move so he was hidden behind Harry.

June's face turned as grey as that of a stone angel. 'Please, mister. Go, go now!'

Frank was sliding his belt from his waist, his eyes glittering behind hillocks of fat, his menacing look aimed at the boy. 'I'll teach you to bunk off school!'

He attempted to snatch Tommy from where he was hiding behind Harry but missed. A quick sidestep and he was up against Harry's chest, a solid barrier to the small boy he'd been aiming for.

His bushy eyebrows met in a menacing vee shape. He threw his arm wide and threatening in front of Harry.

'I've warned you, mister. Out of my way.'

'I can't do that.'

'Then I'll 'ave to make you do it!'

Shielded by Harry's big body, June had snatched her son, protectively wrapping her arms around him. Her terrified face stared at the two men over the top of Tommy's woolly curls.

Fury etched on his face, Harry pointed at the iron trap. 'I buried a fox today.'

Frank laughed. 'That was a stupid thing to do. That pelt is worth ten shillings or more.'

'You'll set no more traps on my land.'

Another laugh from Frank, though more reserved than before. Obviously he was having second thoughts. 'And who's going to stop me?'

'I am.'

Harry braced himself for impact but kept his voice calm, appealing one more time for the man to see sense. He knew he wouldn't. He'd met his kind before.

'I've no wish to come between you and your woman.'

'My woman! Hah! She's anybody's woman. Been with a black man and he left her with that brat in her belly.' He pointed at Tommy.

Despite telling himself he didn't want to get involved; despite telling this brute he had no wish to interfere, he wanted to smash Frank's nose all over his face. His sense of what was right wouldn't let him back down.

'You've a filthy mouth.'

'Maybe I have, but that's none of your business.'

Frank Steele lashed out with his left fist but didn't see the right-hander coming. He staggered backwards as Harry's fist smashed into his nose, leaving Harry feeling greatly satisfied.

'Now, will you look,' he exclaimed. 'You've made me act when really I had no intention of getting involved.'

Frank was looking at the hand he was holding up in front of his face, staring at the mass of blood, snot and bone as though it could not possibly be his.

To his credit, he recovered swiftly, his face crumpled with hate.

Harry readied himself as, roaring like an angry bull, Frank Steele lunged forward.

He didn't give him the chance to land a blow. The punch that had landed on Frank's nose had made him unsteady on his feet. It was now time to take full advantage of that. Bending his elbow and holding his fist way back in order to give more power to the blow, Harry delivered the sucker punch.

Tommy's mother screamed and screamed, but Harry only heard his own blood rushing into his ears. His blow had landed on Frank's jaw, and now his hands were around Frank's throat as he pushed him backwards into the privy. Frank's legs flailed wildly. One minute his arms whirled like the sails of a windmill, the next scrabbling at the hands around his throat.

Harry heard nothing of the woman's screams or the gurgles from Frank Steele. In his head, he was killing whoever had fired that shell into the barn, killing men and horses. Anger remaining from those crueller times surged like a crimson tide inside his head. His hands squeezed more tightly.

Frank was pushed back into the narrow confines of the privy. He tried to turn away from the strangling hands. In doing so he turned so that he was facing into the lavatory.

Harry pushed forward his advantage, kicking Frank's legs from under him so that he fell, his head hanging over the pan.

The final act had to occur. He couldn't resist. Reaching over the supine form, he pulled the chain.

Frank lay there, gasping for breath, the strength in his legs all gone.

Harry backed out of the privy.

'Whatever's going on here?'

He knew that voice, felt almost guilty that she'd turned up.

On backing out of the privy, he saw Sister Edith Harrison, prim and pristine in her uniform, amazement written on her face.

A triumphant looking Tommy explained. 'Frank was going to beat me and my mum with his belt.'

Driven by rage and triumph, Harry had been elated. The twin feelings diminished under the studious eye of Sister Harrison. He put into words exactly what had driven him to act the way he had. 'I couldn't let it happen.'

Was that a smile of approval on Edith's face? He knew it was.

Behind him, Frank crawled out of the privy dripping wet. He staggered to his feet, gave Sister Harrison only the most cursory of looks. The anger still simmering in his eyes was for Harry, who stood like a colossus between Tommy, his mother and the lout who had dared chance his luck.

As a last act of defiance, Frank spit blood and phlegm. It missed his face but landed on his shoulder.

'Water gypsy, that's all you are. And a tramp at that. I'll get you. As for that cow and her brat...' Fuelled by spite, he attempted to resume the fight, but Harry stepped into his way.

'Ah. I see you're still bleeding some; and you still need your mouth washing out.' With that, he pushed Frank back into the privy, held his head down the lavatory and pulled the flush for the second time. 'I think you could do with a rest after all this,' he murmured. He grabbed a handful of Frank's hair, jerked his head back, then forward so his forehead banged on the back of the wooden seat. That was when he finally let Frank's body slide to the floor – his eyes rolling in his head, just this side of being unconscious.

June turned frantic. 'Sister Harrison! Has he killed him? Has he?'

Edith was not in the least bit appalled at what she had just witnessed. In fact, she felt something akin to pride. Her faith in Harry Hunter was proven.

'Unfortunately not.' Sister Harrison's steady gaze transferred to Tommy. 'I came to see Tommy.' She grinned. 'Though seeing his rosy cheeks and shining eyes, I can't think that there's much wrong with him. Unless it's overexcitement.'

June was trembling, but her son's eyes were shining. His adoration was strictly for Harry.

'I knew you was tough!'

Harry accepted Tommy's exclamation with a single grunt. He hunched his shoulders, so they fitted more comfortably into his jacket and turned to go.

'I'd like a word before you leave,' said Sister Harrison.

Did he really see her face was glowing every bit as much as the boy? Of course he did.

'It was a fair fight and I was defending this mother and her son from a bully.'

'Of course you were. Just to get things clear for the report I intend giving to the police and a magistrate friend of mine. I dare say Mr Steele is well known to them and likely due another stay in prison at His Majesty's Pleasure. The time for you to leave is long overdue, Mr Steele. Now get going.'

'You've no right...'

Frank Steele's protest was dismissed with a wave of a hand and an imperial gaze.

'Are you deaf, Mr Steele, or just stupid? Perhaps six months in prison wasn't enough. Perhaps sixteen would make more sense.'

Frank's face crumpled.

From head to toe, Sister Harrison's stance was the one adopted when she was directing the running of a ward. Firm and unrelenting.

No more did Frank Steele look threatening. He had the look of a beaten man under threat of imprisonment. Sister Edith Harrison was bound to have connections. Her sort always did.

Buoyed up by both a strong man and a strong woman, June shouted at him to get his things together and go.

'But without this,' growled Harry, tugging the trap from its hook and throwing it onto the ground. 'I'll be throwing it into the canal along with the other one. You'll have to dive in if you want it back.'

He knew of course that Frank wouldn't do that but would beat a hasty retreat. However, it was his belief that that Edith's threat scared him more than he did.

* * *

Just to make sure Frank Steele had gone, and despite the rain and heavy clouds, Edith stood with Harry under a tree just along from Fisherman's Row. They watched Frank Steele's motorcycle disappear up the lane that led to the main road.

'I do hope he's gone for good,' murmured Edith.

'After that earful you gave him? And the threat of imprisonment? Of course he is.'

Eyeing his profile, she couldn't help but imagine the hidden features. Was that really what that hair was all about, hiding scars or ugliness.

The rain showed no sign of easing off.

'I'm going to get very wet.'

Harry did that thing again of shrugging his shoulders into his coat. 'I wish I could offer you an umbrella, but I don't own one.'

She laughed. 'Neither do I, come to that. I really should pay more attention to Lord Baden-Powell. His motto for the Boy Scouts is to be prepared. It seems neither of us are that.'

'You're not a Boy Scout.'

Her blue eyes sparkled, and her cheeks dimpled when she smiled.

'I'm not a vet, either, which was why I was going to ask you... My eldest cat, Perry, is off his food. I could bring him in for you to look at. If you don't mind, that is.'

Her face had a fairy-tale sweetness.

'Old animals don't need so much food. Let him do what he likes.'

'I shouldn't need to be told that,' she said, reflecting on the number of elderly patients who admitted to not having the appetite they once had. He was quite right, of course, but she wanted another reason to visit him without making it too obvious. Or should she make it more obvious, visit him even when not invited? Dare she hope?

Harry peered up at the sky. 'There's more rain to come.'

'Rain or no rain, I'd better head back.'

She was just about to leave the minimal shelter of the tree and head for her bicycle. Harry's hand coming to rest on her shoulder stopped her.

'I have a sou'wester on the boat. Wait here and I'll get it for you.'

He didn't wait around for her response, he was off, his feet splashing through the puddles, Talbot limping along beside him.

'What are you doing?' he asked himself as he rummaged around in the place where he stored items that might be needed.

His scrutiny strayed to the biscuit tin. In a way, he felt strangely treacherous to the remains he had carried around all this time.

'It might be time to go,' he said, his statement directed at the tin.

Although he was willing to accept that things had changed, it was not easy to let go of the past and the people he'd known there.

What was it that had changed? That was the question he asked himself.

Thinking back to that night when Talbot had licked his face, he realised that up until that point he'd shunned company. Since then, what with Talbot and the people he'd met in Norton Dene, the loneliness he'd suffered but never knew that he'd suffered, had dissipated. Sister Edith Harrison had a lot to do with that, and he was grateful to her. Grateful enough to ensure she stayed dry on her journey back to the hospital. Grateful enough to encourage their friendship and wherever it might lead.

He came back promptly enough without the dog but carrying a waterproof. He came behind her, wrapping the garment over her shoulders, helping her fasten it at the front. His final action was to place the hat onto her head.

27

Clifford Fletcher was a man who liked winning. He also liked accumulating. Getting to the top of the heap sometimes meant greasing a few palms or paying local lowlife for what you wanted done. What he didn't like was fresh air and going out after dark. He left that to the likes of Frank Steele, who'd sent word he wanted paying before carrying out the job he wanted him to do. So here he was, all secretive and suchlike, waiting for Frank to turn up. Not a likeable man. Hit his woman about so he'd heard, but there, what did that have to do with him?

It was a known fact that ex-con Frank did a bit of poaching and a bit of sheep rustling. He also laid traps for foxes and rabbits. Rabbit meat was cheap enough, but the pelts of both them and foxes fetched a good price with furriers or a woman who wanted to add a fur collar to her coat.

Basically, he would do anything for money, but at present Clifford was losing patience. The bloke should have showed up by now. He had heard that Frank had had a mighty row with his missus. He was always having rows. One more or less wouldn't make that much of a difference. The silly cow would take him back. That was the way it was between men and women – except for his wife, that was. She had a heart of stone as far as he was concerned. She loved her dog Polka.

Midnight had come and gone. A mist that was halfway to becoming a fog was rising from the canal, softening hard shapes and smothering others. There was no moon, no warm squares of light falling from cottage windows and no wayside lights by which the creeping figure might better see his way. The dark block that was the narrowboat, lying like a sleeping leviathan, showed no lights either.

When Frank finally turned up, Clifford slithered away.

'I'll leave you to it.'

'Where's me money?' Frank whispered.

Clifford handed over the agreed sum. He hoped it would be the last and that Harry Hunter would leave, never to be seen again.

Frank had come as prepared as it was possible to be. The only light he had was thrown by the rusty bicycle lamp he'd thought ideal for the purpose. The light flashed along at ground level, following the tufted grass, bindweed and buttercups growing out through the wire netting at the bottom of the fence.

He found the gate to the field, which he promptly climbed over, congratulating himself that, although a bit on the lumpy side, he was still agile enough to clamber over, although he dropped like a brick on the other side.

Had he been heard? Being heard was always going to be a problem, especially when there was a dog on board the boat. A dog's ears were hundreds of times more acute than humans and the last thing he wanted was to be heard and have his head punched around by Harry Hunter for the second time.

The bleary gleam of the bicycle lamp landed on a run where a duck and her youngsters were hunkered down. He turned the light quickly away.

He felt his way. What he was looking for was something that would catch light easily without the hutch or kennel's inhabitant making a song and dance about it. He also wanted a hutch built from the most fireworthy bits of wood – scrap stuff long dried out and fit only to lay beneath coals and see them flare.

The kennel he chose was small and held just a single dog which was lying on its side, eyes closed and seemingly unaware of his presence. The wood the structure was built from was brittle and dry. One match and it would swiftly be ablaze.

The darkness hid his triumphant smile.

Before getting out the matches, he ripped up some of the dry grass from the adjacent lumps, plus a few small sticks, pushing the whole lot beneath the kennel before lighting a match.

The first match caught and the dry grass turned scarlet. A second match and the grass began to crackle and twist with flames. The dog did not disturb.

'Sleep on,' he murmured and couldn't help grinning. He didn't care about dogs. Didn't care much about Tommy's mother. The truth was that he didn't care much about anyone except himself.

Tiny flames licked through the dried grass and twigs, growing bigger as they fed on the fuel. The dry wood of the hut blackened and began to smoke. Still the dog did not disturb, but the other animals would once they smelled the smoke.

With the help of the ancient bicycle lamp, he retraced his steps back to the gate. All was well – but only for a moment.

Suddenly, something white flashed ahead of him and he heard a heavy beating sound. He cried out when he felt disturbed air rushing into his face, saw great wings and thought the devil had finally come to claim his soul.

The heavy wings batted at the space in front of him, the head and beak of a swan aimed like a dart as it ran straight for him, poised for attack!

Hearing the swan's muted alarm call, the ducks began to quack, and the sound of barking came from kennels at first and then from the boat.

A light went on and dark figures moved, leaping off the boat, the dog jumping over the gate.

'Bugger!'

The gate was barred to him; he swerved, not sure he could leap the boundary fence but damned sure he was going to give it his best effort.

Having no time for second thoughts, he threw himself over the barbed-wire fence. Threads of jumper were snagged, but he'd cleared it. So had the dog.

As it got closer, he could hear its breathing and the rustling of disturbed leaves and foliage.

Accepting he could not outrun the animal, he turned to face it. His back was against the broad trunk of a tree. He thought about turning the lamp off but reminded himself dogs had a strong sense of smell. It would track him no matter where he went.

He placed the lamp between his feet so he could see the animal coming, then reached into his pocket and brought out the knife.

* * *

With wild desperation, Harry beat at the flames with his coat. Smoke, gritty and acrid on the tongue, was finally all that remained of the kennel he'd so lovingly made. Nothing was left except blackened wood and inside an expectant mother who had passed peacefully away.

He waited for Talbot to come back, his eyes scanning the direction in which he had run. Although getting on in years, the dog was still strong and had a keen sense of smell, but he was not so agile as he used to be.

It was half an hour before he saw him creep under the barbed-wire fence. The dog was limping, walking a few paces, then holding up his paw.

Fearing the worst, Harry ran his hand down the front of the dog's chest and felt the stickiness of blood adhere to his fingers. Whoever had started the fire had been armed with a knife.

His priority was to deal with Talbot's injury and then he would bury the bitch and the puppies still inside her that would no longer be born. He'd earmarked one of those for Tommy. Sadly, that wouldn't happen now.

His jaw tightened with anger. His fingers curled into his palms, making tight fists.

Despite the damage and the tragedy for some of his charges, he felt a strange kind of triumph as well as sadness. His faith in animals had come to his rescue. The strong beak of an angry swan, even the strength in a swinging neck, was capable of serious injury. Whoever was responsible for lighting the fire was likely to be suffering. He guessed the perpetrator to be Frank Steele. He hoped the swan had done a great deal of damage and that Frank was sporting a fine injury. Vicious birds, swans, but you had to admire them.

28

Ma Skittings had a routine when it came to cleaning at the coach house where Doctor Brakespeare lived. Sometimes it left her enough time to give Mrs Cross a hand at the vicarage. Not often, but time enough so they could sit down and gossip over a pot of tea.

She knew Mrs Cross wasn't there today and that the vicar would be alone – no doubt composing the Sunday sermon or the parish magazine. He might also be producing posters to put up around the town advertising the soup kitchen.

Folk who'd fallen on hard times were thankful for the cooked meals given free to the needy. The mines had reopened, but the wages had been cut. Although Ma Skittings had great respect for the Compton-Dixon family – her niece had married into the family after all – she didn't approve of wage cuts.

'Mark my words, there'll be more unrest and another general strike.'

That's what some people said. Others said that the miners were being infiltrated by communists.

Ma Skittings had lived long enough to know that hard times came and went. However, she would have liked an explanation from the family as to why they'd treated the miners like this.

The chance would come today.

Housework at the coach house was finished. Now, she got going in the vicarage.

The pot of tea would be made and with the vicar's permission, she'd asked her niece, Lucy, to join her.

But first she had to get everything done and because she was in a hurry, not everything went smoothly. As she flicked a feather duster around the vicar's study, a few papers fluttered off and fell to the floor.

'Blast.'

Bending down was not her favourite task. Her body was too roly-poly nowadays for bending so she only did what was strictly necessary.

In what order had those papers been?

She picked them up one by one. Most of them related to parish business, scheduled christenings and weddings. No funerals, for which Ma Skittings was grateful. The least popular of church services seemed to come in droves, then there were none, and then along came another batch. All to do with growing older, of course – and wasn't she one of them!

She much preferred christenings and weddings and there were a few of those in the offing, in fact she'd been present at one of the births and news of others were widely known.

And weddings. Young folk of the town stepping out together. Courting, then getting engaged.

Smiling to herself, she shuffled through the papers. There were three that looked to be happening fairly shortly.

The fourth one gave no date. Just the names of the bride and groom.

When she read those names, her jaw dropped and then she smiled.

The vicar and Doctor Brakespeare were going to tie the knot at long last.

Hearing the sound of the vicar out in the hallway, she piled the papers back where she'd found them.

'I'm in here, Reverend. Just finished in your study,' she said, coming out into the hallway.

'Lucy not arrived yet?'

Her face felt stiff from smiling, and she answered that no, Lucy had not arrived yet.

'It seems her path has crossed with that of Doctor Brakespeare. She's gone out to see her ladyship on a hospital matter, I do believe.'

'Then you might want to share a pot of tea with me and my Lucy.'

'I might indeed,' he said with a smile.

Ma Skittings continued to beam at him, so much so that he asked her if anything was wrong.

'No,' she said brightly. 'Nothing at all. And everything is bright and beautiful in your world?'

'Yes,' he said looking a bit puzzled by her comment. 'Yes,' he repeated, 'Everything is fine.'

* * *

It had become monthly routine for Frances to call in and examine Lady Araminta Compton-Dixon. In the past, her visits had mostly been for the benefit of Devlin, but since his marriage to Lucy, he had declared he had no need of being mollycoddled. 'I have a wife and a mother to do that. I am as well as can be expected.'

The sunbaked stone let out heat where it was not covered by a purple flowering wisteria that still glistened with raindrops.

Frances found Araminta in the drawing room. Her hair was a bit awry and the hem of her dress covered her feet, making Frances think she was not wearing any shoes.

Of late, Araminta's hair had thinned and was as white as a dandelion clock.

'So how are you today?'

'Sit down. Please.'

'I've come to examine you.'

'I've ordered tea. I want to talk to you.'

Noting a certain resolution on Araminta's face, Frances did as ordered.

'I had a wash before you came.'

Not quite seeing the point of this, Frances's eyebrows rose. 'Were you cold?'

'I had a wash, not a bath.' She sounded vexed.

'I see.'

'No. You don't. Not really. You do know I tend to mess about in the stables?'

'I heard from Lucy that you like horses.'

'Well, that's as it may.'

Frances was confused. Araminta was getting on in years, but she'd never heard her talking like this. There was something odd about it.

'You know all about Harry Hunter, my late husband's illegitimate son, I take it?'

'Gregory told me.'

'He's very good with Captain, my old hunter. All the other horses are gone now, but I can't bear to get rid of him. Not yet.'

Frances settled herself down to listen.

'I understand the soup kitchen is proving very popular.'

'It is.' Frances frowned. She wasn't at all sure where this was going.

'I'm grateful for you helping the miners out.'

Although it was in her mind to say so, Frances refrained from mentioning the reduction in wages that had led to the hard times the miners were suffering.

Not that she needed to. Araminta began talking about it.

'The sad fact is that the export market for coal is greatly diminished.' She paused, her mittened fingers, rings on three of them, played with the frayed lace of her mittens. 'The fact is that on the advice of my brokers, I sold off half of my interest in the coal mine. It was a condition of that sale that the new investors control the business, including the matter of wages.'

There was an obvious question that had to be asked.

'Does Devlin know?'

She shook her head. 'I'm afraid to tell him. As you know, his interests are in quarrying. He's had little to do with the coalmines.'

'Will you tell him?'

An elusive look came to Araminta's face. 'He'll find out soon enough. When I'm no longer here.'

Her voice had dropped to barely above a whisper.

Frances frowned. 'If you're talking about dying as a consequence of your health, I think I should be the judge of that.'

A slight and sugary smile touched on Araminta's thin lips.

'I'm an old woman, Doctor. I was in my late thirties when I had Devlin. Time has been kind to me, but there is a point of no return, a time when one senses the pearly gates are in sight. I'm feeling...' She flicked her fingers through the halo of white hair so at least one side of it was tucked behind her ears. 'Well. Never mind what I'm feeling. What will be, will be.'

Frances made an immediate decision, got to her feet and unbuckled her medicine bag. 'I still think I should examine you...'

'No!' Araminta's tone was quite adamant. 'I just know, but I wanted to tell someone about the surprise that will await my son, even more so the men who have given me such loyal service. Please tell them, Doctor. Promise you will tell them.'

Frances nodded mutely.

'And, also, Harry Hunter. I want him to know too. I want him to know how much I regretted his mother being married off to a brute.' She shook her head. 'My husband should not have done that.' A faraway look came to her eyes. 'Still, justice was done, I'm glad to say.'

Frances presumed she was speaking of her husband, but it might just as well have been the man Harry's mother had been married off to.

It was as though Araminta was reading her thoughts. There was such a glittering in her eyes, like dark stars suddenly exploding.

'Both of them,' she said firmly but quietly. 'Justice was done to both of them.'

Frances was handed a copy of her ladyship's will before she left.

'I want an independent witness to my wishes.'

Feeling extremely unnerved that Araminta had refused to be examined, she left under duress.

'I here and now register my disapproval.'

Araminta shook her head and said nothing.

It was only then that Frances felt a shudder of apprehension course down her spine. Old people coming to the end of their lives sometimes showed increased instinct. Their bodies were wearing out and their minds seemed to know it – as if silent, unseen messages were passing between each of them.

Time will tell; she told herself as she drove home to the coach house.

* * *

On seeing her car, Gregory came out from the vicarage, imposing in black at the top of the steps.

She left her bag in the car and ran up the stairs to greet him, throwing her head onto his shoulder.

'Our secret is out,' he whispered into her ear. 'I think Mrs Skittings read the draft banns I prepared. So brace yourself...'

The sobs came out thick and fast.

'Darling? What's wrong? It's not the end of the earth if she knows, is it?'

Frances rubbed her cheek against his and gave him a brief résumé of what Araminta had said.

For a moment, he said nothing, and then: 'If she's made her mind up, then there's nothing we can do about it.'

'What will be will be.'

'Yes, my love. What will be, will be.'

There was deep meaning in those words. She knew he wasn't just referring to Araminta. It was also for them.

29

Careful to avoid the rampant brambles, Edith leaned the bicycle against the fence opposite the boat and looked into the field. Patches of blackened grass twisted bits of metal and shards of sooty wood evidenced where the fire had taken hold.

Poor Harry, she thought. His heart must be singed too. This was his baby, the child of his heart and it saddened her.

Turning back to the boat, she closed her fist and rapped on the coach roof. 'Anyone home?'

She held her breath until he appeared, his hair dishevelled and accompanied by the smell of soot.

'I heard about the fire. I came to see how you were.'

She couldn't be sure, but she thought he looked thoughtful. He also appeared to be grinding his jaw.

Somehow, his silence made her feel awkward.

Saying hello and shoving off was not good enough. She sought the sound of his voice. 'Do you know how it started?'

What she'd like to believe was that it might have been a stray spark and therefore accidental.

Thinking of the atmosphere in the Jolly Boatman and what Harry had divulged, she had to admit to herself that there were darker motives.

What he said next confirmed her worse fears.

'Someone started it. I almost caught him.'

She took a deep intake of breath, partly shocked surprise, but also her estimation that he was not a man to be dallied with. He was a strong man. He could take care of himself. The Great War would have taught him that.

'Did you recognise him?'

'I've an idea, though can't prove it. He'll be marked though.'

'You hit him?'

A wide grin divided his thick moustache from his beard. 'No. He was attacked by the cob.'

She laughed, but only a little. Something quite serious seemed to be hanging in the air between them. Or perhaps it was a scene in the book she'd been reading the night before which had been more than romantic. Steamy was the right word for it. How delicious it had been.

'Talbot was injured. A stray bitch I'd rescued died,' he added more sadly. 'She was expecting puppies.'

'I'm so sorry to hear that.'

He nodded silently, his gaze switching from her to some spot further along the canal, where a pair of swans were swimming.

She wanted him to face her again, to see the colour of his eyes. Were they blue, or were they a kind of plum colour? She decided they sometimes looked like plums because they were deep set. Either way, she didn't care what colour they were – so long as he looked at her again.

'Would you come with me to the pub again tonight?'

The question took her off guard, and she nearly choked before she answered.

'Yes. I would. Shall I see you there?'

He nodded. 'Wait for me outside. Seven o'clock.'

'You blame Clifford Fletcher for what happened?'

He turned to her then. 'Enough to delve a little deeper.'

Then he turned.

She reached for the handlebars of her bicycle. 'I'll see you then. I do hope Talbot makes a complete recovery – if you want me to take a look at him...?'

His voice came loud and clear from down in the cabin. 'No need. I can manage.'

When she got to the row of terraced cottages where weeds sprouted from the base of rough stone walls, a Douglas motorcycle leaned awkwardly among the weeds, its headlamp staring skywards.

A shiver ran down her back. Frank was back. Absurd after the hammering Harry had given him.

The garden gate hung askew from its hinges. She was sure it hadn't been so bad as that on her first visit here. Not that it overly concerned her, not like the motorcycle.

Showing fear did not come easily. Her reputation was that of a woman you respected if you knew what was good for you.

You are made of stronger stuff, that's what she told herself as she headed for the front door. Just before getting there, she swerved onto the narrow path that led through the snicket, an arched entry in the middle of the rank.

Out back a line of washing hung sullenly from the clothesline. Looking beyond that, she saw no movement at the top of the garden or around the brick-built pigsty.

Voices within the cottage rumbled and sharpened. An argument was in process, a man's angry voice, a woman's voice, an attempt to placate and then to question. Something about money.

The man's voice rose in line with increased anger.

'Mind yer own business!'

What would it take to see Frank Steele disappear over the horizon and never darken June and Tommy's door ever again?

'Frank, what have you done?'

The sound of a slap, a woman's cry amid the clatter of scattered pots, pans and crockery.

'Just keep your bloody mouth shut!'

Edith hammered on the open door. 'Mrs Newman? It's Sister Harrison here. I've come to see if Tommy is all right.'

The back door was slightly ajar. One push of her gloved hand and it opened wide.

Mrs Newman was sprawled on the floor, surrounded by saucepans and broken crockery.

Edith was aware of Frank's clenched fists, the stance of a man who was a slave to violence.

'It was an accident,' June whimpered as Edith helped her to her feet. A piece of broken crockery had broken the skin beneath June's eye.

She helped her to a chair. 'Sit down.' She barked an order at the loathsome man whose face was still riddled with anger. 'A bowl of hot water and a flannel. Can you manage that?'

For a moment, she thought the kettle of hot water would be thrown at her. He just stood defiant, as though willing her to force him to obey.

Frank Steele did not know with whom he was dealing. Sister Harrison was having none of it.

'Oh, for goodness' sake! Get out of my way.'

Barging past him, she poured water from the kettle into an enamel bowl. There was no face flannel but there was a fairly clean tea towel. In the absence of soap, she added a few nubs of soda.

As she bathed the wound, her eyes flickered in his direction. She noted a line of purple bruising up each arm, plus a range of scabby indents on his hands.

Seeing her scrutiny, he folded his arms, hiding his hands beneath his armpits. The scabs on his hands were hidden, not so the bruises which looked as though he'd been beaten. In her estimation, they were defensive wounds, those likely to occur when both arms are held across the face.

Sarcasm smirked her face and seethed in her voice. 'Been in the wars, have you, Mr Steele?'

She felt June tense beneath her healing touch.

June lied as she'd been ordered to do. 'He fell down.'

Smile at him. Make him feel awkward. 'Really? Is that right, Mr Steele? I see many old people who regularly fall. But surely, you're not that old – are you?'

He became immediately defensive. ''Course I didn't. Don't listen to 'er. She don't know what she's on about! I got into a fight. That's all.'

'I was here when Harry Hunter gave you a pasting. If I recall rightly, he hit your jaw not your arms or your knuckles. I would call those defensive wounds.'

''Tweren't that fight. It were another.'

'Who with?' Edith murmured softly, unable to prevent the accompanying chuckle. 'Or what with?' she added more softly.

Frank threw her a look that could slice butter before stamping upstairs, crashing around up there, before coming back down wearing a greatcoat, a haversack slung over his shoulder.

'I'm off. I won't be back,' he shouted at June.

A glare bounced from one woman to another before he slammed out of the door.

'He's got somewhere to go,' said June at the sound of the motorcycle. 'A job at the docks in Bristol. And he's found lodgings.' She rolled her eyes. 'Thank God!'

Edith responded. 'Thank God indeed. Did he get round to telling you the truth about his injuries?'

June shook her head.

'Then I will tell you.'

By the time Edith had finished the story, both women were laughing like rain pouring down drains, unfettered.

'No wonder he didn't tell me.'

No, thought Edith, but Harry had guessed.

30

It wasn't often that Frances and Gregory were invited to tea together on a Saturday afternoon at Orchard Manor. No reason had been given.

After a hard week at the hospital, Frances was feeling more than ready to relax.

A blue silk tea dress that she had seldom had occasion to wear was taken from the wardrobe. So was a pair of her favourite ankle-strap shoes with a Spanish heel – low enough to facilitate her driving there.

Gregory looked splendid in off-white flannels he usually wore when playing cricket, paired with a striped blazer.

'Let us suppose that it is purely a social occasion.' She looked him up and down. 'We certainly look as though we're out on a jolly.'

Gregory was more sanguine. 'I sense purpose in her summons. Both of us at the same time. So not church business. Not hospital either. She tends to be singular about those things.'

They were shown into the drawing room at the rear of the house, a place of faded wallpaper and gilt-framed ancestors. Most visitors had experience of the reception rooms at the front of the house. Few were invited to the room at the rear, where Araminta sometimes adopted male attire more suitable for dealing with animals – horses especially.

'Make yourselves comfortable.'

Araminta tipped a grey-whiskered terrier off the sofa.

The sofa was comfortable and neither Frances nor Gregory were so bad-mannered as to brush lingering hairs away.

She sat herself down in a velvet-covered Victorian nursing chair that was quite low and suited her short legs.

Frances thanked her for inviting them. 'It's a while since I've had an excuse to wear a tea dress.'

A stick of a woman with iron-grey hair and pursed lips burst through the door and placed a tray of sandwiches and slices of cake on the table.

'I'll bring the tea things along on a separate tray,' she barked. 'I've only one pair of hands.'

With that, she was gone but only momentarily before it burst open for the second time and another tray was placed on the table.

'Thank you, Minette. That will be all.'

In the pursuit of a reason for the visit, Frances asked if Devlin, Araminta's son, was in good health. She answered that he was fine. So was Lucy.

'Everyone is in fine fettle.'

Gregory was direct and to the point. 'Nice as it is to take tea with you, we were a bit surprised.'

'You mean it doesn't happen that often.'

'I wasn't being rude.'

'I know you weren't.'

'So what's this all about?'

'Concerns,' said Araminta, shoving the tea tray to one side.

Gregory took a guess. 'Is this to do with Harry Hunter?'

Araminta replied that it was. Her long, elegant fingers began tapping in sequence on the chair arms. Every so often, they tightened. It was as though she was trying to hang onto something.

'Perhaps you also know that my husband left him a parcel of land. A waterlogged piece of land.'

Gregory answered quietly. 'I had heard it said.'

A bemused smile came to Araminta's face. 'Being the subject of rumour – whether true or otherwise – is a cross the landed gentry have to bear.'

Frances refrained from making comment, simply because what Araminta had said was true. There were always rumours about the history of wealthy families.

Fingers still tapping, Araminta went on.

'My husband was careful with whom he had extramarital relationships. He was never what could publicly be regarded as a ladies' man. Out of courtesy to me, I think, he kept his affairs private. And for the most part that was how things were. Except for one, the one who gave birth to Harry.'

Frances had the distinct impression that Araminta was still bitter about what her husband had done, bitter also with the woman who had given birth to Harry.

In a sudden fit of movement, her ladyship began pouring tea and passing round sandwiches and pieces of cake. A way of suppressing any emotion from showing on her face.

'I have every intention of honouring Harry's wishes.'

Frances frowned and shook her head. 'I still don't understand what it has to do with us.'

Araminta bypassed her question and looked searchingly at Gregory.

'I'm not sure that he bears any resemblance to my husband or to my son. Though I would like to know – before I go.'

Frances opened her mouth, intending to say that Araminta was in good shape for her age.

Araminta raised a hand. 'Don't patronise me, Doctor. If I could choose, I'd ask to be shot – like an old horse.'

Understanding what she was getting at, Gregory spoke. 'You want reassurance that it is him.' He paused. 'You want to see his face.'

She didn't move. Didn't speak at first, and then, 'I'm near the end of my life and although I was baptised a Christian, I'm not sure about the existence of heaven. If it does exist, I would like to meet up with my husband again. I miss him,' she said softly, her eyes downcast, eyelashes feathering her pale cheeks.

'Then you must believe in heaven.'

Her mauve lips teetered on the verge of a smile. 'I'd like to think so, but just in case, I would like to see Harry's face, to see if there is any resemblance to my late husband.'

'But you've met Harry.'

'Yes. But...' Her eyes sparkled like droplets of morning dew. 'All that hair. I've seen his eyes, so enticing, electric. The man I married had charisma, I doubt I would have married him if he had not. I doubt also that so many women would have surrendered to him if he had not. I want to know what

Harry Hunter looks like beneath all that hair. I want to be taken back in time to when I was a young girl and in love with a man so many were in love with.'

'I understand,' said Frances and reached for Araminta's hand. She looked at Gregory. 'If we can convince him to shave, we will. Won't we?'

Gregory responded. 'Nothing like being put on the spot.' He nodded. 'I'll see what can be done.'

There were times when it was impossible not to look at each other without betraying their deepest feelings.

Araminta was one of the more astute observers. 'So when are you getting married?'

There was no getting away with half-baked denials.

'Soon,' said Gregory, reaching for Frances's free hand. 'Soon.'

'Before I die if you could. So there you are. That's the timetable. Stick to it, or I'll come back and haunt you!'

31

Noise fell out of the pub door, along with those who had drank their fill. Nobody seemed to be going in. Nobody seemed to be waiting. Just her. No sign of Harry.

An old man, a pewter tankard clutched in his hand, sat on the bench outside.

'Too 'ot in thur,' he said, tipping his hat. 'T'ain't much better out yur,' he added, wiping his hand across his forehead before taking a deep swig from the tankard.

After agreeing with him, Edith's attention switched to a plush-looking car parked outside the pub that she recognised as belonging to Clifford Fletcher.

A small movement inside the car caught her attention. Closer inspection revealed a dog, paws scrabbling against the closed window, its tongue hanging out.

'That poor creature,' she exclaimed, not hiding her indignation. 'How could anyone be so stupid as to leave the creature – any creature – shut behind glass on a warm evening.' She addressed the old man. 'Am I right in thinking that this is Mr Fletcher's car?'

The old man squinted before declaring that indeed it was.

'He's left his dog inside.'

The old man bent his head, peered in that direction and squinted again. 'Seems like it.'

'It's far too hot to do that. I wonder how long it's been in there.'

The old chap struggled to his feet, his head poking forward on the end of a long neck from a hunched back. Like a tortoise. 'It was in thur when I got yur.'

'And what time was that?'

'Well…' The old man pursed his wet lips, his bleary eyes wandering as he sought a reasonable excuse that wouldn't incur a glare that could curdle milk. Nobody willingly crossed swords with Sister Harrison. And everyone knew her – or of her.

He settled for saying that it must be hours ago.

'Though I couldn't swear as to 'ow long.'

There was nobody else around, nobody to see what she had in mind to do next.

She was aware that Doctor Brakespeare didn't lock the door of the car, so it was a safe bet that this one wasn't locked either.

She tried the door handle, found it stiff, but a little more pressure and it made a clunking sound as the catch gave and the car door opened.

The dog leapt into her arms, scattering her face with wet kisses and trailing his leash behind him.

Before she had chance to grab it, it ran off towards the canal.

She ran after him, calling, 'Come back.'

The dog careered onwards, finally heading through a clump of weeds onto a narrow split of mud where the canal wall had been damaged. From there, it was easy for him to get to the water. She found him there lapping at the water as though he would drink the whole canal dry.

'Edith.' Harry appeared, looking slightly bemused. 'You're a fair way from the pub.'

His obvious amusement annoyed her.

'Then it's a good job you're not there yet.'

She regretted sounding so accusing. This wasn't at all how she'd intended behaving this evening.

She explained about finding the dog shut in the car.

'He was in a state of panic. I heard from an old man outside the pub that it had been in there for some time.'

Thirst slaked, the little dog came bounding back from the canal's edge. Sniffing happily at the reeds and grass, it jumped up at her. Muddy paw marks were added to the white and yellow daisies scattered all over her dress. She'd been proud of how fresh it had looked but swallowed her dismay, told herself that the pawmarks weren't that different to the daisies. Harry bent his knees and knelt in the dirt. The dog went to him.

'Cruel bugger,' said Harry, rubbing behind the little dog's ears.

'It was Clifford Fletcher's car.'

'Which figures this is his dog.'

'Poor thing. Look at its muddy feet. I suppose I'd better take it back, though I doubt its owner would want muddy pawmarks over those plush seats.'

'Doubt he'd miss the poor thing.'

'Indeed.'

'Could do with a new home.'

'Possibly.'

'He couldn't love the dog the way young Tommy Newman loved his dog.'

'I doubt Clifford Fletcher loves anyone – except himself.'

'I would guess you're right, Edith.'

She loved the way he said her name. Yes, there had been men in her life, but none of them had uttered her name like he did.

They stood there quietly, the dog on the ground in between them, looking up as though awaiting their decision on what should happen next.

They were in tandem in their thinking, which made her ponder eventually uttering a suggestion that she was sure he would share.

'I wonder if he would miss him – if we didn't put him back in the car.'

Their eyes met. One side of her mouth lifted in a mischievous smile. Never mind his hairy face, she didn't need to see his mouth to know he was of the same mind.

'We are united, I think. Now we test our theory,' said Harry, stroking a hair away from his eyes. He bent down and picked up the muddy end of the dog's lead. 'Here, little dog. Come with me.'

The three of them regained the towpath, their footsteps heading for the field.

The path was stony underfoot, but Edith didn't care, in fact she was quite elated.

'You're going to steal the dog and give it to Tommy.'

'Rescue. I'm going to rescue the dog and give it to Tommy. Can you think of a better future for the poor creature?'

She shook her head. 'No. I think it's a wonderful idea.'

They stopped at the gate to the animal sanctuary he'd created. A hand-painted notice had been nailed to the gate. It said 'Harry's Lot'.

'You've given it a name.'

'Yes.'

'Why lot?'

She fancied the edifice of a smile behind that mass of facial hair.

'Lots of reasons.'

They both laughed at his joke.

'That man Weaver is to blame, the one Fletcher sent along to make me an offer. Lot, because if it went to auction it would be termed that. Lot, perhaps because this is my lot in life. Lot...' His voice trailed off.

She didn't press him.

'I have a spare kennel,' he said when she gave him that silence to fill. 'One that survived the fire.'

Enough golden light remained for her to see that he had made good progress in rebuilding the kennels and cages.

They made their way into the field, past the ducks and the swans to the tumbledown shelter at the far end.

They paused at the burnt-out wreck of the kennel the pregnant bitch had inhabited. The blackened pieces of wood still carried the smell of smoke and soot.

Her stomach churned.

The remains of a straw bale, dirty and ancient, provided enough bedding for the dog to be comfortable.

The door to the shelter was in two parts. The upper part hung loosely on one hinge. The bottom half was firm enough on both its hinges.

'In there, girl. There's food and water enough for all night.'

She trusted his judgement.

It came as no surprise that the dog showed no sign of missing her owner and seemed content that her belly was full and cool air was blowing in over the top of the dilapidated door.

'I'll see you tomorrow,' whispered Harry, stroking her head behind the closing eyes. 'Now be good. Don't make a noise, and guess what? I'm bringing along somebody who's going to love you. What do you think of that?'

The dog, curled into a ball and made snuffly noises and closed its eyes.

They left it there, slid the bolt across the door on the outside and headed back to the towpath.

Now it was just the two of them.

For a while they walked slowly, Harry seemingly immersed in thought.

The sun dipped into a blazing pool of gold behind the railway embankment.

She wanted to remind him that he'd asked to meet her outside the pub, wondered whether he'd forgotten.

'I haven't forgotten that we were going to go to the pub tonight.' He stopped in his tracks and turned to face her. 'By rights, I should go by myself. Dragging you along wouldn't have been fair.'

'I don't mind,' she blurted, barely controlling the impression that she would go with him anywhere.

'Violence might have ensued – correction – violence *would* have ensued. Clifford Fletcher was behind the burning. I'm guessing Frank Steele lit the touchpaper.'

'Yes. He did.'

She went on to tell him about calling in on June Newman and the injuries to Frank's arms.

'How would you know if someone had been attacked by a swan?'

'Think about it. When it flew at you, you would hold up your arms – like so.' He crossed his arms in front of his face. 'With a bit of luck, you won't get a face injury, though there is no guarantee. Your arms would bear the brunt of the attack.' He shrugged. 'Never get between a swan and its mate. Or its cygnets. You'll be sure to come off the worse.'

'Attacked by a swan. Will he ever live it down?'

He laughed, not just a chuckle, but a full-throated laugh.

She was mesmerised by his profile when he threw back his head, like a lion does when it's about to roar. Laughter was preferable, rumbling up from the depths of his chest.

How pleasurable it was with their laughter lingering and their upper arms brushing together.

She looked up at him; her face shadowed on that side turned away from the sunset.

'What will you do next?'

She thought she saw a chewing motion around his whiskered mouth and a narrowing of his eyes.

'He killed some of my animals.'

'You're not going to kill him, are you?'

She shivered at the way he held her gaze and kept her waiting for a response.

'I will be having a word with him.'

'Now? At the pub? I thought he'd left.'

'His sort hangs around, waiting for crumbs from better men's tables.'

'Please don't do anything stupid.'

Seconds grew into anxious minutes. Holding her breath, she awaited his response.

She imagined rather than saw the resultant smile.

'I'm sorry for dragging you out on the promise of agreeable company. Were you looking forward to it very much?'

She cocked her head to one side in a challenging manor. 'I was, though that would have depended on what sort of evening it would have turned out to be. And that, Harry Hunter, would all have depended on you.' She shook her head. 'I don't want to bear witness to violence.'

That silence again. Would he offer to escort her home – at least as far as the bus stop?

She made a snap decision, took a couple of steps in the direction of the lane which led up to the bus stop. 'I'd better go. I'm on duty tomorrow.'

'I've a bottle of port on board the boat. Would you care to take a dram with me?'

Her heel caught and she toppled slightly. He caught her, cupping her elbow in his hand.

'Are you all right?'

'Yes.' His palm was warm – no, not warm, hot as though he'd warmed it by a fire purely for her pleasure.

He led her to sit on the roof of the boat.

'I often sit up here and contemplate the stars. See that one there? Three in a row. That's Orion's Belt.'

She knew the constellation, but it was pleasant to hear him pointing it out to her.

She settled down and waited whilst he went downstairs. Some of the stars seemed to be winking at her – as if they knew why she was feeling happier than she ever had in her life.

Blow Clifford Fletcher. Blow Frank Steele. Tonight, it was just the two of them, sitting on the cabin roof of a boat named *Talbot* beneath a canopy of stars.

Toasting each other with the tots of port should have been a straightforward affair. A cool breeze chose that moment to send Harry's fuzzy growth blowing like a widow's veil between them, the tail ends tickling Edith's nose and tangling in one of her pearl drop earrings.

Laying aside their drinks, their fingers fumbled together to let loose the hair. Edith held her head sideways so his hair didn't pull so much on her ear. Harry got closer to help alleviate the tugging on his beard.

But that closeness also brought a moment when his lips brushed her cheek, then his fingertips tickling beneath her ear. Then his lips on hers.

Now this, thought Edith, *is what I've been waiting for.*

Confidence gave birth to being outspoken, to chancing her luck.

'Harry,' she whispered. 'Do you know what would make a repeat of this evening that much more perfect?'

Their breath mingled.

'Tell me,' he whispered.

'You having a shave.'

32

Mrs Abbot had her own stool in the post office. She'd demanded it because her legs were bad and getting worse. The time she spent sitting on that stool was getting longer, but the postmistress knew better than to comment. Aggie Abbot watched and listened to everyone who came in and out and talked about them all. The postmistress was a retiring soul and had no wish to be the subject of her vicious tongue. Her job was to be a stalwart of service to the community, so she kept mum.

Aggie had few real friends, just people who preferred to keep on friendly terms for the same reason as the postmistress. Ma Skittings was one of them, a long-time friend, who, like Aggie, knew a few secrets some in the village would prefer were dead and buried.

The door to the shop suddenly opened. Gasps sounding as though they'd escaped from a leaky bellows blew around the post office. Harry Hunter had come in to collect his pension. The floor crammed with boxes of vegetables, the walls lined with shelves facing the post office counter, there was little room for no more than six customers. The new arrival in his bulky coat and rampant head of hair, made it seem substantially smaller.

There was silence. Other waiting customers stood aside as he made his way to the counter and presented his army pension book.

'Will that be all, sir?'

The postmistress was always polite, her voice having no edge of emotion or opinion, mainly because she didn't have any.

'Thank you.'

The bell above the door jangled as he heaved it open and Clifford Fletcher entered.

'Hunter!'

Clifford Fletcher had not even granted Harry the courtesy of a Mr.

Harry, his eyes fiercely blue let him pass.

Clifford Fletcher, as self-important as ever, puffed out his chest and addressed the postmistress. 'The wife's made a poster. A reward to whoever finds her missing dog. Fond of it she is. Five pounds to anyone who finds it.'

A murmur of interest circulated. Five pounds was a lot of money. Few people made that in a week.

The postmistress came out from behind the counter. Her face remained impassive as she took the sixpenny fee from Fletcher and with bits of sticky tape, placed the missing dog poster up in the window.

Harry glanced at it. 'Five pounds. Is the dog really worth that much to you?'

'I could ask the same of you, about that field. Had a bit of a fire, so I hear.'

His smirk bit Harry like a rabid dog. Using both hands, he grabbed Clifford by his coat lapels.

'Keep away from my field, Fletcher. And keep that other dog of yours, Frank Steele, away from me. I'm warning you.'

The glass rattled in the door frame as he slammed it shut behind him.

* * *

The straight and narrow path had never been much to Frank Steele's liking. Or perhaps fate didn't want him on it, giving him a push just when he thought he had things sussed.

The woman Frank Steele had moved in with in Bristol had thrown him out after he'd punched her in the face, breaking one front tooth and making her lip swell up like a balloon.

Insult had added to her injuries when he couldn't get weighed on for a few days' work at the docks. What made matters worse was that he didn't go out of his way to find fresh employment. This woman was no June Newman, no mouse to be taken advantage of. It went so far and that was enough.

'You're not lazing around my place all day.'

He didn't think this fair. Not being inclined towards honest work, he'd been giving her some of the money he'd earned from a bit of breaking and entering, going back to Norton Dene and doing 'favours' for the likes of Clifford Fletcher.

He'd enjoyed lighting that fire and on the other occasion had enjoyed letting go the lines on the boat and seeing it drift out towards the weir and the three-foot drop to the other side. He hadn't reckoned on Harry waking up and being such a strong swimmer, or his dog being clever enough to take a line and help as though he understood what was going on.

The only animals he had time for were those whose meat or pelts he could sell. Strictly speaking, it was poaching, but he was hardly the only one doing it. Poaching was ingrained in folk around here. If you couldn't afford a bit of meat for the pot, you stole it.

He'd poached most creatures. Rabbits, foxes, stolen sheep, stolen chickens, salmon, trout and anything else that swam in the canal, though the salmon were only in the river. He had to walk a bit further to get there.

The canal was home to a flock of mallards and moorhens. There were plenty of them along the canal and the nearby river. Ducks were succulent and easy to catch, which made him wonder what a swan tasted like. Nice bit of meat on them, he reckoned, more than on a duck, perhaps as much as on a goose. What he would like to do to that bloody swan!

It was nothing compared to what he'd like to do to the man who had dented both his pride and his chin, the man who had shoved his head down the lavatory and pulled the flush. He was a water rat. Nothing but a water rat.

After being thrown out of his lodgings, he was back in Lower Foxford with evil intent towards Harry Hunter, but also with the intention of sweet-talking June Newman into taking him back. Given time, he might also be able to persuade her to get rid of the kid, send him into care or preferably off with those other kids – orphans and bastards mostly – being shipped out to Australia.

He did not intend to go empty-handed when he visited June. Most women liked to be brought presents, though he had no intention of taking her anything that would cost money. Why do that when he could get something she would really appreciate for free?

With that in mind, he'd gone to the river under cover of dusk to see if there were any salmon or fat brown trout loitering around the base of the weir. Before going there, he'd paid a visit to Clifford Fletcher. It wasn't the first time he'd called at the house. Caroline Fletcher had once answered the door, a small dog in her arms. He'd tried to be charming, but she'd wrinkled her nose and told him to see her husband in his office and never to darken her door again. Obviously a cold fish. Preferred dogs to a good-looking bloke like him.

On this occasion, Clifford was home, though reiterated that Frank should only call at the office.

'The wife's short-tempered at present. Her bloody dog's gone missing. Had me posting these notices all over the place and putting up a fiver reward to anyone finding it.'

Frank had glanced at the poster, immediately recognising the dog Mrs Fletcher had held in her arms on a previous visit.

'It might be down in that field with the hairy monster.' He said it jokingly, but Clifford was in no mood for his brand of humour.

'Keep your bloody voice down.'

Frank, stupid as ever, repeated himself in a softer voice.

'What about—'

'Try something else. But be careful. If you get caught I don't know anything about it. Is that clear?'

Frank had set off back down the lane to the canal whistling all the way. He'd no plans as to what other inconvenience he could contrive with regard to Harry Hunter. What he did know was that Clifford Fletcher wanted him gone and that he would be paid well if he succeeded.

Poaching or fishing on the river without a licence was an offence, but keeping on the right side of the law had never been a high priority as far as Frank Steele was concerned.

Flies were skimming the surface of the water and the brown trout were coming up to suck them down into their hungry little mouths. It wasn't long before he had three of them, which he stuffed into a canvas nosebag he'd taken from some drunken gypsy fellah.

Three trout. Two he would sell so he could buy himself a few ciders, the other he would present to June as a peace offering.

At the thought of drink, he licked his lips. It had been twenty-four hours since he'd sunk six pints of cider and he reckoned he was now due six more.

The lights of the Jolly Boatman were blinking into existence as the dusk deepened.

Looking in the other direction, he saw smoke curling up from the metal stack of the narrowboat. There was no sign of either the tramp or his dog.

A steely determination came upon Frank then to chance his luck and see what mayhem he could produce, perhaps even start another fire? It wouldn't be expected, so all the better to start it now.

Keeping to the hedges and ragged walls at the side of the towpath, the nosebag of fishes bumping against his thigh, he headed towards the ramshackle gate that opened into the soggy field.

There was a gap between the shrubs rambling over the jagged wire fence with just enough space for him to squeeze through.

The kennels and runs seemed strangely empty and it did occur to him that Harry was already making plans to leave. Clifford Fletcher would be bowled over by this, but Frank didn't want the man to leave until he'd earned more money from Fletcher and had his revenge on the scruffy bugger on the boat.

Only one run seemed occupied. He tucked his hand in his pocket as he got closer, feeling for the box of matches he always carried and wishing he'd brought the bicycle lamp.

At exactly the right moment, the moon came up from behind the trees. The whole field was bathed in silver and more especially the occupant of the kennel in front of him.

He curbed the chuckle that rose in his throat, aware that the slightest sound carried better at night than it did in daytime.

By moonlight, he immediately recognised the dog belonging to the Fletchers. The five-pound reward was his. He was about to lift the latch that held the door shut, when a sudden thought struck him. Returning the dog to its rightful owner and receiving the reward was all well and good, but he also wanted revenge. If he played this right, he could kill two birds with one stone. Tell Clifford of the dog's whereabouts but remind him that this was a licensed animal and dog stealing was an offence. Get the police involved, he thought, an evil smile spreading across his face.

With the plan settled in his mind, he crept away. First, phone the police from the phone box at the bottom of the lane that led up to the main road.

After that, he would treat himself to a few pints of beer whilst awaiting the arrival of the police and the arrest of Harry Hunter.

* * *

June had landed a night's work behind the bar at the Jolly Boatman. She saw Frank before he saw her.

'You all right?' asked Mrs Fletcher on seeing her turning pale.

'No. Not really. It's him.' She jerked her head to where Frank was swilling back his second pint of beer. 'Do you mind if I go home? I mean, I don't want any trouble and he's bound to start when he sees me.'

'Out the back way, love. It's not that busy, so I can manage OK.'

June thanked her, grabbed her coat and shot out through the back of the pub.

Once outside, her heels clattered on the cobbles as she ran for home. The first droplets of rain that had been threatening for days spotted the dry ground but didn't turn into a real downpour.

Coming out from behind the pub, she was about to scurry off towards home when she saw Clifford Fletcher's car pull in and Frank strut out of the pub door.

Clifford slapped Frank on the back in a matey manner.

The old fear returned and her first instinct was to run for home, but the sudden jangling of a police bell stayed her. A black police car careered down the lane leading from the main road and parked beside Clifford's car.

The police, Clifford Fletcher and Frank huddled into a group, avidly discussing something, though she couldn't hear what it was.

The big surprise was Frank being in the company of police officers. He hated them, called them bluebottles.

Bluebottles. Swat them like flies. That's the best for the likes of them.

And you should know, she thought to herself. Frank had been confined to a cell on more than one occasion, mainly for being drunk and disorderly – or so he'd said. Sometimes she suspected he'd been arrested for something worse than that, but he'd admitted nothing.

The police, Frank and Clifford Fletcher headed off away from the pub. They were heading along the towpath in the direction of Harry Hunter's field, the one coveted by Clifford Fletcher. Before they got there, they would be passing the boathouse, also owned by Clifford Fletcher.

A light flicked on from the upstairs window. A figure passed between the light and the window, throwing a shadow on the yard outside.

June headed there.

Just for once, the door was locked against the world. June glanced in the direction where the men had disappeared. They were beyond hearing her, dead set on whatever they were up to. She decided she had to follow.

As usual, Clifford Fletcher was full of his own self-importance, striding along at the head of the little band, Frank and the police following on.

Frank had one hand in his pocket, his head jutting forward like a tortoise that's just coming out of its shell. He was wearing a tight smile and his hand was fingering the sand-filled cosh that he carried in his pocket. He had every intention of using that cosh on Harry Hunter and the sooner, the better.

Once there, Clifford Fletcher hammered on the side of the boat with his fist and shouted. 'Come on out, Ben, Harry, whoever you bloody are. We want a word with you.'

The senior policemen eased him to one side. 'Excuse me, sir, but that's our job.'

Harry appeared, looking too big to have fitted behind the small cabin door. His frame filled the space. He nodded a gruff greeting.

Clifford Fletcher couldn't help the twisted sneer that came to his face. 'With or without a beard, get your stuff. You're going to jail for dog stealing.'

'That will be enough of that, Mr Fletcher.' The policeman carried on, 'Excuse me, sir, but we have some questions for you.'

Harry eased himself up top and shut the door on Talbot, who was behind him down in the cabin growling fit to burst. Neither of them liked uninvited strangers on board.

'Can we get onto the path?' asked Harry, showing no sign of panic. 'There's not much room on here and you're upsetting the dog.'

The policemen said that that was all right.

'But just don't try anything,' growled Frank Steele, his eyes glinting with violence.

One of the policemen pushed Frank back with his outstretched arm. 'That will be all, Frank. There's no need for unnecessary force. The gentleman is coming quietly.'

'He'd better,' Frank snarled.

Once on the towpath, Harry stood taller than everyone else, though Frank puffed out his chest and squared his shoulders, aching to use the cosh that was burning a hole in his pocket.

Clifford undid the gate into the field, heading to where Frank had reported seeing the dog. 'There!' He pointed at the dog, who, in return, showed her distaste for her legal owner, snarling and showing two rows of very sharp-looking teeth. 'That's the little... That's Polka. That's my wife's dog. I want this man arrested.'

The two policemen looked thoughtfully down at the little dog.

'It doesn't seem to like you much. Snarling and snapping like that.'

'So does the wife! She snarls and snaps a bit too. Get it?' Clifford chuckled at his own joke and Frank, keen to curry favour, followed suit.

The policemen refrained from commenting, but asked Harry where he'd acquired the dog.

'It was lost.'

'Are you saying it was homeless?'

'I suppose I am.'

Clifford protested. 'That's rubbish! It's my wife's dog and was wearing a collar. And it had a tag with our name and address on it. And may I remind everybody, the dog was taken from the back of my car. That's breaking and entering.'

'Was your car locked, sir?'

'Well, no. All the doors and windows were shut.'

'Were the windows broken?'

'Well, no...'

'Wednesday was a warm night, yet you still shut the dog in.'

'I parked in the shade. The doors were shut but when I returned the back passenger door was open and the dog was gone.'

'And this was from outside the Jolly Boatman.'

'It was.'

'Did you have much to drink?'

'What's that got to do with anything? I can drink as much as I like.'

'More's the pity,' muttered the policeman. 'Mark my words, the day can't come quick enough when driving after downing a few drinks is banned.'

'That's ridiculous. How will anyone get home from the pub?'

After suggesting that customers would have to walk, the policeman asked Harry a question.

'You know that, as a licensed animal, stealing does warrant an appearance before the magistrates?'

'The dog was not wearing a collar. And anyway, it wasn't me that found it. It was a friend.'

The policeman got out a notebook, licked the end of a pencil and prepared to write. 'What was the name of this friend, sir?'

'Sister Edith Harrison.'

A pair of hairy eyebrows rose in surprise. Pencil and notebook were put away.

'We'll have a word with her.' He turned to Clifford Fletcher. 'Quite honestly, if Sister Harrison says the dog was running lose and she thought it was a stray, then I'd be inclined to believe her. She's as honest as the day is long. Besides which, she's the one person in Norton Dene who I would be loath to cross.'

'Brought my Ruby into the world,' said the other policeman, his earlier stridence gentled by the thought. 'This town's got a lot to thank her for.'

'So what happens now?' Clifford Fletcher did not sound happy.

'Well,' said the policeman as he adjusted his chin strap. 'I suppose if you are definite about it being your dog, you can take it home.'

'I am definite. But what about him? Are you going to arrest him?' He pointed at Harry.

'He says he found it, sir. It would be a different matter if you can prove otherwise. If that was so, he'd be up before the magistrate, though should you wish to give him the benefit of the doubt, you could make a private arrangement as recompense. The choice is yours, but I would point out to you that the magistrates would look favourably on such an upright witness as Sister Harrison. Besides, if you think about it, it is her who first found the dog wandering, so by rights it's her that should be arrested.' He shook his head. 'I wouldn't advise it though.'

Clifford, sensing a chance to get rid of his wife's dog without him seeming the guilty one, looked at Harry. 'In that case, I would be quite willing to let bygones be bygones as long as you move on. Leave here. Get going and the sooner, the better. I can make it worth your while,' he added.

Harry said nothing.

Clifford stopped what he was going to say next about some people not pulling their weight in this world, not investing in jobs that would help the employment situation and suddenly looked to where smoke plumed upwards from a smoky campfire. 'And whoever's camping out in that place can go too. Now, let's be having this bloody dog. Frank, do me the honour of getting that dog out of there.'

Frank, as toady as ever, bent down, undid the wire holding the door of the pen shut and did as he was told.

Seeing as it had never met Frank, the dog allowed itself to be lifted out.

'Here you are, Mr Fletcher.' Frank handed the dog over.

The moment Clifford's hands were around it, the dog barked, then snapped its jaws around his hand.

'Oooow!'

Clifford dropped the dog and before anyone had chance to grab it, it was gone, disappearing into the gathering darkness and the woodland on the other side of the fence.

'Blasted thing!' Clifford clamped his hand around the wound in a bid to staunch the blood.

Harry had turned his back on them all and was already heading back to his boat, his dog, his supper and a half tumbler of whisky.

'Hey! Not so fast.' Frank grabbed hold of his shoulder.

Harry stopped.

'We've got a score to settle, you and I.'

'No we haven't.'

A heavy hand landed on Frank's shoulder. 'Frank Steele, if you don't wish to land up in a cell overnight at her majesty's pleasure, then let the man go. I want no brawling tonight.'

Fists flopped to Frank's side as though they were made of jelly.

'Time to go.' The way the policeman said it was an order, not a suggestion. 'The dog's gone and that's that.'

Harry climbed onto his boat without turning his head.

Clifford stood on the path, chest pouting like a fat pigeon. 'Mark my words, I will get you for something, Harry Hunter. Best you get out of here and don't cross your betters. The land is mine – or will be, and I'll tell you this, the first thing I'll do is to tear down that sign and rename it. Something like "Sweet Meadow" would do. A nice little private housing estate that'll have people queuing to buy. I provide what people want, Mr Hunter, and in the end, I always have my way.'

A sudden streak of lightning lit up the sky. The river path finally emptied, and Harry was once more alone. The sound of great wings sounded from overhead, followed by the swishing of moving air as the two swans landed in the field bequeathed to him by a man he'd never known but wished he had.

33

A storm threatened, the air bristling with humidity prior to a thunderstorm.

Frank Steele wiped the sweat from his brow with the back of his hand and gritted his teeth.

That tight sod Clifford Fletcher had only given him a pound note for his trouble. He'd reminded him that the reward for the return of the dog was five pounds, but Clifford was having none of it.

'You found the stupid bitch, but then you let her get away. So a pound for your trouble, Frank, and just remember the likes of you are two a penny. I can get plenty of muscle to replace you any time I like.'

He'd driven away, leaving Frank clutching the pound in his hand in front of the Jolly Boatman. Frank was thirsty. He went inside and ordered himself another pint.

He looked at the woman behind the bar. She was plump and might almost be pretty if only she was smiling instead of scowling at anyone who wanted serving.

When he smiled, thinking he could get the best of her, she sneered back. He turned away, peering over the rim of his beer mug in search of another woman more worthy of his attention. The few women that were there had no teeth and their hair in curlers.

At least June still had most of her teeth and didn't go outside the house with her hair in curlers.

Another pint served by the sour-faced woman and he remembered the trout and the idea to give it as a peace offering to June. Who knew, their relationship might be rekindled. It was worth a try.

Another pint or two and he'd try his luck.

* * *

Flashes of lightning lit the sky.

Tommy wasn't ready for bed but sat on the step outside making rabbit snares. He was good at catching rabbits and skinning them too. In the past, his mother had made rabbit stew from his bounty. Rabbits were now needed to feed Polka, as well as filling his mother's stew pot. He'd had to leave the dog with Harry for the time being until sure that Frank was not coming back. More afraid than he cared to admit, Tommy could not face seeing another dog abused. He hated Frank for kicking his dog and for hitting his mother. Even in his dreams Frank was the bogeyman, the stuff of nightmares. Tommy still woke up in the night covered in sweat. In the darkness of his cramped bedroom he fancied a shadow forming in a corner, growing taller until it was hanging over his bed. Daylight brought respite and reality. Food on the table took priority and his mother would be thankful. With that in mind, he stuffed the lures into his pocket.

He'd seen the police car come down the lane so rather than walk along the riverside path, he cut up the dirt track leading up through the woodlands, then downwards alongside the field.

At the edge of the field, hidden by the trees, he heard everything and almost cheered when he'd seen Polka bite Clifford Fletcher. He only wished she'd also bite Frank Steele. He certainly deserved it.

He hadn't dared cheer her on as she'd made her bid for freedom, though his spirits soared when he felt a wet nose against his thigh. Polka had found him.

She'd licked his face and wagged from the head down.

'You're safe now,' he said to her. 'You're safe. And nobody is ever going to hurt you again. Got that?'

Another lightning flash. Thunder began to roll. Tommy and Polka skipped and ran across the field, Polka jumping up and down beside him or chasing at shadows or jumping through the long grass that sprouted from the nooks and crannies at the base of the wall bordering the path.

Once he'd made sure Polka was fed and watered, he skipped along the towpath, for once looking forward to getting home.

Sight of the motorcycle leaning against the front wall and the good feelings vanished. He gripped the top of the garden gate at the sound of raised voices. He recognised his mother's voice, but also that of Frank Steele.

He sank down on the towpath side of the garden wall, uncaring of the nettles, the brambles and the prickly weeds that grew there.

'No,' he whispered, shaking his head, heart full of despair. 'No. Please, God, no.'

Frank's voice was loud and angry. 'I've brought you some trout, ain't I?'

'And you think that gives you the right to move back in?'

'This is my place. I pays the rent.'

June retaliated. 'Sometimes you do. That's when the money don't go over the bar of the Jolly Boatman.'

Tommy gulped, shut his eyes tight and made a wish for Frank to go away. If only Harry was here, but he wasn't. There was still time for his mother to fall in love with him – if the police didn't carry him off. He'd hoped that might happen, though Harry had given no sign of being interested in his mother. It was just a pipedream.

Hot tears spilled from his eyes and ran down his face. He swallowed them when they got to his mouth, sucking them back with great gulping noises.

If my father was here now... A slight soughing of the trees turned into a sound like a saw cutting through wood. The wind had increased, strong enough to fill the sails of a boat, the kind he liked to think his father had worked on.

Thinking of his father and what he might have done in these circumstances led Tommy to a decision. He could not and would not stay under the same roof as Frank Steele, especially now he had Polka to look after.

Raindrops as big as pennies became wind-driven, rattling against the old windows like handfuls of gravel.

Tommy sat down in the dirt, back against the wall, hands clamped against his ears. He couldn't chance Polka being kicked and abused in the same way Patch had been. He'd so wished he could have protected his little dog, but he was only a boy. When he became a grown man, it might be a different story.

The shouting blasted out from behind the cottage windows.

'I know you, June Newman. You're carrying on with that bloke, ain't ya! Did he tell you 'e'd 'ave a shave in the 'ope that you'd fancy 'im? I bet he did, and you're going to 'ave him living here. I'm right, ain't I? I'm bloody well right!'

'That's not true,' Tommy heard his mother shout back. 'I've had nothing to do with him.'

'Then I'm willing to move back in.'

'Please, Frank. I don't want any trouble.'

Frank emitted a deeply drunken laugh. 'Well you're going to get some, girl...'

Tommy couldn't stand it any longer. He couldn't bear hearing the fear in his mother's voice and he knew from experience what was likely to happen next.

He buried his face in his arms, and although she wasn't with him, he made his new dog a promise. 'I won't let him hurt you, Polka. We're going to run away and be happy. It'll be all right. You'll see.'

Tall grass hid his progress from the front wall of the cottage down to the canal, where poppy heads clouded the air with fine seeds.

Talbot, the boat Harry lived on, was in darkness. That was fine and meant to be, thought Tommy as he quietly retrieved the dog from its kennel. The dog sneezed. Normally, Tommy would have laughed, but this was a scary occasion and he dare not make a sound. They were going to run away. They were going to be happy and that was all that mattered.

But where would he go?

'That's it,' he whispered into Polka's ear. 'We'll run away with the raggle-taggle gypsies. My mum used to sing about them.'

Gypsies were a regular sight around the town and here in Foxford.

The peg seller had been around yesterday afternoon, teeth missing from the front of her mouth and her black hair slicked back with goose grease beneath a multicoloured headscarf.

His mother had bought a few pegs and crossed the woman's palm with silver to tell her fortune. He had no idea what she'd foretold, only that his mother was happier after it was done.

Once she'd called on every house, the gypsy woman had rejoined a tousle-haired boy waiting for her by the reed beds. He'd been holding a piece of rough hemp attached to a heavy leather head collar. The skewbald young horse, its cheeks whiskered, its legs feathered with long hair, had been munching the grass at the side of the path.

Their selling of pegs and plastic flowers finished, they'd headed off in the direction of the meadows further along the waterside where the canal and the river divided into two.

He knew where they would be camped.

His skinny legs propelled him along at speed, his feet splashed through puddles, Polka squirming in his arms.

Forked lightning made the sky seem as though it was cracking open, like old walls on a derelict house. Thunder followed. The rain came down in sheets as though somebody had turned a tap on in heaven. The downpour was so sudden and so heavy he could barely see where he was going. He was soaked through, but still he kept going, rain dripping from his hair, his eyebrows, his nose and his chin.

He began to shiver and the weight of the dog was making his arms ache. If Frank hadn't been there, he would have headed for home and the warm supper likely to be waiting for him. But Frank *was* there. He couldn't go back. He could never go home again.

He didn't know how long he walked. All that he did know was that his legs were heavy, his shoes and socks waterlogged, and he was close to giving in.

The trees around him afforded no shelter against the weather. His sodden clothes felt as leaden as his legs and his stomach was beginning to rumble.

The rain eased just as it had done earlier. The sound of water running through mud and gullies and over stones was all around him. He was tired and hungry, the night was dark and wet, the dusty ground now a quagmire beneath his weary feet.

Coming out of the trees, the clouds parted and for a moment there was starlight. The puny light picked out the scene in front of him, a clearing where a fire had been lit beneath a tarpaulin awning supported on rough poles stuck into the ground.

Wooden gypsy caravans were ranged around the edge of the clearing, their shafts lowered, the tips resting on the ground. In the gaps between, hobbled horses neatly nipped at the abundant grass and drank from buckets filled with rainwater.

There were people – men, women and children – gathered around the glowing embers of a fire over which hung a cast-iron pot. The smell from the pot elicited a low growling in his stomach.

It must have done the same for Polka because she let out a large yelp.

'Shhh. You have to be quiet.'

He wasn't sure yet what he was going to do. He'd heard that gypsies sometimes stole children, forcing them to live with them. In his case, they didn't need to steal him; he would go willingly.

He'd never really spoken to gypsies before. They flitted in and around the river, knocking on doors, trying to sell what they could. His mother reckoned they could tell the future.

'Palm reading. That's what they do.'

He wondered if palm reading was easy to learn. Reading a book was quite hard until you got the hang of it. He presumed palm reading was something like that but with only one page instead of lots of them.

The gypsies scared him. They scared everyone.

Needing to think about what to do next, he hid in the long grass behind a blackthorn bush. The smell of food cooking was very enticing.

As yet, he wasn't quite brave enough to go in and ask for food. He was tired and worried, firstly about his mother but also about his dog. Polka was getting hungry and the remains of the digestive biscuit he had in his pocket was not going to last long.

Running away had seemed so terribly easy, but as Tommy snuggled down as best he could, sheltered and hidden, he began to have misgivings.

For a start, he was wet through. What if there was more rain and the river overflowed its banks. He might well drown and his mum would be very upset if that happened. And what about Polka? The little dog was asleep at present but had only dropped off out of sheer tiredness. A little time and she would be yapping loudly, demanding food and to be let loose from Tommy's arms to play in the grass.

Soon the gypsies would have finished their food and bedded down for the night. With a bit of luck, there might be something left at the bottom of that pot and at some point he had to ask them if he could stay. For now a little sleep and perhaps a biscuit and he would be ready to confront them.

He pulled his coat collar up and snuggled the dog inside. The warmth of her body was comforting. Gradually, his eyes closed and he slept.

He awoke to somebody shouting, 'Oi! Oi! What are you doing 'ere?'

A rough hand was shaking his shoulder. He almost wet himself. The worst thing possible must have happened. It was Frank! Frank had found him, but when he looked up, he saw a face that was far too dark a complexion to be that of Frank Steele.

'What you doin' 'ere, young lad?'

The man had an odd accent and smelled of horse dung, woodsmoke and fresh hay.

Tommy jerked into wakefulness, the dog stirring against his chest, tail wagging and mouth open as though she were laughing. Tommy sought the lie most likely to get him what he wanted.

'I ran away from an orphanage. Nobody wanted me, even them. So I ran away.'

The man seemed to think about it and for a moment Tommy worried that he wouldn't be believed.

The rough hand dragged him to his feet. 'You wouldn't be the first. What's yer name?'

'Tommy.'

'Hungry?'

He nodded.

The sallow-faced gypsy ushered him towards the glowing embers of the fire, where a woman was using a ladle to fill the many bowls being offered up.

'Here, lad.'

A bowl of something hot and steaming was thrust into his hands, as well as a wooden spoon.

Tommy set too with the spoon and Polka yapped with delight in response to being given meat sliced from what looked like a clay bowl with prickles sticking out of it.

The man who had found him seemed oblivious to the pouring rain as he told everyone that his name was Tommy and he'd been in an orphanage.

'At least that's what he tells me.'

'Heard that one before.'

There was laughter but also murmurs of approval.

As the fire began to die down, they gave him a blanket and a red velvet cushion embroidered with silvery stars and told him he could sleep there close to the fire.

He curled himself and Polka into the blanket, his cheeks reddening from the warmth of the dying embers of the fire.

With the coming of darkness, somebody began singing and somebody else began playing a guitar.

The food, the warmth and the music were so comforting that it wasn't long before Tommy's eyes began to close, Polka making small snuffling noises against his chest.

Once he was asleep and without him knowing, Luther, the man who had found Tommy, was asked his plans for the boy.

'You heard him. He ran away from an orphanage. I'll not turn him away.'

'As long as the coppers don't come looking for him. How do we know he's not lying?'

'Do we care? He's only a boy, but he's still got the right to live the life he wants to live. Anyway, by the looks of him, I'm inclined to think he's telling the truth. Half black, ain't he? And we all know how anyone a bit different is treated.'

They all agreed with Luther that he probably had been in an orphanage and none of them condemned him for running away.

'If he wants to stay, he can. Give it a few days. He might get fed up and run back again. Once he knows how we live... all this fresh air and cooking outdoors is too much for some.'

34

At first, she'd thought that Frank was dead. Like him, she'd been unprepared for the blow that floored him from the iron frying pan she'd left on the table.

June stared open-mouthed at Sister Harrison, who promptly asked her, 'I thought he'd gone for good.'

'So did I. He came back.' June eyed the new arrival with curiosity. 'You're out late, Sister Harrison.'

Was that a guilty blush June saw?

'I know it's late. I came as soon as I could. I saw Harry Hunter outside. He came along to say that Tommy's dog has gone missing, and he thought he saw Tommy earlier on his way to the field. I heard raised voices and thought I'd better intervene.'

'You certainly did that,' said June, looking down in astonishment at the supine form spark out on the kitchen floor. 'Is he dead?'

Sister Harrison bent from the waist and peered at her victim a bit more closely.

'He's still breathing. I can see his nostrils moving.'

'Should I call an ambulance?'

Edith did a quick check, delicately lifting his eyelids between finger and thumb, checking his pulse. 'No. I shouldn't bother.' She saw June's fear-filled eyes. 'I know you're considering his behaviour when he comes round.'

June shivered when she nodded. 'I'll be for it. You can bet on that.'

Her right hand brushed against her cheekbone and the faint yellow of a fading bruise.

Sister Harrison put the pan back down on the kitchen table. 'Call the police.'

'They might arrest you.'

Her rescuer frowned. 'I very much doubt that. In fact, they wouldn't dare.' She grinned. 'Sergeant Paling suffers from piles. If he's not careful, the next time he receives treatment from me, it might be more painful than it could be.'

'Fletcher wants that field from Mr Hunter and as long as he's paid, Frank will do whatever he's asked. That's why I think he came back. One more job for Mr Fletcher.'

Sister Harrison raised her eyebrows. 'Was it indeed!'

She thought of Harry, a man of strong build who had fought in the war. He'd survived, not just by luck, she fancied, but because he had an astute mind and a fighting spirit.

She commented further. 'He'll have to get up a bit earlier in the morning to get it off him. I don't think he's any chance whatsoever.'

The two of them regarded Frank thoughtfully. Edith Harrison thought of the men she had known. People looking at her would be surprised to learn that she too had once been involved with men like him. Not now, though. She'd risen above that, but the memories brought bitter bile to her throat. Due as much to luck as judgement, she had risen above that type of man. June had not been so lucky.

'He's coming round.'

Edith considered their position. How much better it might have been if he'd died. It was a terrible thought, but the police would have believed two women accusing Frank of attacking them. Two weak women pleading self-defence. She smiled at the thought.

Frank groaned, moved onto his side, hands flat on the floor, elbows bending.

Fear returned to June's face. 'What do we do now?'

'Leave it to me.'

Retrieving the frying pan from the table, Edith stood over him, a picture of menace with the flying pan held high.

'Time you cleared off, Frank. We never want to see your ugly face around here again.'

Shoulders squared, he was halfway to getting up – and still defiant. 'You can't make me.'

The iron frying pan threw a shadow over his fleshy face.

'I believe I can.' She nudged June to say something. 'Go on. It's your house. Your name on the rent book now. Isn't that right?'

June took a number of deep breaths before finding both her courage and her voice.

'It's either that or we get the police here and say you attacked me,' she blurted, the words rat-a-tatting out like bullets.

Looking a little surprised at first, Frank – on all fours now – sneered. 'Don't make me laugh. The police don't like to get involved with couples.'

'I'm not your wife.'

'All the more so,' he said sneeringly, his head turned sideways as he struggled to half stand, using the back of a chair to get to his feet.

Wearing the look of a woman used to being in charge, Edith Harrison brought her face level with his. 'We're not going to tell them you attacked June. We're going to tell them you attacked me, a much-loved and respected member of the community. I can assure you they'll take a very dim view of you doing that. Many in this town owe their lives to my ministrations. Bear that in mind, Mr Steele, and tread carefully, or you'll find yourself bundled into the back of a Black Maria in double quick time. A stint in the cells might make a man of you. A different man from the one you are at present.'

Frank's jaw dropped. He'd had enough dealings with the authorities to know that she was speaking the truth. Also, like many others, Sister Harrison's commanding presence put the fear of God in him.

He managed one last effort to wriggle out of the situation. 'You'd be lying.'

'Takes one to know one. Now, I know it was you who started the fire.' She smiled somewhat maliciously. 'And so does Mr Hunter. It can't be too long before he pays you a visit to discuss the matter. I also want to know everything about what you were doing along at the field with the police.'

'It was nothing. Nothing much at all. The bloke had Fletcher's missus' dog that was all.'

'Mister Fletcher doesn't strike me as a dog man.'

June frowned. 'It ain't the same dog my Tommy has been going on about, is it?'

'Fletcher wanted Tyler – or Hunter – whatever his bloody name is – arrested for stealing the dog.'

June frowned. 'Why would it suit him to do that?'

Edith smiled knowingly. 'Because Clifford Fletcher is a cunning devil but a bit lazy. He wants that piece of land but with as little difficulty as possible. It he can have Harry move on or flung in jail, leaving the path clear for what he plans to do, then so much the better. Jail or moving on, it would make no difference to him. What Clifford Fletcher fails to realise is that if anything happened to Harry, the field would revert to Devlin, his half-brother. And it wouldn't do to cross swords with the Compton-Dixon family.'

Frank was hardly the brightest star in the sky, but he did take in what had been said. The family was historically powerful. Clifford Fletcher had wheedled modern wealth in the aftermath of the killing spree that had been the Great War.

'Well, Harry certainly won't be going to jail.'

There were times when she was on the ward that she had need to pull rank. That was what she did now, folding her arms, head held high and her gaze sharp enough to cut through Steele. She would have things her way. That was the meaning in that look.

'Well, Mr Steele. Once we let Mr Fletcher know you've told us his plans, he'll never employ you ever again, especially when we inform her ladyship. Did you know she owns the lease of the pub? Clifford Fletcher could be out on his ear if she gets wind of this. So you might as well leave Foxford. For that matter, it might also be wise to leave Norton Dene.'

Frank winced as he rubbed the area of his head where the frying pan had landed. 'I can't leave yur. I got a living to make.'

'No longer, I fear. I think it would be for the best if you leave, or did he pay you that well, more than you were paid on the docks?'

Frank chewed his lip as he thought about it, jaw moving side to side as though chewing thoroughly before swallowing. 'No. The swine didn't pay me for finding the dog. He said 'e would but 'e didn't. Just a pound – a snotty one-pound note. I'm worth more than that. I've been loyal to that geezer; done everything he wanted.' His voice rose. Ire had replaced any loyalty he might have felt. Not much of it, in Edith's estimation.

Edith took pleasure in saying what she said next, which she knew would make up Frank's mind to leave. 'Mr Hunter's dog was injured that night when you set the kennels on fire. There was also another dog there about to give birth. Her puppies never got born. They were all burnt to death. Now think carefully, Mr Steele. How do you think Mr Hunter is feeling? How likely is he to seek revenge once he knows you're hanging around?'

Frank's jaw had stopped the masticating action. His jowls hung loose upon his jaw. He couldn't care less about the dogs, only about his own skin – and earning money. 'They're only dogs. Animals.'

June, empowered with a new courage she hadn't known she had, prodded him with the rolling pin. 'You wouldn't have cared tuppence if you had known they'd all died. Would you, Frank?'

Edith leaned in too, pleased to heap praise on the man she was falling in love with. 'Harry Hunter has a passion for animals. It makes him angry if they're treated cruelly. I think it's time you made your way back to Bristol. You can easily lose yourself there.'

Sweat staining his shirt, Frank thought about what might be coming his way. Fleeing the scene was preferable to facing Harry Hunter.

One hand rubbing his head, the other reached for his coat. He'd barely fetched it from the back of a chair when June flung him his canvas knapsack.

Mind made up, he nodded at the two women who stood with arms folded, heads held high. 'I'll be off then. No regrets.'

'No regrets? That's a laugh. My only regret is that I met you,' said June.

She held the same stance as the woman beside her. Stalwart. Defiant and unassailable.

They saw him stagger a little as he headed down the front garden path to the gate.

Halfway down the path, June shouted out to him. 'Hey! Frank. You've forgotten something.'

He turned round, then was hit backwards as a brown river trout clouted him in the face.

'Take your fish with you. And don't come back.'

Edith nudged June as they watched until the chugging of the motorcycle diffused into the rain-soaked night.

'Good riddance to bad rubbish.' It was expressed with great sincerity.

Edith thought of the night she'd sat with Harry on the cabin roof and stared at the stars, listened to the sound of water as some unseen creature slid from the bank.

Another night, please. Another sky full of stars.

Patience, she told herself. *You must have patience.*

Friendships over the years had come and gone and she had no close confidante to hand. No sister. No female friend to give advice. She was in dire need of someone she could confide in. The hospital was where she had the most discourse with other women and human beings in general. There was only one whose opinion she would value.

Tomorrow, she thought. *Tomorrow I'll take biscuits and tea into Doctor Brakespeare, and for once we will touch on personal matters.*

35

June tapped the cheap wooden clock Tommy's father had won on a darts stall at a fairground they'd gone to many years ago.

In response, the minute hand shivered slightly and moved onto the next number. It was gone nine o'clock and still there was no sign of Tommy.

'I'll murder you when you get home, you little sod.'

She took another look at the covered plate she'd placed on top of a saucepan full of hot water to keep it warm.

Darning and ironing awaited her attention, she didn't feel inclined to do it. It was almost as though she was rebelling against the household chores that defined a woman of the twentieth century. Although women had got the vote, she couldn't see that their lives had changed that much.

One thing she did accept was that she had stood up to Frank Steele and, with Sister Harrison's help, had banished him from her life.

Frowning, she took another glance at the clock. The minute hand still wobbled uncertainly between the numbers on the dial.

Just to be sure, she looked behind the chair in the kitchen to see if Tommy's satchel was there.

It wasn't.

She decided that he must be out somewhere along the canal.

With that dog, she thought, the one Sister Harrison had told her about.

The story had amused her and only added to the happiness that had come her way now Frank had left.

On opening the door, the rain battered in, soaking her dress and speckling the flagstone floor with raindrops.

Where was he? She feared for him being out in this downpour.

Muttering threats under her breath that she had no intention of carrying out, she pulled on a cardigan and headed out.

What was left of the hollyhocks, some of them over seven feet tall, were bending in the wind, ragged blooms of apricot and red flying away like embers in smoke.

No birds swam on the rippling waters of the canal and the reed beds rustled like sheaves of rusted metal. She turned to face the wind, instantly narrowing her eyes against the grit and sand it was blowing before it.

'Tommy? Tomm... eeee!'

Her voice wasn't entirely lost on the wind. A moorhen heard and made a dash for the water, the wind-driven rivulets skimming the surface behind her.

She leaned on the wall at the front gate, looking up and down the path. For one frightening moment, she wondered about the canal; could he have fallen in?

As she turned her back to the wind and leaned out of the gate, she chanced to look down to where ragged tufts of grass grew at the base of the wall.

Tommy's satchel. Alongside it were half a dozen rabbit lures. This could only mean that her boy had gone rabbiting immediately following school. And returned in time to hear Frank and her arguing.

'Tommy!'

Her heart lurched in her chest.

Panic-stricken she went over what had been said, then, with a jolt, she realised that it wasn't what was or wasn't said, the very fact that Frank was in the house was all it needed for her son to misunderstand. Oh God, was it possible that he'd assumed Frank was moving back in? It was more than likely.

So if he had misunderstood and run off in a panic, where had he gone?

She looked wildly around her, unsure of where to look for him, which way to go.

Rain beat into her face, soaking her hair and her clothes as she ran along the riverbank telling herself not to worry, that she was panicking unnecessarily. Perhaps Harry had seen him getting soaked to the skin and had insisted on giving him shelter, telling him to wait until the rain eased off, though judging by its ferocity it wasn't likely to be any time soon.

And what if he was hurt? He might need a doctor.

Harry's boat was tossing up and down on the turbulent water, like a bucking horse, unwilling to be ridden. There was no chance of reaching and hammering on the side of the boat. She shouted, but her voice was lost on the wind.

With the toes of her shoe, she dislocated a stone from the soggy ground, aimed it at the boat and threw it. Despite the storm, nobody could have failed to hear it drop heavily onto the cabin roof.

A shaft of muted light fell out from the boat's interior.

'Mrs Newman?' Voice raised with surprise, Harry took in her appearance, soaked to the skin, water dripping from her hair, her nose and her chin.

'Tommy. Have you seen Tommy?' Her voice was barely audible, whipped away as it was by the wind.

Harry climbed out into the cockpit where the tiller was rattling in its mountings.

'Not since yesterday. The dog was in its pen. If Tommy did wander down here, I didn't see him.'

She threw her hands over her face. 'I'm beside myself. This weather isn't good for him.'

He looked at her, then around him at the stormy scene.

Buffeted by the wind, the single glow from the narrow windows moved from side to side, towards the bank, then away again.

'Don't try to come aboard,' he shouted. 'It's too dangerous.'

He leapt off the moving vessel, carefully choosing that moment when it was closest to the bank.

His coat billowed behind him like a sail. His hair writhed around his head like Medusa's snakes.

He dared say what June was thinking herself.

'Is it possible the wind would snatch his breath?'

What he was in fact asking was if the poor boy was likely to collapse.

Every fibre of her being shivered with the pressure of having to respond that such a dreadful thing was possible.

He voiced what was on her mind. 'Best to contact the hospital.' He took hold of her arm. 'We'll phone first. Do you know how to use the telephone?'

Using a telephone was alien to her and she said so. 'But I'll do anything I have to do.'

Getting as far as the Jolly Boatman took effort. Harry had it in mind to use the phone at the bottom of the hill. Or ask Clifford Fletcher to use the one in the pub. Surely, he wouldn't refuse the pleas of a worried mother?

Twigs and small branches were being wrenched from trees. Climbing up the lane to the main road would not be easy. That's if they could get through to the hospital in the first place.

He could see the lane from where they were, a black everlasting hole spanning upwards through the trees. Completely black, though suddenly a flash of headlights appeared, disappeared, and appeared again.

Just as they got to the phone box, a car emerged from the tunnel of trees.

Stepping out in front of it, he waved his arms for all the world like a human windmill, leaving it with no option but to come to a stop.

They explained that Tommy was missing, had a bad chest and might have collapsed. They needed to phone the hospital.

'You'll be lucky. All the lines are down.'

'Can you take us there? It is an emergency.'

* * *

Sister Harrison poked her head out of the front door of the hospital in the hope that the unseasonable downpour had at last abated. Borne on a storm wind, rain whipped into her face. It was very late but she feared if she didn't leave now she'd be on night duty. In her estimation she had done enough already.

Her cloak would be a must. An umbrella was debateable. It might keep the rain off, but it might also blow inside out and collect what she'd prefer to keep off.

The two lamps perched on the pillars to either side of the gate were intermittently visible, a little light. She had it in mind to have Walter get the pony and trap out. She'd still get a soaking in the open trap, but at least she might get home quicker.

A small square of amber light showed in the nightwatchman's window away to her right. Like the lights at the gate, the glow was intermittent thanks to the branches of trees wildly dancing around in front of it.

If she was going to venture to his front door, she would need her cloak – unless it came to him that she needed him. But then who in their right mind would want to journey to the other side of town on a night like this?

Cloak first.

She was in the process of going to the staffroom to collect it, when a pair of car headlamps lit up the front gate.

At first, it seemed as though the vehicle was passing by, the headlights searching along the lane that ran away from the main road and along to the quarry.

The lights swerved, glancing off the wet road, like fallen eyes seeking their way to the entrance.

Shielding her eyes with one hand against the rain and unaccustomed brightness, she glimpsed a sign on its roof. A police car.

Rear car doors opened and two people came rushing towards her. Another figure alighted from the driver side, pulling the peak of his hat lower over his face. Another policeman got out from the passenger side.

She recognised June. Recognised Harry. What were they doing here together at this time of night?

June almost fell over her feet, so desperate was she to ask for their help. 'It's Tommy. He's missing. I'm afraid for him, what with his bad chest.'

Their estimation seemed a bit mangled, but in this weather, Tommy was best indoors not gallivanting around with a blasted dog.

The policeman who had got out of the car shouted that he would help them look for him.

'I'll get my cloak.'

Rain dripped from the peak of the police sergeant's helmet and ran down his face.

The two women got into the back seats. Harry turned away.

'I'll search on foot,' he called over his shoulder when Edith suggested he join them.

She noticed his voice carried despite the strength of the wind.

Edith regretted his decision. It would have been nice to feel him tightly packed against her.

'You'll get soaked through.'

Her exclamation fell on death ears. He'd already turned away, melting into the darkness.

The police officer suggested they do a slow drive around town.

June shook her head. 'He never goes into town. He wanders and takes his dog with him.'

'Would he have gone off with strangers?'

Edith wound an arm around June's shoulders, felt her wetness and her shivering. She guessed that the shivering was not necessarily because she was sodden. Having a child go off with strangers was always a mother's worst nightmare.

'I don't know.'

Her teeth chattered.

Edith pulled her closer. 'Don't worry. It's a question that has to be asked.'

June's teeth stopped chattering as she thought about it.

The policeman encouraged her. 'Any strangers at all.'

'Strangers? A gypsy woman came selling pegs. I bought some. She told me my fortune as well.'

'Was anyone with her?'

'I think there was a young man with a horse down on the towpath waiting for her.'

Just as June had predicted, there was no sign of Tommy along the road into Norton Dene, nor in the town centre.

'You think he'd have wandered through the woods? Along the canal?'

June mumbled a soft cry of 'Yes.'

The wind whipped leaves and twigs across the road in front of them and the windscreen wipers hissed at top speed across the windscreen.

There was a minor lane down to the towpath. The police car bounced up and down over its uneven surface.

June checked to see if Tommy had found his way home. She dived in quickly and just as quickly out again.

'No,' she shouted, shaking her head fervently.

The lights of Fisherman's Row were left behind as they headed up the lane to the main road, beam of headlights piercing the total blackness.

It was a relief to get back to the main road, where the streetlights helped relieve the darkness. The bad weather had kept everyone indoors – except for one.

His tall figure was unmistakeable. Beside him was Talbot, his dog.

The police car pulled up beside him. 'Nothing?'

'Nothing.'

'Thank God for these gaslights.'

There weren't that many, but the policeman was right. Unfortunately, his relief was short-lived.

'First the phone lines, and now the power lines are down. Don't rate this new-fangled electricity meself. Most of the lines are trailed across the trees around here. Formula for disaster.'

With only headlights, the car made slow progress, so much so that they stayed level with Harry, who, despite the weather, took big, confident strides as he leaned into the wind and rain.

'Will you be able to see the turning?'

Sister Harrison was not a driver, but having been a passenger with people who were, she had some idea how it was done. Perhaps it was a skill she would take up in time.

'Here!'

Driven too fast, the car overshot the turning.

The steering wheel locked, the car skidded.

'Drive into the skid,' shouted the police constable sitting in the front passenger seat.

His colleague did just that, but no matter how hard he tried, he failed to keep it on an even keel.

It took both men manhandling the steering wheel to being the car to a halt.

Relieved, Edith threw back her head and closed her eyes.

The front door was tugged open from outside. When her eyes opened, there was Harry. Relief flooded over her.

Addressing the two uniformed men, he ordered them to relax their grip. 'Take deep breaths. And loosen your grip on the wheel or your knuckles will be bursting through your skin.'

They got out and although they suggested Sister Harrison and June stayed put, they were having none of it.

June was frantic. 'I need to find my boy.'

Edith lay a reassuring hand on her shoulder. 'They'll find him.'

We must find him, she thought. *No child should be wandering around in this weather, more so one who suffered from a bad chest.*

One of the policemen brought out a flashlight from the boot of the car.

Harry took it from him as he might a rattle from a baby and headed for the lane.

The policeman tried to snatch it back. 'Where are you going?'

'Down that lane there. It leads to the river. The river runs alongside the canal.'

'I can drive down.' He repeated the attempt to snatch the light.

'No you can't.' Harry clutched it with a grip of iron and aimed it at the murky place where the lane began. 'Look at the state of it.'

He was right. Mud had slid from the banks at the side of the lane and now lay two or three feet high in the middle. Access was further curtailed by a number of spindly fallen trees which lay across the mud.

'We need to keep together, at least until we get to the bottom of the hill. Only then do we fan out.'

Harry's commanding orders were unchallenged.

June shouted. 'Tommy! Tommy! Are you there?'

The shout was lost in the wind and rain.

Nobody protested when Harry took charge, bidding them be careful as they made their way downhill. Just as in the Great War, his command was obeyed.

* * *

In the spot close to the swelling river, Tommy woke up to mayhem. Horses were screaming and people were shouting and running around all over the place. He heard cracking sounds and the rushing of water, the pelting of rain against sodden leaves.

'Get up, boy. Get out of here.'

He felt very much colder and as he got to his feet could see that the fire that had burned so brightly was no more. He shivered. If he'd been wet before, he was far wetter now. The cold penetrated his wet clothes, clamping around his chest, causing him to cough.

In his mind, he saw his mother's gentle face and heard her say that cold and damp were no good for him.

At this point, the river and canal ran alongside each other. Taking advantage of the river's natural flow, the canal had been dug out of the earth in the eighteenth century.

It was the river that had overflowed its banks. The rain was teeming down and the wind was tearing twigs and even branches from the trees. Water was swirling all around him and people were running everywhere.

Polka was up to her belly in water and although his arms still ached from the night before, he had no choice but to pick her up.

The men were shouting, waving their arms, tugging at the shafts of their horse-drawn homes.

'All the kids get to high ground. The rest of you help get these horses hitched up. We have to save the vans.'

The vans referred to were the brightly coloured caravans, travelling homes pulled by gallant piebald and skewbald horses.

Water and people swirled all around him and nobody was paying him much attention.

Polka lay heavy in his arms. He knew he had to save her and himself. His first thought was to retrace the route of the previous evening back along the river, crossing onto the towpath and following the canal home.

'Not that way,' a man shouted when he attempted to do that. 'It's flooded. Go up. Up.'

It was so dark, he couldn't work out which way was up until he thought about the way he'd come, which was on his right when facing the river, so behind him had to be the right way to go.

The route away from the river was slippery and he couldn't see where he was going. Only by the pace of his feet and the angle of his knees did he know for sure that he was going upwards, away from the river.

Brambles and other spiky-leaved bushes scratched his bare legs where his socks had crumpled into his shoes. The ground became steeper and uneven, small rivulets of water dislodging stones and carving out gullies that he could not see.

He stopped and turned in an effort to see what was going on behind him. It was difficult to make out what was happening. There was movement and noise from horses and people scrambling to get to higher ground.

'To the road,' somebody shouted.

He didn't know where the road was, and judging by what he could see, the lane would shortly be crowded with people, horses and their precious caravans.

It seemed they had forgotten him, left him to his own devices.

For a moment, he stood petrified, unsure where to go or what to do. Craving their company in this dangerous situation, his instinct was to join them on the narrow lane that wound upwards away from the swirling water.

Staggering sideways against the rivulets going downhill, he groped his way with one hand, his other clinging desperately to Polka, who was whimpering beneath his arm.

He felt a draught of air and the smell of manure as a panicked horse kicked out, the feathery fronds of its leg tickling his face, its hoof making a whooshing sound and just missing his head.

The lane was narrow and horses and vans were packed tight across its width.

Tommy staggered backwards and, as he did so, Polka slipped from his arms.

She headed for a thicket deeper into the trees.

Tommy, frantic now, followed her.

Legs scratched from the whipping fronds of shrubs, he carried on until he found her cowering beneath a bush.

Frightened he might lose her, he grabbed a chunk of her fur, took off the belt from his trousers and placed it around her neck.

Polka barked and tugged against the restraint, pulling him away from the lane and through the bushes.

Twigs slashed at his face as Polka pulled him onwards through the slushy mud and myriad streams rushing downhill to join the river.

'Polka. Polka...'

He wanted to be the one in charge, but his strength was all but gone. The dog was having it her way, meandering beneath bushes that he had no option but to barge through.

Too fatigued to resist, he gave in to her fervent tugs and staggered after her, his legs aching, his body hot now despite his soaking-wet clothes.

His knees wobbled and still holding onto the end of the belt he fell forward onto stony ground.

As he struggled to his feet, his hands felt more stones and when he began to move forward, there were even more underfoot. He didn't know for sure, but it seemed he'd located a stony patch through the foliage. He also noticed that the ground was not so steep, merely a slope, whereas up until now it had been a steep climb.

Indistinctly, he could hear the gypsies some way behind him, making their way up the hill. He considered joining them, then thought about his mother. It hadn't occurred to him before that she might be worried.

The decision was made. He was going home – if his legs could make it. If he could find his way.

Suddenly overcome by weariness, he sank to his knees in a mossy area underneath a fir tree. Polka's body warm against him, his eyes fluttered, then closed.

* * *

Mud squelched with each footstep, the ground slippery and soft.

The flashlight was growing dim, so once he'd shone it ahead and assessed the way he was going, he turned it off to prolong its battery life. Harry shouted at the others to stay close, close enough to hear their efforts, their feet squelching into the mud. Close enough to smell their dampness and their sweat.

Before leaving the boat, he'd seen that both the water in the canal and in the river was rising. The canals had been designed so that excess depth was syphoned off into the river. The narrowboats only needed about four feet of water.

He hoped that the excess would tumble safely away over the weir. That's what it was there for, so the river level would be maintained and the village would not be flooded.

Following his nose in the darkness, he felt the ground beneath his feet becoming steeper.

Every so often, June shouted her son's name.

He sensed that Edith was the closest behind him and it made him smile. She was a tough one all right. In charge of everything she did, he thought, including the patients she cared for. By hook or by crook, they'd get better if she had anything to do with it.

He'd met the gypsies on their way hereabouts. Not being in the market for pegs or paper flowers, he had bought some herbs from them. Like him, they lived in tune with nature, kept themselves to themselves.

He knew where their campsite was situated. He also knew they wouldn't wander too far from it but would wait on high ground until the river had receded and wait for the ground to dry before returning to their regular pitch.

It was a long way down to their encampment and it would be a long climb back up.

Judging he was roughly a quarter of the way down the lane, he turned the flashlight back on.

'Oh. There you are,' gasped an exhausted voice from behind him. The senior police officer appeared from behind Edith. 'Wicked night.'

Harry grunted a response. Yes, the weather was wicked. So was the mud, but he had endured worse. Nothing could be as bad as France. Nothing as bad as Flanders. Nothing as bad as...

'Edith. Are you all right?'

She shouted back that she was.

The light picked out a wall on his left side and woodland on the other. He recognised elm, lime and beech trees, the needled branches of a Scotch pine and junipers. Bushes heaved to one side in the strong wind and the sound of water dripping from leaves tinkled like bells.

Seeing nothing of note, he turned off the light.

For a split second, he thought he heard something else besides raindrops.

He turned on the light again and flashed it over the Scotch pine, a great big tree with widely spreading branches.

The wind stirred everything with noise, but his ears were keen. Yet again he thought he heard something.

He stepped away from his companions, aware that Edith was not far behind him. Not even wearing boots, he thought. How do women walk through rough terrain in the ridiculous shoes they wore? Truth be told, he admired her. She reminded him of some of the stalwart nurses who'd manned the field hospitals behind enemy lines. Supposedly safe. A red cross emblazoned on the roof. For the most part, they had been safe, though not always. He'd seen it attacked from the air. Nurses, doctors and injured men had been killed and that in a war behind them. What about the future? Progress might make those who attacked from above more deadly than they were now.

There was no doubt in his mind that he was attracted to Edith, though up until now had not been able to understand why. This mud, this darkness, this foul weather went some way to clearing his mind.

The trenches had been foul, putrid with stinking mud and rotting corpses.

By contrast, Edith was clean, soft, pristine – the opposite to the filth he'd endured.

The realisation shone like the beam of a lighthouse in his mind. He'd long been on the rocks. Bit by bit, he was treading a different path, one taking him further from the past. One that was healing his soul.

He shook it all away. *Stick to the job in hand.*

'Is anyone there? Tommy?' His voice thundered out into the trees.

There was no reply. That old instinct of working out where you were and what might be ahead of you, kicked in. He'd learned a lot in the army, not just about killing. It was instinct that helped you stay alive.

He raised his arm bringing everyone to a halt.

'Silence. Stay still.'

His companions did as ordered.

During a lull in the wind, he heard a sound, a low keening like an animal crying.

Taking greater strides, careful not to crash to the ground, he clambered over the remains of a stone wall.

Even when the light flashed over him, the sleeping boy did not stir, but the dog whined and yapped in equal measure.

Back in professional mode, Sister Edith Harrison pushed him aside. The boy moaned as she tested his pulse, felt his face for fever or, indeed, the chill of death.

'He's alive, but we need to get him to the hospital as quickly as possible.'

Harry bundled both boy and dog into his strong arms.

It was a long climb back up to the main road and the awaiting police car.

There was only room in the car for the police officers at the front, Sister Harrison, June and her son at the back.

The dog was left with Harry, who tucked it inside his coat, where it snuggled against his hard chest.

'You're coming home with me,' he said to it.

* * *

Two hours later and they'd made it.

The storm was abating, but now and again returned, a reminder that storms tend to circle overhead and come back for another bite.

After the dog was fed and watered, Harry considered his options. His plans were somewhat in disarray. Where was that revenge he'd harboured all these years? Where was that deep need to make the Compton-Dixon family suffer for all that he'd suffered, for taking on the identity of a man who had died rather than be himself? It was complicated, but he'd found something he hadn't expected to find. He'd found somewhere he belonged and perhaps someone he wanted to be with.

36

It wasn't often that Frances Brakespeare was lost for words. Sister Harrison had telephoned her from the hospital and given a brief résumé of the emergency.

Mabel, the car, always seemed to know when it was an emergency. Despite it being close to midnight, she had started first time, though the noisy engine had awoken Gregory. He'd come storming out in his dressing gown. Having received a brief explanation, he told her to wait and that he wouldn't be long.

He'd returned fully dressed in clothes that didn't match but had been close at hand. The balaclava he wore made him look like a medieval monk.

On the way to the hospital, Doctor Frances Brakespeare had explained as much as she knew – which wasn't much.

'Sister Harrison was there – and Harry Hunter.'

'Ah, yes.'

'You don't sound surprised.'

'Even if I was, I know I won't be for long. You, my darling, are bound to fill me in on the details.'

Love and amusement embellished the words. Frances couldn't help but be affected.

There was a moment's silence before she admitted that Sister Harrison had confided in her.

'She's been out with him a couple of times. I also suspect that there is more than one reason she usurped the district nurse's round, though only when it included Fisherman's Row. Harry's boat is down there too.'

'Sister Edith Harrison is in love? I don't believe it!'

'Like a lot of other people, you're fooled by her crisp shell. Don't be. There's a furnace burning beneath that stiff exterior.'

'Perhaps they're a pair well met,' he said softly, not without amusement.

Gregory stayed behind in her office, promising to put the kettle on the gas ring whilst Frances went with a very bedraggled Sister Harrison to check on the boy.

Tommy was sound asleep, though not before fretting about his dog.

'He was fine once I told him that the dog was with Harry.'

Frances smiled. 'It seems our Mr Hunter is trusted by many people.'

Her pointed look brought a pink flush to Sister Harrison's face.

'I hear he calls you Edith. I don't recall you allowing anyone to call you Edith.' *Even me*, she wanted to add but held back.

Pretending she hadn't heard, Sister Harrison stuck to the job in hand.

'The boy is recovering well. His mother, Mrs Newman, is a little worried about payment, though I had already told her there was no need to worry about that. She and Tommy are on our parish panel list.'

'All's well that ends well. And Gregory has put the kettle on. Would you like one?'

A great tiredness seemed to take hold of her senior nurse. Hair usually perfectly coiffured stuck flat and lifeless to her head. Her clothes were mud-spattered and creased.

'I would prefer to go home, get some sleep and change.'

'Then I will drive you there. We'll drop Gregory back on the way.' *Though he's more likely to come on the whole journey*, she thought.

Gregory did indeed accompany them on the whole journey.

'Shame we had to leave the tea. We could have had a nice chat to wrap things up.'

Frances's eyes slid sidelong. It was too dark to see his face, but she had caught something in his voice that made her think he was up to something. Gregory could be like a mischievous schoolboy at times, making leading comments that would eventually get him the answers he wanted.

'I dare say we'll get round to that. For now, I think Sister Harrison needs her bed. Isn't that right, Sister?'

Gregory concurred. 'Of course.' A short silence and then, 'How about the three of us have dinner together at the vicarage? Perhaps Harry too? Might as well lay something on for the big hero, and he was a hero, wasn't he?'

There was no way Gregory could perceive that Sister Harrison's spirits had been energised with his suggestion. But Frances guessed it and added her own reason for them meeting up.

'To celebrate a satisfactory conclusion. I think it's a grand idea. Do you think so, Sister Harrison?'

The moment appeared to be the right one.

* * *

The man who had passed himself off as Ben Tyler and now was most definitely Harry Hunter gazed at his reflection in the jagged scrap of mirror, the only one on the boat.

The wreath of hair hid most of his features except for his nose and his eyes. When was the last time he had seen his shaven face? There had been a time when shaving was compulsory, a necessary adjunct to the wearing of a uniform.

The mirror misted up thanks to the steam coming from the kettle he'd placed on the range. He placed it onto a cast-iron trivet. It needed to cool a bit before he added some to the lump of shaving soap he'd bought at the store in town. Shaving brush and razor too.

Taking up the scissors he used to trim animal hair and cut lengths of wound dressings, he prepared to cut into hair that hadn't been trimmed for years.

The first cut would be the hardest to do. His hand trembled at the thought of it.

Dinner at the vicarage. Who would have thought it? There was no going back. The die was cast. The time had come to work out where he truly belonged.

37

The moment Gregory opened the door, he found himself staring into a face he'd seen on a painting and in photographs up at Orchard Manor.

As they shook hands, he looked him straight in the eye. 'Harry Hunter. My eyes are open. It was hard to see the resemblance under all that hair growth.'

Harry frowned. 'Resemblance?' He wanted Gregory to say that he looked like his father, but then, he would never have known him.

'You look like your brother.'

'My half-brother.'

Gregory kissed Edith on her powdered cheek. 'Is this really Sister Harrison? I would never have known,' he commented, one corner of his mouth upturned in a cheeky grin.

'I'm not on duty this evening,' the well-respected nursing sister returned. 'And tonight, I am Edith.'

He recognised the emotion behind the look that passed between the couple. They were like pigeons that had come home to roost; comfortable with each other, just like him and Frances.

Frances got to her feet when they entered, greeted Edith and then turned to Harry, the collar of a white shirt contrasting with the dark jacket he wore.

He looked straight at her when he said, 'I apologise for my subterfuge. I was not myself.'

Frances smiled and took his hand. 'I'm a doctor, Mr Hunter, and served in the field hospitals. I saw things that have stayed with me to this day.'

Gregory, peacemaker that he was, filled their glasses with measures of sherry.

After they'd all taken a sip, Gregory asked if anyone minded him saying a prayer. 'I'm not usually one for saying grace over dinner, but this is, I think, a special occasion.' He grinned suddenly. 'I promise I won't let it grow into a sermon.'

A titter of laughter ensued before heads bowed.

'Lord, it's been two decades since the most horrific war in history began. Give understanding to those who still carry the burden of those years, inside as well as out. And, Lord, can I please implore you not to let it happen again. Amen.'

The evening light seemed to turn golden as the amen sounded.

There was general conversation over dinner, the tale of Tommy running away with the gypsies, which sounded quite romantic, though it had been far from that.

Harry asked Frances what made her decide to become a doctor.

'I thought that might have been obvious,' she replied softly. 'My fiancé. I came back. He did not.'

'And you never thought you'd love anyone else?'

Frances smiled and exchanged a glance with Gregory.

Without pursuing Frances's approval, Gregory said, 'We have come to a decision.'

'Has a date been set?' asked Edith.

'We're waiting for a period of time when we're not weighed down with commitments.'

This was a doctor and the vicar before her, but all the same, she cocked an admonishing eyebrow. 'Your professional commitments are immaterial. You're the lucky ones and as such should be concentrating on committing to each other.'

'You have a point,' said Gregory, heaving a sigh. 'Duty done, it's time for devotion.'

'We've all served our country. Now it's our time. The war is what started me on my career.'

Edith found that she firmly believed it. Rarely did she allow those images of injured men to regain a section of her mind and her feelings.

'All that filth and mud those poor men were lying in before they came to the King Edward the Seventh. I wanted to make a difference. To have things for patients as they should be. Cleanliness is next to godliness. That was what my mother used to say. I disagreed with her on a lot of things, but not that. Cleanliness is healthy.'

When Frances looked at Gregory, he was sitting with his hands clasped between his knees, staring downwards, thumb of one hand stroking the other.

Suddenly aware that she was staring at him, he chugged back the last of his drink, got up and poured himself another.

Harry declined. His eyes were unblinking and fixed on Edith.

Frances was thinking of Ralph. What would their lives have been like if he had survived? Would she have become a doctor? Or a housewife and mother, no different than thousands of others. There was no way of telling.

'Did you lose someone close?' Frances asked. 'Someone who never came home?'

There was a look on Edith's face that could only be described as irritation. 'No. I did not. You may have noticed, Doctor, that I've never been very lucky in love. I would like to be.' She shrugged. 'But there you are.'

'People don't realise that those left behind feel guilt because they came home. That's what I felt about Ben dying and me still being alive. Taking on his name was my way of keeping him alive. It also made me want revenge against a birthright that put me outside the Compton-Dixon family. I know it sounds odd, but having Ben's ashes buried in the family tomb was my revenge for my mother's death and the assuaging of my guilt that I was still alive and he was dead. Hard to believe, don't you think?'

Gregory shook his head. 'No. I don't think so.'

Frances's thoughts immediately returned to her own background. Her mother too had been made pregnant by the master of the house. After giving birth, Frances had been left in the workhouse, her mother forced to leave the country and live on the other side of the world.

Returning to the here and now, she listened to what Harry was saying with great sympathy.

'I have thought about moving on and taking my troubles with me.'

Edith's voice rose in protest. 'No!' Her alarm was obvious. He couldn't go. She didn't want him to go.

Harry pondered what he was letting himself in for, but the urge was too strong. His smile was for her. 'There's too much keeping me here.'

Hidden beneath the dining table, Frances reached for and clutched Gregory's hand.

He looked at Harry. 'I hope that we can all remain friends. Can we drink to that?'

Of course they could.

* * *

Back on the boat, the man who had insisted on being called Ben Tyler for a time lay awake thinking about Sister Harrison – Edith as he preferred to call her.

There was an intrinsic connection between him and Edith that was as tenuous as silk, as strong as iron. It was there just beneath the surface, no more than a whisper on the wind.

For the first time in years, he truly felt some break between the past and the present, like a piece of ice cracking on a pond in February and floating away. Tomorrow, he promised himself he would finally put the unquiet spirits to rest.

* * *

It was Sunday. Ma Skittings had removed a bunch of dead flowers from the wrought-iron floor-standing holder. She was throwing them on the compost heap when she saw Harry Hunter ducking beneath the lychgate. He was a tall man. A handsome man. Just as his father had been. That strong jaw, the high cheekbones, the deep-set blue eyes. The likeness continued with his broad shoulders. Strong from head to toe and without the overlong hair it was easier to see the likeness in the clean lines of his shaven face.

He did not enter the church but stood sentry-like at the entrance, unblinking eyes fixed on the road outside. He moved aside to let the early arrivals file into the church. Bracing his legs, he went back to his original position.

Brushing the residue of the flowers from her hands, she made her way to where he stood, like a colossus guarding a treasure.

She'd left the fresh flowers in a bucket to one side of the church door, a summer mixture of blue, pink, mauve and white. No yellow. Yellow was the colour of spring. Spring had passed. Early summer had arrived.

He didn't seem to notice her when she bent down to pick up the bouquet. The flowers were meant to join those already decorating the nave and the empty area beside the pulpit, adding both colour and perfume.

One more bouquet. Straightening, she eyed the fresh blooms, thought how beautiful they were and how they gladdened the heart.

And conveyed a message.

She addressed Harry. 'We've too many flowers. Would you like these?'

He looked at her as though only just realising she was there.

'You might want to put them on your mother's grave.'

She saw the confusion on his face.

'Were you never told that she was buried here?'

He shook his head, a look of alarm on his face.

'They said he set fire to the house after he'd killed her. I'd left home by then, so… I didn't know…'His voice flittered with words. 'If I'd known…'

Ma Skittings jerked her head. 'Come with me.'

He'd been waiting to see Lady Araminta Compton-Dixon, but the thought of gazing on his mother's grave was too compelling to ignore. He followed her.

They stopped in front of a single grave, its headstone soft grey and still shiny. There was a marble urn in front of her name, and it was bursting with flowers.

Such was the shock, that his breath was knocked out of him.

When he finally found his voice, he thanked her.

'For showing it to you?' She shrugged.

'For the flowers. For looking after her grave.'

Hers was a contemplative look that eyed him from beneath the brim of her best Sunday hat. She shook her head. 'I didn't. It's her ladyship's orders. She blames her husband for your mother's death. Every week since her passing, she's ordered that flowers be placed on her grave. Her homage, recompense for the mistake her husband made in marrying her to a man she should never have been married to.'

He was still staring at the headstone and the flowers after Ma Skittings had moved away.

The sound of a car jerked him away from his contemplations. Her ladyship had arrived.

He went back there, meaning to say a lot but saying nothing.

When her ladyship noticed him, her hand went to the throat. He sensed a deep gasp. Her eyes were round with surprise. Her son and daughter-in-law were ranged behind her. They said something, but she did not acknowledge them. Instead, she stared, not hearing anyone asking her what was wrong.

He didn't know if he was doing right but decided it was something he had to do; stand in front of her, have her gaze on his unshaven face.

Her hand dropped from her mouth and a look of understanding came to her eyes.

'Yes,' she said softly. 'You look like him.'

* * *

He'd stayed for the service, standing next to her ladyship and his half-brother in the family pew.

'All is well,' Gregory whispered to Frances once the service was over.

'So I see,' Frances remarked.

Sister Edith Harrison had joined the crocodile of worshippers as they filed into the nave and out into the daylight.

Harry and the family had exited their pew first. He turned as they filed up the aisle and saw Edith, waited for her to catch up, put his arm around her and followed the others.

Sunday lunch at Orchard Manor, an invitation to stay overnight. A bed would be available.

Edith had voiced the fact that she was on duty the following day so would need an early night.

They were dropped off at their separate destinations in her ladyship's chauffeur-driven car.

'They're getting married,' Edith said suddenly. 'The vicar and Doctor Brakespeare. They're getting married.'

The hint was there. He heard it in her voice.

Not yet, he thought. It would not be proper to propose just yet, but he could see their future together.

'They deserve each other. Just as we do.'

It was as far as he would go – for now. There were a few loose ends to tie up, and then...

* * *

The towpath in Lower Foxford was clear of rubbish and the green water pouring over the weir did so like a tinkling fountain and not the rushing torrent it had been during the storm.

Dusk was creeping across the land like a grey veil. Trees soughed in the breeze, droplets of dew tinkling like rain.

Some way in a meadow or thicket, a vixen called to her mate.

Standing next to the tiller in the one-man cockpit, Harry prised open the biscuit tin. It was not an easy task, the thin metal flexing as he tried to prise it open. Damp and time had rusted the two surfaces with gritty determination.

Resorting to the cockpit toolbox, he pulled out a screwdriver. The sharp tip made easy meat of the problem. Lid and tin separated to expose all that remained of a man who had once lived and breathed.

For a moment he stared at it. The tin had become part of him, an essential part of the life he'd led, the war he'd fought. He no longer asked himself why Ben had died. There was no way of bringing him back. He was gone, and God bless the man.

The water was inky black and very still. Not a ripple, so still and black that its glossy surface reflected the stars hanging overhead in an indigo sky.

A perfect night. As close as anything could be perfect for what he had to do.

Leaning over the side of the boat, he paused only to close his eyes and say a few words committing Ben to the hereafter.

The words faded and drifted. His hands trembled slightly as he shook the contents from the tin. Faint scummy whirls remained on the surface, gradually spreading thinner and wider, fading and drifting just as his words had done. A few minutes and they were indistinguishable, mere detritus on a muddied surface.

Ben Tyler was gone. The real Ben Tyler was gone. Harry Hunter had survived the war and was still here.

His work done, he sat aloft for a while, staring at the rising moon, a glowing disc behind the furthest treeline. The disc was not dissimilar to the halo around a saint's head depicted in coloured glass on a church window.

But the trees were not saints – and for that matter neither was he.

He'd vowed to have revenge on the Compton-Dixon family. At one time, that revenge had been cold as frost in winter. It wasn't like that now. His mother was long dead and belonged to a different time. He'd come through a war when many others had not and for that he was grateful.

* * *

MORE FROM LIZZIE LANE

The next book in the gripping Orchard Cottage Hospital saga series from Lizzie Lane is available to order now here:

https://mybook.to/OrchardCottageBook5

ABOUT THE AUTHOR

Lizzie Lane is the author of over 50 books, including the bestselling Tobacco Girls series. She was born and bred in Bristol where many of her family worked in the cigarette and cigar factories.

Download your exclusive bonus content from Lizzie Lane here:

Follow Lizzie on social media here:

facebook.com/jean.goodhind
x.com/baywriterallatı
instagram.com/baywriterallatsea
bookbub.com/authors/lizzie-lane
goodreads.com/lizzielane

ALSO BY LIZZIE LANE

The Tobacco Girls

The Tobacco Girls

Dark Days for the Tobacco Girls

Fire and Fury for the Tobacco Girls

Heaven and Hell for the Tobacco Girls

Marriage and Mayhem for the Tobacco Girls

A Fond Farewell for the Tobacco Girls

Coronation Close

New Neighbours for Coronation Close

Shameful Secrets on Coronation Close

Dark Shadows Over Coronation Close

Tough Times on Coronation Close

Bad Company on Coronation Close

The Strong Trilogy

The Sugar Merchant's Wife

Secrets of the Past

Daughter of Destiny

The Sweet Sisters Trilogy

Wartime Sweethearts

War Baby

Home Sweet Home

Wives and Lovers

Wartime Brides

Coronation Wives

Mary Anne Randall

A Wartime Wife

A Wartime Family

Orchard Cottage Hospital

A New Doctor at Orchard Cottage Hospital

Family Affairs at Orchard Cottage Hospital

Bleak Times at Orchard Cottage Hospital

Echoes of the Past at Orchard Cottage Hospital

The Kowloon Series

Doctor of Kowloon

Escape from Kowloon

Standalone Novels

War Orphans

A Wartime Friend

Secrets and Sins

A Christmas Wish

Women in War

Her Father's Daughter

Trouble for the Boat Girl